TYDELL - WAR OF THE TIERS

BY

DANIEL BERRISFORD

CONTENTS

Prologue 3

Chapter 1 — Life In The Bottom Tier 6

Chapter 2 — The Hunt Begins...13

Chapter 3- The Force Of The Law 17

Chapter 4- One More For The Road 23

Chapter 5- Time For Sign Up 27

Chapter 6 – The Arrival 42

Chapter 7- Conversations..51

Chapter 8-Forgetting The Past 62

Chapter 9- Building A Team..70

Chapter 10- The Moment..77

Chapter 11- Heigl..79

Chapter 12- Moving On 83

Chapter 13- Coming Back Stronger...................................97

Chapter 14- First day back 103

Chapter 15 – Meeting the boy..112

Chapter 16- Barrack Thirteen 120

Chapter 17- The King 127

Daniel Berrisford © 2021

Chapter 18- Fallax's fall out 130

Chapter 19- Gathering Supplies. 141

Chapter 20 - History..169

Chapter 21- The Rise and Fall 189

Chapter 22- Escape 211

Chapter 23- Twists and Turns..............................227

Chapter 24- Division..255

Chapter 25- Impact..270

Chapter 26- Making amends 296

Chapter 27-Knowledge is Power 306

Epilogue 371

PROLOGUE

Wind whistled through the gaps in the weathered wooden slats of the shack, a frail structure standing defiant against the blistering gusts—unusually blowing in from the west.

Romius sat on the porch in his rocking chair, his weapon propped within arm's reach. Eyes closed, he listened to the soft chime hanging from the door, its music partially masked by the growing breeze.

His home stood a mile east of Tydell—a small city nestled in the valley between two towering mountains. Tydell was one of Thearon's oldest cities, perched at the northern edge of the Exia Desert, a place where few dared settle. Life here was harsh, the land barren, but Romius didn't mind. He welcomed the isolation. The fewer people around, the harder it was to be found—or so he liked to believe.

The shack was nothing more than a single room with a bed, a stove, and a desk—a bleak existence. But trying to topple a government rarely led to mountain mansions; it usually led to an early grave.

As the sun dipped behind the colossal rock formations, Romius rocked slowly, the evening breeze running through his unkempt beard. A rare calm washed over him. He had spent a lifetime dealing death, earning the name *The Man with the Steel Skin*. One day, his past would find him—he'd always known that.

A faint disturbance stirred far in the distance. His muscles flexed beneath the hooded cloak draped over his broad shoulders, a twinge of ache reminding him of the years he carried. He was still strong—tall, muscular—but age had crept in: grey streaking his beard, a receding hairline hidden by a clean shave.

The wind stilled, the chimes fell silent. Then a new sound rolled across the valley. The ground trembled, dust rising from the west. Romius's eyes narrowed.

Fallax.

Two hundred soldiers of the Thearon King's Guard marched aggressively across the cracked valley floor, swinging around from the stone buildings to the north. He had ten minutes, maybe less.

Even now, part of him considered facing them head-on. It wasn't impossible. With Domir—his double-headed, razor-edged battle axe—he stood a chance. But his true edge came from being the last Steelmancer.

Rising with a groan, he stepped inside. His desk was littered with loose papers. Shoving them aside, he uncovered a small silvery-blue cube that pulsed with a limitless glow. He slipped it into the pouch at his belt.

In the doorway, his sleeveless cloak billowed in the dying wind. Hood drawn up, red bandana pulled high to mask all but his eyes, he inhaled deeply.

Silver light flared in his gaze, smoke curling upward. The glow ran down his arms, bright veins tracing the muscle, the Steelmancer's power awakening.

The army stopped fifty feet away.

One last deep breath…

CHAPTER 1 — LIFE IN THE BOTTOM TIER

She continued to clamber up the seemingly endless flight of steps, pushing her way through the bustling crowd, clutching the sack of cleaning supplies that hung heavily over her shoulder. Alicius did everything she could to provide for her children. This job was finally the first tangible reward for all her efforts. She always made sure to look presentable—her thick autumn-coloured hair clean and swept back into a neat ponytail. Her apron was freshly washed, and she wore shirts she had carefully bought and mended from the market stalls.

Becoming the cleaner for a prominent soldier in the Tydell city guard still didn't afford her the luxury of new clothes, let alone a way out of the poverty-stricken slums of the tenth tier—the absolute bottom of the valley. The Tydell social system was brutally clear: the higher your tier, the wealthier your life.

Finally, she reached the ninth tier. The only consolation was that the tiers grew smaller the further up she climbed. Soon she had scaled up the tiers high enough and arrived at the door, intricately carved with elegant patterns. She had been here only once before, when she secured the job.

She had been lucky to get the opportunity; the father of her son's friend was a master black smith and provided weapons for the Captain that lived here. He had set up the interview. She knocked on the door, the in-house chef let her in. It was modern and large, that meant a lot to clean.

Ξ

Alicius swept the living room floor of Captain Gremallax; dark oak flooring, wine and alcohol rack built to the wall, kitchen work tops with stone only found along the eastern coast, rather expensive to transport. If all this didn't state how wealthy this man was then the view she was admiring did. The luscious fields of shrubbery and foliage to the west of Tydell. Most homes had west facing windows due to the fact the east was a barren desert with little life. However, to the east, the Tydellese prided themselves on the plant life that flourished along the mountains.

"Enjoying the view, miss?" Captain Gremallax's voice broke the silence as he entered the living quarters of his sprawling mountaintop home, carved into the jagged north mountain ridge. His tone was sharp, and he regarded his personal chef similarly, who soon scurried out of the room after delivering some unwelcome news.

"I'm dreadfully sorry, sir. I'll get back to cleaning right away," Alicius apologized. Her unnaturally large, chocolate eyes and flawless porcelain skin seemed to catch him off guard, and his anger softened.

"No, no, it's alright. I can't blame anyone for admiring the sights of the Great City of the North. I've grown too accustomed to this view myself. I should stop and appreciate my luxuries more often."

Alicius thought his arrogance overshadowed his tall, hulking frame, though the navy blue and gold Tydell Captain's uniform he wore was crisp and pristine. He was the epitome of a handsome man in his late thirties—square jaw, muscular build, and piercing bright blue eyes.

"It really is beautiful, sir. You should be proud," she replied cautiously.

Gremallax gave her a slow, flirtatious grin. "You're the new cleaner! My assistant never gave me the pretty woman's name."

What an overly confident chauvinist, Alicius thought. *Just keep going for Oliax and Eryx.*

"Alicius, sir. I must apologize, but I really need to continue if I'm to finish before sundown."

"A southern name, but no accent. Shows signs of a good education. What's a posh southern girl doing cleaning houses up here?" His question dredged up memories of her past in the Thearon capital, Poltan.

"I taught myself Tydellese so my children would have a better chance in life here," she said, fighting back the tears threatening to spill from behind her composed facade.

"That's very honorable. I have some free time and will be here for the rest of the day. When you're finished here, you can leave and be with those children of yours. I'll see you tomorrow, Alicius."

"Thank you so much, sir," she replied. He turned and headed toward his home office, while Alicius worried quietly for that poor girl.

He might be a captain living high in the upper tiers of Tydell, but he understood how the poor lived. Alicius hadn't left her children with maids, nuns, or even at school—it was too costly. Oliax and Eryx were left to fend for themselves in the dark, narrow streets of the Tydell slums.

Ξ

Eryx drifted through the bottom-tier markets of Tydell, moving with the casual patience of someone who belonged here. The place was alive with sound and colour—vendors calling out their deals, the clatter of cart wheels over cobblestones, the hum of bartering voices. The air carried the mingled scents of ripe fruit, sharp spices, and grilled meat, each one teasing his empty stomach. The market was a labyrinth to strangers, but to Eryx it was as familiar as his own hands. He knew which alleys hid shortcuts, which stalls kept loose watch over their goods, and where the shadows lingered just long enough to disappear into.

He strolled toward the southern stalls, where food traders gathered in tight rows. It was the perfect hunting ground. He had no coins in his pocket, but that wasn't a problem—it hadn't been for months. In that time, he'd grown deft at snatching what he needed, quiet and quick.

His mother's new job was helping, but the little they gained wasn't enough. The extra food he stole meant they could save coin instead of spending it, edging them one step closer to leaving the bottom tier behind. They'd been stuck here ever since they fled Poltan six years ago, when he was just fourteen. Now, nearly a man at seventeen, he'd shot up to a solid six feet, his frame beginning to show the promise of muscle, though still wiry. A shadow of a beard clung stubbornly to his jaw, his green eyes sharp under unruly curls, his wide nose giving his boyish face a stubborn kind of charm.

He crouched between two stalls—dried meat to his left, citrus fruits to his right—and tore off a bite from a strip of beef he'd already lifted. His gaze stayed locked on the basket of fresh produce across the lane. Like a predator watching prey, he studied the rhythm of the attendants, waiting for that perfect moment when distraction would open the door.

"Eryx, why are we in the markets?"

The voice made him jolt. He spun around to see Oliax standing behind him, hands on her hips.

"Oliax! You're supposed to be home," he hissed.

"Well, I got bored. You always get to go out, so why can't I?" she whined, her tone pure mischief wrapped in youth.

At seven, she was too clever for her own good, always tagging after him when she could. She was bright but still innocent, too young to remember their escape from Poltan. To her, the narrow alleys and grit of the bottom tier weren't a prison—they were just home, a place surrounded by the endless walls of the Exia Desert.

"Go home," Eryx said, softening his voice. "I'll be back before Mum gets home. I'll even bring you some grapes."

She eyed the beef in his hand, lifting an eyebrow. He sighed and handed it over. Her stern little glare melted into a grin, and she skipped off toward home.

Eryx turned back to the basket across the lane, the fruit practically calling his name. The moment was coming— he could feel it.

CHAPTER 2 — THE HUNT BEGINS

"General, is it truly necessary to wake me at such an ungodly hour?" King Leax's voice was soft as ever, though it carried the weight of irritation. Age had not been kind to him—his eyes were sunk deep into a face lined by decades, his wide nose bridging over a thick white mane that framed his jaw.

"I am deeply sorry, Your Majesty," General Fallax replied, bowing his head. "But the Karathi have begun to move at the borders. I need your approval to engage."

Fallax was regarded as one of the noblest men in the realm. From a lowly foot soldier, he had risen to command the Thearon National Guard. Years of war had carved themselves into his rugged features, yet even with hair greying at the temples and lines etched across his brow, he could still best a man half his age.

"Of course, General. Do what you must—this was inevitable," Leax murmured, still shaking off the haze of sleep. "The Karathal government is making sure we, as a sovereign state, do not grow too ambitious and press for more land."

"Thank you, Your Majesty. I will begin recruitment in the northern towns and cities at once," Fallax said. "The

Exia Desert will slow their supply lines; the terrain should buy us time."

The King gave a tired nod of dismissal, and the general bowed once more before turning on his heel, already planning the defence of the border.

Ξ

Fallax knew he didn't need to travel north himself, yet the weight of unfinished business pulled at him. The man with the "Steel Skin" had escaped once before—years ago now—after slaughtering his men and leaving him for dead. Time had dulled neither the sting of that defeat nor the anger it left behind. When word reached him that the assassin had resurfaced and was making for Karathal, Fallax swore he would not let the man vanish again.

He walked the length of the palace hallway, letting his gaze sweep over the golden lantern brackets and the deep red velvet carpet. It would be a long time before he saw such comforts again. Ahead lay a harsh journey north, the command of an army in one of the world's most unforgiving landscapes, and a hunt for Thearon's most dangerous fugitive.

He summoned his second-in-command. "Tell the men to ready the horses. We leave for Tydell before noon. War is upon us."

The officer snapped to attention, then hurried into the courtyard, barking orders at the troops. Even with the Tydell City Guard and fresh recruits from northern towns and villages, Fallax would still march twenty thousand soldiers from the National Guard to the border. Karathal was ten times the size of Thearon, and with that came ten times the men. If they were coming, he had to be ready.

Ξ

Karathal lay to the north of Thearon, vast and powerful—one of the largest nations in the world. Its sprawling cities, steeped in centuries of culture, made it a coveted place to live.

A century and a half ago, Thearon had fought for its independence from Karathal. In truth, the victory changed little in day-to-day life; the two countries were still separated by the harsh, unyielding Exia Desert. For two and a half years, the Karathal government resisted, but in the end, they conceded, granting Thearon its sovereignty.

The Thearish people had long made their homes along the fertile southern coast, where the land yielded crops year-round beneath warm, gentle skies. Over time, however, many had migrated north, closer to the Karathal border. While Thearon retained its own language, the closer one travelled to the frontier, the more common it became to hear Tydellese—a hybrid tongue born from the mingling of the two cultures.

Karathal, however, had not forgotten Thearon's defiance. They would take no chances in allowing their former vassal to grow too strong or too ambitious. Their recent troop movements along the border, laced with intimidation, made their intent all too clear.

CHAPTER 3- THE FORCE OF THE LAW

Eryx steadied himself preparing to snatch the basket, *One…Two…*

"Oi, I don't think so son!". Eryx turned as Eroge jumped on his back. "you truly are an imbecile" replied Eryx then laughing as his best friend dismounted from his back. "what's taken you so long, you said you would be here when you finished work?", "My dad made me finish the throwing knives order we had. Look, I made an extra for us to practice with". Eroge was the same age as Eryx. He was a Blacksmith apprentice at his family's business. Eroge pulled a six-inch throwing blade from his coat pocket. It glistened in the evening sun, curved to perfection, so it could glide through the air. It was some of Eroge's best work.

"How have you not got the basket yet, you soft arse" Eroge joked to a nervous Eryx. "I was waiting so you could see the master at work" an unconvincing retort.

He crouched slightly, weight shifting forward. The stall owner turned toward a new customer—perfect. Three… GO.

He darted in from the side, hand closing around the basket's handle in one swift motion. A sidestep, a pivot, and he melted into the press of bodies in the market.

Behind him, Eroge was already puffing, his heavier frame struggling to keep up.

Eryx moved like smoke, slipping between shoppers, careful not just to evade the stall owner's eyes but to avoid becoming a recognizable thief. He cut left into the shaded section of the market, then broke into a full sprint.

By the time they reached their usual hideout at the foot of the mountain, the adrenaline had faded into breathless laughter. Among the rock pools, they tore into the stolen fruit, juice running down their chins, the thrill of the chase still lingering between them.

Ξ

Alicius arrived home to the warm, eager embrace of her little girl. Oliax's wide grin and bright eyes—so like her own—met her at the door. She was a miniature reflection of Alicius, from her delicate features to the way her smile lit the room.

"Where's your brother?"

Silence.

"Was he at the markets again?"

Oliax gave a small, sheepish nod.

"That foolish boy," Alicius muttered, setting down her sack of cleaning supplies with a thud. "He's going to get himself arrested." Frustration simmered beneath her voice. She knew Eryx meant well, but stealing was never the answer. He could get a job, come with her to clean houses—anything but theft. His father had been the same, forever testing limits, dancing too close to trouble. But he was long gone, and those memories should have been buried with him.

"He'd best be back before the lanterns are lit," she said, half to herself, "or I'll kill him myself."

Oliax giggled, unbothered by the threat, and began helping her mother prepare tea.

Ξ

"So, this is made from ninety percent Thearon steel?" Eryx asked, turning the blade over in his hand.

"Some of the purest weaponry I've ever produced," Eroge replied with pride. "Light enough to fly, strong enough to pierce stone."

The massive man reclined in the fading sun, ginger whiskers catching the light. His long, untamed hair framed a face that rarely saw a comb. Eroge didn't waste vanity on himself—every scrap of care went into forging deadly masterpieces.

WHACK!

The throwing knife buried itself deep into the stone wall. Eryx tugged it free with effort, the blade unmarred.

"You've outdone yourself," Eryx said. "The way it cuts through the air—so fast I can just—"

Slow, deliberate clapping cut him off.

A man in his mid-thirties, dressed head to toe in black leather, leaned casually against a rock. "Playing soldier, are we?" His voice dripped with mockery. "A master thief and a skilled fighter."

He pushed away from the rock, his long leather trench coat swaying. Behind him, a group of heavyset brutes fanned out, hemming Eroge in. Even if the big man wanted to run, there was no room to escape.

The stranger's hand shot out, clamping around Eryx's throat. "I think you've realized you've stolen from the wrong person, boy." His breath was hot, his grip iron. "You'll repay me in fingers."

Heat rushed through Eryx's body. Fight or flight roared in his ears. His fist moved before his mind caught up— crunching into the man's nose.

"Eroge, go!"

The blacksmith's apprentice bulldozed through the men blocking him, all brute strength now.

Four of them turned to Eryx. He weighed his odds— slim. Then he remembered the knife in his hand. He kept it low, hidden behind his back, before hurling it at the first man who charged. His aim was wide, and he spun toward the wall, scrambling up. He made it four feet before rough hands dragged him back down.

The leader loomed over him, blood streaking from his nose. "First you steal from one of my stalls, now you impale my men?" He sneered. "You'll lose more than fingers."

Confused, Eryx glanced over to see one of the brutes writhing on the ground, the blade jutting from his shoulder. He could have sworn he'd missed.

"Get me that knife."

One of the men yanked it free and handed it over. The leader pressed the cold steel to Eryx's neck. His pulse hammered so hard he thought his chest might burst. All for a basket of fruit. Now he was going to die.

He closed his eyes, bracing for it—

"Damiax, put the boy down," a commanding voice called out. "I'm sure you have better things to do than harass children."

Sergeant Urasmus strode into view, Eroge panting and red-faced behind him.

Damiax scowled, dropped the knife, and leaned in close to Eryx. "Keep one eye open, boy. You won't be so lucky next time." His hand whipped across Eryx's face in a brutal backhand before he stalked off with his crew.

Urasmus and Eroge rushed over. Eryx's left eye was already swelling—black by morning.

"You, son, are a blithering idiot," Urasmus said bluntly. "Stealing from Damiax the debt collector? You're braver than I am." He shook his head, hauling Eryx to his feet. "Let's get you home. Your mother's tongue will cut you deeper than I can. And next time, don't send your mate to find me—poor bastard looked ready to collapse."

Eryx knew the sergeant well. The veteran often patrolled the markets and the Bottom Tier—the most dangerous part of town. Short, broad, with a moustache as white as his hair, Urasmus was in his fifties and carried the stubborn, sinewy strength of a man who'd never stopped working.

The three of them made their way toward Eryx's home—a leaning shack that barely deserved the name.

CHAPTER 4- ONE MORE FOR THE ROAD

Romius stood in the doorway of the tavern cellar, a dark figure framed in the flickering lamplight. His black cloak hung loose around his shoulders, the hood casting a shadow over his brow, while a deep crimson bandana masked the lower half of his face. Only his eyes were visible—cold, metallic, and unblinking.

The eyes of a Steelmancer.

To most men, that sight alone was enough to inspire fear. To the four men in this cellar, it would be the last thing they ever saw.

Romius's purpose was clear. Kill every man in the room. There was no hesitation anymore—killing had long since become second nature. The weight of it didn't touch him; the act was as routine as breathing.

He pushed the door open, and the faint silver light in his eyes brightened.

Four men. Three seated at a table, one standing guard near the stairs. The guard's gaze locked on him, his training kicking in faster than his fear. In a heartbeat, the man drew his side sword and brought it down in a sharp arc.

Romius didn't flinch. His left arm rose to meet the strike, and in the instant before the blade made contact, his skin shimmered, hardening into living steel. The sword hit, screamed in protest, and bent uselessly around his forearm. Romius didn't even blink.

The guard had just enough time for his eyes to widen before Domir—Romius's curved battle axe—came slicing through his skull from behind. The lifeless body crumpled to the ground, the silvered axe head dripping.

One down.

The three at the table were already half-rising. One, braver or more foolish than the others, tried to speak. "Listen here, you twisted murderer. You won't get aw-"

His words ended with a wet thump as his head slid clean from his shoulders. The throw had been perfect—Domir sailing end over end across fifteen feet to claim its mark. Not that distance mattered. Thearon steel bent to Romius's will; the weapon would have hit its target no matter where it had been thrown.

The last two men scrambled for the cellar door in a blind panic. Romius moved faster. His hand clamped around one man's throat, lifting him off his feet, while his boot slammed into the other's gut, sending him sprawling. The one in his grasp didn't last long—Romius twisted, a sharp snap echoing through the cellar. The body fell limp to the floor.

With a thought, Domir returned to his grip, and in the same motion, he drove the axe through the final man's back. The scream was brief. The body went still.

The cellar was quiet now, save for the steady drip of blood on stone.

Romius exhaled once, calm and measured. The job was done.

He ascended the stairs, each step heavy and deliberate, before stepping into the warm, noisy air of the tavern above. Without removing his hood or bandana, he sat at the bar and ordered an ale.

To anyone else, it would be unthinkable—how a man who had just slaughtered four lieutenants of the Poltan City Guard could sit there so calmly. For Romius, the answer was simple. It no longer fazed him.

The ale arrived. He drank. Then he rose, tossing a few coins onto the bar.

It was time to head north. Cross the border. Return to his homeland.

The Thearon capital had nothing more to offer him. Twenty years of pursuit had been more than enough—

and the forces hunting him were closer than ever. But Romius was ready.

He always was.

CHAPTER 5- TIME FOR SIGN UP

It took all of two seconds for Alicius to notice the swelling around her son's eye.

"What on earth have you been doing?!" she demanded, then turned to the sergeant with a sigh. "I'm so sorry, Sergeant—what is it this time?"

This wasn't the first time Eryx had drawn the attention of the law. He and Eroge found trouble almost daily, but this time they'd been spotted—by the wrong men.

"Nothing too serious, Miss," Urasmus replied smoothly. "Just a bit of loitering. The eye? That was from a bit of rough-and-tumble with that big fella he's always with. Isn't that right, Eryx?"

Eryx blinked, surprised that the sergeant was covering for him. He gave a quick nod, and Urasmus answered it with a discreet wink before turning back to Alicius.

"Truth be told," the sergeant continued, "I think this lad would do well in the City Guard. Give him something productive to do with his time."

Eryx opened his mouth to protest—only to catch Urasmus's pointed look. A look that very clearly said: *Question me, and I'll drop you in it, big time.*

Ξ

"What am I going to do, Eryx?" Alicius exclaimed, rubbing her forehead with thumb and finger as she perched on a chair in the kitchen.

"I think Urasmus may be right. The army is probably the best thing for you." Her voice wavered, and the thought made her uneasy. Eryx shot up, panic in his eyes. "No! Mother, you can't make me go. I promise I'll stop stealing and get a job!"

It didn't matter whether Eryx truly wanted to work or not. His father was gone, leaving no business for him to inherit. That was the way of Tydell: sons followed in their fathers' footsteps. And what man would hire a stranger over his own son? That left only one path—joining the City Guard.

"Son, please understand… this is for your own good. I'll speak to Captain Gremallax and make sure he keeps an eye on you." Alicius saw the fear reflected in her eldest's eyes. She felt cruel, almost heartless, but it was necessary. Eryx would enlist the next morning.

He spent the entire night turning over plans to avoid the army, but every scenario ended in either death or imprisonment. *I'm going to end up dead no matter what,* he thought, finally surrendering to his fate—and at last, he managed to sleep.

Ξ

Eryx walked up to the sixth tier to enlist in the City Guard. The climb halfway up South Mountain was long and tiring, but it gave him a view of the city transforming beneath him. The streets grew tidier, the homes larger, adorned with intricate designs and lavish details. One day, he hoped to live somewhere as luxurious as this.

He followed the cobblestone streets through the bustling trade section until he reached the small stone building. Inside, a man sat at a desk against the back wall, while a woman in front of him recorded details. After Eryx gave his name and age, she let him pass straight through.

"Sit down," the man demanded abruptly. Sergeant Holiax didn't want this to drag on longer than twenty minutes.

"Why are you joining, then…" He glanced at the form the woman had handed over, scanning for Eryx's name.

"Eryx. Not much choice, Sir. No father to work for, and a mother who wants me out of the house," Eryx added with a joking lilt, hoping to elicit a laugh. There was no reaction—not even a hint of a grin.

"Urasmus told me your situation last night. You are in no position to be fooling around, trying to crack jokes." Eryx felt the tension thicken, a lump rising in his throat.

He rubbed the back of his neck, the awkwardness pressing down on him.

"Erm… I really need this, Sir. I'll do whatever it takes to prove my worth."

Holiax's lips twitched into a smile. It wasn't the smile of a man impressed, but of one who knew exactly what challenges lay ahead for Eryx.

He exited the stone building they sunk into the mountain, out into the glistening sun. Eryx could feel the impact of this decision. A turning point in his life. The thoughts swirling around in his mind as a shady but familiar face strode past.

Damiax grabbing hold of a beggar and dragging them into a dark crevice between the rock formations. Eryx tried to avoid him at all costs, especially after what had happened the previous day. The villainous character caught a glimpse of the teen. Eryx ran.

Ξ

Alicius arrived at work early, hoping to catch the Captain before he left. She knocked, even though she had a key—she wasn't about to barge in on a potentially naked man. The door opened to reveal a man with a ripped torso, peeking out.

"You're rather early… or dreadfully late," he said, winking at her.

She brushed off the comment, partly because it was unprofessional and partly because she was distracted by what she saw.

"Sorry, sir. I thought I'd make up for the lost time from last night."

"That was a gift, not a 'go away and make up for it later,' you remarkably committed woman," he replied.

He gestured for her to enter, subtly directing her to take a seat, which she did. Perfect opportunity.

"Would you like a hot beverage, Al?"

Who does this man think he is, giving me a nickname? Her thoughts faltered under the piercing blue eyes and rugged features of the topless Captain.

"Oh, no thank you, sir. I do, however, have a question to ask," she managed, refocusing.

"Go ahead," he said.

"My son is signing up for the City Guard today. I was wondering if you could keep an eye on him. I know it's unprofessional, but he's young and a little…," she hesitated.

Gremallax cut her off with reassuring words. "Of course, I will. A caring and beautiful mother like you deserves to know her son will be safe."

Whether he said it to increase his chances with her or was genuinely sincere didn't matter. She was simply relieved he had agreed to oversee her son's time in the City Guard—for now.

She thanked him and left the room to begin her extensive cleaning duties. She glanced back towards the room, Gremallax still admiring her from the doorway.

Ξ

Eryx's heart pounded as he bolted through the crowded streets of the sixth tier, Damiax's shouts echoing behind him. Every step sent pain lancing through his legs, but years of running, lifting, and scrabbling over fences in the back alleys of Tydell had built him for exactly this. He vaulted over a low cart with a strength that made him feel almost airborne, landing lightly on the cobblestones and keeping his momentum.

Damiax wasn't far behind, but Eryx's endurance carried him forward when others would have faltered. He twisted sharply down narrow lanes, weaving through merchants' stalls, his lungs burning, yet refusing to slow. The scale down South Mountain loomed ahead—ten tiers of winding streets separating him from safety. Most would have gasped for air halfway down, but Eryx's legs pumped like pistons, his speed unnerving even himself.

A row of steps forced him to leap over the railings, the drop was three men high, his legs enduring the force of the stone as he landed. He could hear Damiax stumbling, cursing, as the distance between them widened. Eryx didn't look back; he didn't need to. Every fibre of his body was tuned to survival.

By the tenth tier, sweat stung his eyes and his chest heaved, but his strength allowed him to shove past merchants and doorways without slowing. He skidded into the wooden building, that was Urasmus' office, chest heaving, arms trembling but steady, his legs still carrying him forward.

"Urasmus!" he gasped, throwing the door open. "He's after me!"

The door shut behind him, muffling the distant shouts of Damiax. Eryx's body trembled with exertion, but a faint grin appeared on his face. He had made it—powered by speed, endurance, and strength that he hadn't even realized he possessed.

Ξ

Eryx leaned against the doorframe, catching his breath. Urasmus studied him with a sharp, assessing gaze.

"You shouldn't have come all the way up here, Eryx," Urasmus said, his tone calm but firm. "Damiax won't give up that easily."

"I... I didn't know where else to go," Eryx admitted, still trembling from the chase.

"Then we'll cut the risk short," Urasmus decided. "I'm sending you straight to the barracks. No detours, no delays. They'll keep you safe—and out of his reach."

Eryx's shoulders sagged in relief. "Yes, sir. Thank you."

"Good. Move quickly, and keep your head down. You're stronger than you realize, but some fights aren't meant to be won alone."

Ξ

Alicius continued to clean the room, her hands moving over the worn wood of the table, though her mind was elsewhere. The captain had already dressed and eaten, his presence filling the small space with a quiet, steady energy.

"I'm about to head off to the barracks," he said, fastening his cloak. "I'll look out for your son, but he'll probably be out on the morning run."

Running isn't too bad, she thought. Hopefully that's all he'll ever have to do. The thought gave her a fragile kind of relief.

"It will do him some good," she replied, pausing in her work. "Thank you for this—it means so much."

He smiled, a slow, warm thing that softened the hard edges of his face. She couldn't help but smile back, almost startled by how natural it felt.

For a moment, neither of them moved. His gaze lingered, as if weighing something unspoken. She felt the warmth of it in her chest, an unfamiliar ache she thought she'd buried long ago.

"Sometimes," he said quietly, "it's easy to forget there's more to life than orders and duty. People like you remind me."

Her fingers stilled on the cloth. There it was again— kindness, without expectation, without judgment. It made her wary and hopeful all at once. Could she let someone see past the walls she'd built? Could she trust someone to stay?

He adjusted his gloves, his movements slower than necessary, as if reluctant to break the moment. When he finally turned toward the door, she caught herself wishing he wouldn't go so soon.

And when the latch clicked behind him, she realized her pulse hadn't settled since he'd smiled.

Ξ

Signed up and transported to the barracks, no time to collect any of his belongings or even say goodbye to his mother and sister.

The barracks were situated north of the North Mountain, on the perimeter of where the land turned from a luscious green to a sandy orange.

He walked over with Urasmus, "Ha-ha, oh dear. You fool. This might just kill you off lad" he had the same reservations Holiax had in the Tydell city guard office. The sergeant gave Holiax a wave to signal he had it from here. They travelled across what looked like a dueling area, it was empty at the moment. It was still early in the morning.

Eryx took a deep breath and entered the arched stone building before him. Two large white numbers were painted on the front. It was modest—seven feet tall and about thirteen in length. He approached his assigned bed.

"Okay, listen here you bunch of morons. New lad, name's Eryx. If he falls behind you are all in bother. So, don't let it happen". The sergeant walked out of the stone barrack. The building held five beds, four occupied and a wash area to the back with sink, lavatory and shower.

"Listen here newbie, barrack thirteen isn't no piss around" said a tall, muscular man who was approaching him. He held out his hand, gesturing Eryx to shake it. "We do our job right then we can enjoy ourselves." His face changed losing its seriousness and the firm grip on Eryx's hand eased. "now the lecture is out the way. I'm Rannax, squad leader, welcome to the team" Rannax's smile dazzled beneath the most impressive moustache Eryx had ever seen, contrasting his shaven head. The man wore a vest that signified his rank, being a squad leader at what seemed to be earlier thirties was signs of ambition in the man. Hence the direct approach about work ethic.

"You need a change of underwear lad? Ha-Ha" bellowed the second soldier. "Bardius, but everyone calls me Bard".

"That's because you force everyone too" replied Rannax looking at Bard with mock despair.

"It's a pleasure to meet you both" Eryx chipped in, not wanting to seem rude. He wanted to go meet the third man in the room, who stared directly at him, but just as he was walking over, leaving the other two to squabble, Urasmus rang a bell apparently signaling training.

Why didn't I sign up later on? I'd have missed all this. Straight into it, no warning, no preparation. He was in single file waiting to take part in his first training session.

He ran at number four, shadowing the unknown man. Rannax led, broad shoulders swaying with effortless power, and behind him, the bulky man with a goatee— Bardius… no, Bard. He was in at number two, his steady stride swallowing the shifting sand beneath their boots.

The barracks were a distant memory now, replaced by the merciless desert. Heat rippled off the dunes like a living thing, waves of shimmering gold that blurred the horizon. Jagged rock formations jutted out from the sand, casting long, cruel shadows that danced as he passed. Eryx could have sworn he glimpsed a house—an illusion conjured by exhaustion—but the desert offered no mercy, no shelter, just sand and sun and the endless, punishing climb.

Time warped around him. He sucked air through his teeth and lungs, each inhale a searing burn in his nose and throat. His heart hammered like a war drum against his ribcage. Twenty-five minutes. At least. Longer than any exercise he'd ever endured in these conditions. Yet the squad pressed on, legs pumping, sand kicking up in tiny storms around their boots, drifting with each step.

He wanted to collapse, to sink into the hot grains and let it all end. Surely that would feel better than this relentless torture. But the man ahead—the one whose face remained calm, almost mocking—glanced back, smiled, even winked. Not a bead of sweat marred him. Not a muscle quivered. What was he made of?

His vision blurred. Sweat stung his eyes, mixing with the fine dust coating his skin. Legs screamed with each stride as Rannax's pace tore him further behind. No other squad had ever run like this; no squad had ever been tested like this. But Eryx forced himself to grind forward, teeth clenched, mind clouded with fatigue and panic. He had always trailed at the back, always failed. But now—this was a fresh start. A chance to prove to himself, to his mother, that he could endure, that he could fight.

A spark ignited inside him. A second wind—or perhaps desperation itself—but suddenly the burn in his muscles dulled to a dull throb, and the air, while still hot and coarse, no longer seemed enough to suffocate him. Step by step, he gained ground on the three ahead, sand rising in a silvery mist around his legs. The landscape grew familiar, contours of rock and sand guiding them back toward the barracks.

They arrived back in the training complex. "Thirteen, first again" Urasmus stated, making notes in his book, "even got the sickly, looking child back with you! Consider me impressed". Rannax turned to Eryx with a smile that said well done. His expression however turned to a look of confusion, it quickly dispersed as he rubbed his eyes removing the sweat that dripped from his forehead. *I'm not the only one who's seeing things, thank Heaphius."*

They returned to the barrack to shower and change for the afternoon. Bard cheered "What a run, boys! Best yet considering the spindly branch kept up"

"Don't be so harsh Bard. You finishing with that potato shaped torso is far more impressive," Rannax said defending Eryx. The two started wrestling half naked towards the shower end of the barrack. It baffled Eryx how two men who seemed so disciplined and determined when out training could be so easily brought to anger and fight like children.

Eryx sat on his bed going through the sack filled with uniform he had been provided. There was some shirts and pants and a pair of shiny leather boots next to the bag. The showers turned on so he looked back up to find that his final squad mate was discussing something that seemed rather serious with Urasmus at the door. By the time the conversation ended the Square jawed man who was physically in better shape than the rest of them collected his things and left the barrack.

No-one said anything about what had just happened, Eryx was confused to why the fittest soldier in the group had left, and why Rannax let it happen. Especially considering that Barrack thirteen was the smallest squad by around six men. Including the man that just left.

"Why has he gone?" Eryx finally questioned, curiosity getting the better of him. "Right freak isn't he" Bard replied. That didn't explain why. "Ignore him, he's going senile" Bard could only be in his late forties but the tone in Rannax's voice suggested it was said to provoke the older man. "That's Jaimius, the quiet type. He comes, stays for a couple months, then goes"

"Tells some cracking tales of old magic and all that malarkey," Bard added. "He was a historian for the King of Thearon, but got caught up in some unsavory things and was discharged from his position," Bard said.

Eryx was still confused but nodded and pretended to understand. He finally entered the showers now that the others had finished.

CHAPTER 6 – THE ARRIVAL

The fields of vegetation stretched in chaotic abundance around Fallax and his small team of captains, who accompanied him to Tydell. Workers moved through the crops like ants, their labour punctuating the air with the smell of earth and sweat. Beyond this pocket of life, the northern towns were scattered and sparse, the rest of the land a barren expanse where only hardy weeds dared survive. Most of the army Fallax had brought fanned out across the region, combing the towns for potential recruits, their presence leaving trails of dust in the dry wind.

This northern city was a world apart from Poltan. The mountains rose jagged and imposing, a stark contrast to the gentle beaches and rolling seas of his homeland. Life here clung stubbornly to the valleys, pockets of green and human activity emerging from the otherwise desolate terrain, supplied by a lush, powerful river that ran from source to sea. Fallax missed the towering structures of Poltan, the organized streets and elevated civilization that made the world feel ordered. Here, the lower tiers throbbed with poverty, buildings huddled against one another as if for warmth, their stone walls scarred by the harsh environment. He adjusted his course, aiming for the foot of the southern mountain.

Fallax dismounted his steed at the entrance to the Tydell City lord's manor. Perched atop the south mountain, the residence exuded majesty, even by Poltan's standards. Its walls gleamed in the sunlight, defiant against the vicious winds that howled along the ridge. Most of the buildings he passed on the ascent had been carved into the mountain itself, blending with its stony slopes. This manor, however, rose independently, a testament to power and permanence.

He raised his hand and called for one of his captains to bring the Craekee—a rare bird bred for incredible speed and precise obedience. He fastened a sealed letter addressed to the king to its leg, signalling his arrival, and set the bird free. The Craekee's small head perched on a neck as long as its streamlined body, feathers shimmering silver like molten steel, unyielding and never shedding. The creature's legs were powerful, ending in lethal talons, and when it launched into the wind, it leapt with explosive force, slicing the air with the grace of a living arrow. To gain even a single feather from such a bird was considered a rare treasure.

Ξ

The guards hesitated at first, their reluctance thinly veiled, until the papers Fallax presented changed their demeanour instantly. They parted with little more than a murmur, allowing the general to pass. The hallway beyond was extravagant, a riot of colour and art, gilded frames and intricate tapestries lining the walls—a display of wealth that felt almost performative. Fallax's boots echoed on the polished floor as he stalked purposefully toward the City Lord's office, every step measured, controlled.

He arrived at the carved wooden door and entered without permission, his gaze sharp and unyielding. "Greetings, my lord," he said, voice steady. "I'm afraid the king has declared that Thearon is to defend its borders, and it requires the assistance of Tydell."

The City Lord, an aging man with a long beard, rubbed at his chin, eyes flicking over the papers. His body slumped in the throne, posture feeble, once commanding strength now replaced by age. His power rested entirely on King Leax's appointment, and the years suggested familiarity and trust between them. Yet Fallax noted how easily the signature was given, the wave of the hand signalling him to leave. There had been no discussion, no challenge. The simplicity of it pricked at his suspicion.

The signature granted Fallax full authority over the Tydell City guard and the right to conscript any man over eighteen. He did not relish such powers, but duty demanded that he wield them carefully. Only what was necessary to protect the kingdom, only the decisions that ensured the country's safety.

As he made his way out of the vast manor, a bureaucrat intercepted him, offering instructions regarding accommodations for him and his troops. They were assigned to an opulent inn in tier two; the upper tiers reserved exclusively for high-ranking officials. Fallax nodded curtly, noting the arrangement without indulgence.

Though the City Lord was barely known to the people of Tydell and even less to the political circles in Poltan, Fallax's instincts whispered caution. A man so easily yielding power might be hiding motives beneath his feeble exterior. He would watch. Carefully. This man could be dangerous.

Ξ

He allowed his men to settle into their accommodations after the exhausting trek to what the locals proudly called the "Capital of the North." The journey had been long, the roads rough, and the air thinner as they climbed higher into the mountains. Fallax lingered on the balcony, gazing down at the valley below. From this vantage, the city spread like a jewel against the barren landscape—a stark contrast to Poltan. Even the language marked the difference; here, they spoke a northern variation of Thearon, unfamiliar but not incomprehensible.

When Thearon had split from Karathal, the lands stretching from the Exia Desert down to the coastal villages had been desolate. It was only after years of population growth, fuelled in part by Karathi deserters, that the northern settlements became more substantial. Yet these gains were largely confined to the coastal cities—and, of course, to Tydell. Tydell remained an enigma, a fertile anomaly amid the surrounding wastelands, capable of producing verdant fields and sustaining life where nothing else could. Everywhere else, the earth was cracked and barren, and the wind carried dust like a constant reminder of nature's harshness.

Fallax, as was customary for the educated southern elite, had studied this dialect and could read it with relative ease. He held a translation book in one hand, fingers brushing its worn pages while his eyes roamed the landscape. The valley stretched beneath him, dotted with the small, organized plots of farmland that clung to the fertile soil. And there—peeking from behind the northern mountains—his target came into view: the training barracks. Mid-afternoon sunlight bathed the grounds, the perfect hour to observe the troops as they began their weapons practice, disciplined lines moving with measured precision.

Ξ

Weapons training had begun. Two trials occupied the day: relentless practice against wooden blocks and the brutal "king of the ring" competition in the heart of the training grounds. Today, Barrack Thirteen would compete, a man short since morning.

Rannax lined up his three-man squad in the sun-scorched, sandy duelling arena. A thick rope traced a ten-meter circle around them, a fragile boundary against the chaos to come.

King of the Ring meant facing Barrack Twenty-Three—fifteen men, six victories deep, and still hungry.

First day on the floor, and Eryx was staring down five opponents alone. Panic flickered across his features, but the calm, lethal confidence of his new teammates grounded him. "Listen, Eryx," Rannax said, his voice low but commanding, "you just stay behind us. Smash anyone who tries to jump on our backs. That's it." Easier said than done.

Eryx planted his feet, gripping the wooden staff with its steel banding, heart hammering. The bell shrieked across the arena, and the fifteen charged like a tidal wave. Rannax's mace rose and fell in a blur, striking knees and joints with surgical precision. The first three men crumpled before they could even react. Beside him, Bard barrelled through six with his massive curved shield, a battering ram in human form.

The weapons had been partially nullified—Rannax wielding a spikeless mace, Bard hefting a shield that weighed twice a normal weapon—but their mastery made the handicap meaningless.

One attacker hurled a dulled longsword toward Rannax's side plate. Reflexively, Eryx jammed his staff between them, deflecting the blow before it could bite. Around him, Rannax and Bard moved like shadows, twisting, bobbing, striking with feral precision.

Victory required forcing the opposition out of the circle—or submission.

The man Eryx had blocked lunged at him again, sword aimed at his face. His stomach knotted. The staff shot up instinctively, colliding with the blade just in time. Shock froze him; he hadn't even consciously moved. Another soldier surged forward, but Rannax's sharp command snapped him out of his daze: "Get your head out of your arse!"

Eryx refocused. Only five men remained. Bard pressed two against the rope with relentless strength, their swings useless against the curved iron wall of his shield. Rannax turned his attention to the remaining three, dropping low, sweeping his mace along the sand. Limbs buckled, men collapsed, and Eryx's astonishment bloomed into awe.

Bard toppled his two—but at the cost of his footing. He was dragged along the sand, growling in frustration. Rannax, unflinching, dispatched one man, mace intercepting a wooden axe mid-swing, then hurled the soldier out of the circle with devastating efficiency. Two remained, swords drawn, a dangerous stretch of steel between him and victory.

The first lunged. Rannax rolled, the blade grazing harmlessly past his shoulder. His mace snapped upward, striking the man's elbow joint with a crack. The sword fell. Rannax seized the arm, flipped the man over his shoulder, and hurled him beyond the ropes.

Before he could recover, the fallen soldier hooked his fingers in Rannax's collar, yanking him backward. The final opponent loomed, sword poised above Rannax's chest. Time slowed. Deep breath. Sweep the leg.

The wooden staff arced through the air, connecting with a sickening thud against the soldier's jaw. He crumpled, unconscious.

Eryx blinked, stunned by the flawless strike. Was he…okay? Motionless, but the circle was theirs. They had won.

Rannax seized Eryx and hoisted him into the air. "COME ON!" he bellowed, a primal roar of triumph. Bard joined, shield raised in celebration. Six more barracks remained, but this victory alone would etch their names into the eyes of the high-ranking officers.

Ξ

Fallax had just witnessed a true underdog battle. He was massively impressed with the three men who against the odds fought their way to victory. He knew that these competitions were all for bragging rights but the squad leaders could also impress and earn a chance of promotion. "What barrack are they from sergeant?" Urasmus responded in his usual tone "Thirteen sir. Unlucky for some. Well unlucky for barrack twenty-three, look like right pathetic losers now."
Fallax continued to admire the trio's display as they set up again to defend their position against barrack eight.

"I will have to keep an eye on that group sergeant!" Fallax stated to Urasmus before walking away to observe some other sessions that were taking place.

CHAPTER 7- CONVERSATIONS

It had been a couple of days since Eryx had entered the army, and, thankfully, for Alicius, her little boy was safe... still alive. The words felt almost foreign in her mind, a fragile reassurance that barely calmed the gnawing anxiety in her chest. Every morning, Gremallax reported back to her before leaving for his own duties, recounting Eryx's progress in careful, precise detail. Each word, though meant to comfort, was a double-edged sword.

She had been given the full account of his first bout—how he had swung his staff, parried attacks, and survived against far stronger and more experienced soldiers. It was a story that should have filled her with pride, yet it left her heart thudding with unease. The vivid description of the blows he had deflected, the thuds of men hitting the sand, and the near-misses made her stomach twist. She knew Eryx was growing into something formidable, but every success in the arena felt like a reminder of just how fragile he still was.

Alicius found herself imagining all the things that could go wrong—the wrong step, a miscalculated swing, a momentary lapse of focus—and her chest tightened with dread. She wondered if he felt the same fear she did, buried deep under bravado and determination. Was he truly ready for this? Could a mother ever stop imagining the worst when her child was thrust into danger?

And yet… there was relief too. Relief that he was learning, that he was working hard, that he was finally finding a place where he mattered and could hold his own. That sense of pride battled with her worry in a constant, silent struggle. Each morning, she clutched the letter or the report from Gremallax like a lifeline, reading it over and over, parsing every sentence for signs of trouble—or triumph.

She had never been far from him in all his life, and now he was out there in a world full of men who could crush him in a heartbeat. The thought of the arena, the roar of the bell, the clash of weapons, made her fingers curl into the fabric of her chair. Every detail of the fight she had heard—every fallen opponent, every parry and strike— replayed in her mind like a heartbeat she could not quiet.

And still, somewhere beneath the worry, Alicius felt a flicker of hope. If he could survive this, if he could endure the trials, perhaps he would grow into something greater than she could have imagined. But the fear… oh, the fear would not leave her, not for a single moment.

Ξ

Another day began to the sound of insults being thrown around the barrack. "Where have you put my towel you lanky moron"

"Why do you need a towel? You don't shower." His new roommates seemed to do this a lot, he was just glad they hadn't started on him yet.

"Come on hairless, get dressed!" Bard bellowed from the shower to Eryx. "Run starts soon, don't want to be behind." Eryx swung his feet over to the side of the bed and sat up. The moment he went to stand up the aching pain overcame both his legs and he fell back down. He winced in agony, how could he be so sore?

"Ah, the morning is the worst. And it doesn't really get much better. Grit your teeth and get in the shower, it will help." His squad leader passing on some not so comforting wisdom. He managed to stand and hobbled over to the showers. The heated water felt soothing on the aching muscles, silvery mist encompassing his body, but as early morning rose, the air was beginning to rise in temperature. Out of the barracks the mountains provided no shade like they did in the valley. This meant blistering heat directly beaming down on to the building and training area.

Eryx stepped out of the barrack door following the other barrack thirteen members. This was the first time he managed to get a look at the layout of the military base. Twenty-six different stone buildings set in a semi-circle facing inwards, towards the mountain. In the centre of the base lay the roped dueling circle, some officer tents, an armory, medical centre and a training courtyard. These were high level facilities. King Leax ensured high quality equipment for his first line of defense.

Ξ

Fallax received a replying message from the king. *'Fallax, I am glad you have arrived safely. I have also attached instructions for the Tydell Captain to foretake, please ensure that information remains confidential and gets to its intended personnel'*. The metallic bird cracked its neck and flew off, presumably back to Poltan under the king's instructions. Fallax pondered over the decision to take a look at the second scroll containing information meant for a lower ranked officer but it was the Kings demand, so he decided against it. He sought out the captain in order to deliver it personally.

Ξ

All lined up, Eryx scoured the other Squads, noticing a depleted Barrack twenty-three further along the line, showing the impact of their duel. The surrounding barracks looked over the three men of barrack thirteen with discontent. Due to the lack of war and border disputes in recent years, the city guard had become a place of competition rather than regimented training in preparation for battle. Squads became their own entities rather than part of the bigger group.

They set off, another enduring test of fitness and mental resilience. Scrambling over the rocky maze and maintaining balance across the sand ridden surfaces. Eryx knew anything but first was a failure.

Ξ

Gremallax sat in his personal office built amongst the other tents. He held the highest rank in the Tydell City Guard but in comparison to the Thearon National Guard he was rather small. Despite his relevance nationally he was still rather important, he had just had the pleasure of meeting General Fallax, *right miserable bastard,* who hand delivered a message from the king himself, personal wax seal and all. He opened the scroll, '*Captain Gremallax, below are clear instructions about…*' the door to his barrack-based office swung open, Urasmus stood in its frame flustered "Sir, you're going to want to see this!"

The two of them jogged to the finish line, surprisingly three exhausted men stood, doubled over sucking in copious amounts of air. "How are they back already?" Gremallax checked his watch. A fancy new device that used the worlds rotation to determine time, only the elite had access to this level of technology. Urasmus looked as bewildered as the captain "Honestly sir, the Craekee has confirmed that every scout post saw them, no short cuts. These jokers can't be human". Gremallax looked closer at the men and noticed that his new love interest's son was amongst the physically exceptional soldiers. "Urasmus, take them with you to patrol the valley, they deserve to skip this afternoon's squad duels for that exceptional performance."

Gremallax turned back, heading to his office to finish that letter, he caught sight of the General looking 'happy' as ever in the viewing gallery. He decided to smile at Fallax but got a stern look in return.

Ξ

Fallax walked down to congratulate the men who completed the run in such emphatic fashion. They had gone before he had chance to talk to them. "I'd like to speak with those men please sergeant" Fallax said in a tone that suggested it was optional however both men knew it wasn't. Urasmus caught up with the trio and instructed them to join Fallax in the Officers tent.

"Come in gentlemen, have a seat." Fallax greeted them as they sat on the bench in front of him. "Listen men. I am General Fallax, leader of the Thearon National Guard. After watching you train I am highly impressed" the tone then got more serious, matching his face. "I will need personal protection while here in Tydell as my usual soldiers are out recruiting. How does that sound?"

The General peered forward, a reluctant grin creeping from his lips. This made Rannax suspicious as did Bard based on the look he threw to Rannax. But better to keep those suspicious types close he thought.

"Yes. We would be honoured sir," lying to the general. "We will serve and protect".

Eryx stood there still recovering from the intense feat he'd just taken. Now he's being dragged into defending the highest-ranking officer in the Thearon army. How does he object? Massively underqualified yet he couldn't object.

"I will arrange the movement of your accommodation to my inn" Fallax stated before tending to some paper work on his desk.

Ξ

The news had reached Gremallax that the General had acquired the services of barrack thirteen. This made him rage. Who did this man think he was, depleting his troops for the sake of having a personal guard. The audacity! He stormed out of his office heading straight for Fallax as the sun began to lower.

Ξ

It would be their last task as a barrack and Eryx had only been in it for a handful of days. They were walking round the north west side of the mountain, passing the barns and farm houses that accommodated the farmers that resided here in Tydell. The walk was not long but it allowed him time to admired the wonderful landscape as well as time to think.

This is nothing like Poltan. Eryx was eleven when his mother woke him in a flustered haste, dragging him out of bed, ushering him out of their home into the back of the carriage. That night is one that sits firmly in his mind. A day he will never forget.

They cornered the last part of the farming sector heading up the dirt track into the compact stone housing of tier ten that littered the valley floor. The valley was very large, he was another ten-minute walk from his neighbourhood.

The narrow streets reminded him of the hallways in his home back in the capital, fine white marble walls and floor, a grand staircase and glass chandelier. He doesn't particularly miss the money or the luxuries that came with wealth. He misses the safety it brought, especially for his mother and sister. They travelled further towards the centre heading for the markets. The ones he had days earlier been loitering in.

"Here we are you bunch of flax heads!" Flax was a recreational drug, used quite commonly amongst the poor. It gave you more energy but was highly addictive and wasn't cheap. "How could he be on Flax, he's far too fat," Rannax chuckled at his own joke while pointing towards Bard. The denser man whacked his friend in the private area with a swift flick of the hand.

Urasmus took back control of the group, "We have to just patrol this area, look out for thieves, illegal substance trading or arms dealing anything else just let go. Not worth the paperwork" he then set off into the labyrinth.

Eryx was left to scout out crime alone but he knew this place like the back of his hand. Out of the three members of Barrack Thirteen, Eryx was the only one who had actually grown up in Tydell. The city's narrow, cobbled streets and the smell of the harbour were familiar to him, a comfort in contrast to the alien world of the army. The others had come from far-flung corners of the realm, each carrying the weight of their past like armour.

Bard hailed from the eastern town of Yelast, a bustling port known for its fish markets and clamour of trade. He had once been a fishmonger, hauling crates of saltwater catch from the docks to the market stalls, shouting prices over the roar of gulls and waves. That life had been honest but hard, until a misstep—or a betrayal—had drawn him into trouble. Tax fraud, Rannax reminded him with a dry grin, "No, actually… that was all you." Bard had laughed it off, but the glint of unease in his eyes suggested that the memory still stung. The incident had pushed him out of Yelast, forcing him to start anew in a city that had no knowledge of his past mistakes.

Rannax, in contrast, was a man of mystery. He spoke little of his own history, his words measured and sparse, revealing only fragments. Eryx knew enough to piece together parts of it: he and Bard had first met in Yelast, and it had been Rannax who had helped Bard move to this new city, arranging lodging and work, ensuring his friend had a foothold in unfamiliar territory. That journey—long days on winding roads, nights under starlit skies, and shared hardships—had cemented a bond between them stronger than mere camaraderie.

Eryx, still new to the group, could sense the depth of their connection. Bard's easy laughter and boisterous energy seemed to spring from the trust and loyalty forged with Rannax, while Rannax's calm, almost impenetrable demeanour was the steady anchor that kept Bard's fire from burning too recklessly. And somewhere in the mix, Eryx was learning to find his own place, relying on their guidance while discovering his own strength.

Eryx had been so caught up in his thoughts that the loud cry brought him back to reality. The sound had come from a street outside of the market perimeters. He wondered into the alleyway that lead to the following street, the darkness initially masked the two figures that were further down. The whimpers continued but were muffled, Eryx encroached to get a better view. One of the figures darted the opposite direction leaving the other slumped against one side of the alley. Eryx reached the man. He was dead.

Ξ

Gremallax came out of the heated debate with Fallax even angrier than when he had entered. His superior had too much authority and stubbornness to release Barrack thirteen from their new responsibilities. Gremallax was irate for two reasons: because of the way the general had undermined his position and that he had disrupted his romantic endeavors by taking on his cleaners' son.

CHAPTER 8-FORGETTING THE PAST

Gremallax stepped into his home, head bowed, shoulders heavy. The weight of the day clung to him like a storm cloud. He had fought—no, *battled*—to keep her son safe, and for a fleeting moment, relief had flickered across him. But it was tinged with guilt. He had only known Alicius a short time, yet he felt the sharp, gnawing ache of a parent's worry as if it were his own. He knew all too well what it was to fear for a child.

Years ago, he had lost his wife and daughter in a house fire. He had been stationed in the barracks when it happened, unaware, powerless. The helplessness had destroyed him, left scars that no blade or victory could ever erase. Now, he realized with a sinking heart that he had placed another parent in that same torment. He had made a promise to keep her son safe—and he had only partially succeeded.

"So…how did he get on?" Alicius' voice trembled, quiet but brittle, as she packed her belongings.

Gremallax hesitated, the words heavy on his tongue. "He did marvellous… however, that's the issue."

Her face fell. "Issue?" Her voice cracked slightly, holding back the tide of tears she refused to let spill.

"There have been… developments in Thearon-Karathal," he said slowly, each word deliberate, "disagreements of such magnitude that the King has ordered the National Guard to intervene." He watched her hands clench, fingers whitening. Her breath hitched, and the first glimmer of tears formed in her eyes.

"The General of the army… he saw Eryx's performance in weapons training," Gremallax continued, his voice quieter now. "And—he has made him… and the barrack—his personal guard."

The words hit her like a physical blow. Alicius sank to her knees, the sound of her collapse sharp against the quiet of the room. Gremallax stepped closer instinctively, though he knew no comfort he offered could fully reach her. Her face, etched with shock and fear, betrayed the knowledge she carried from her previous life. She knew General Fallax. Knew the danger. Knew, with chilling certainty, that her first-born was now bound to a peril far greater than the ordinary training ground.

Gremallax clenched his fists, rage and helplessness twisting in his chest. He wanted to shield her, to absorb the threat himself, but he could do nothing but watch. And yet, despite her tears, her trembling, her fear, there was a flicker of resilience—her maternal instinct, raw and fierce, burning brighter than any despair.

Ξ

First week on the job now he was protecting such a valuable man. Eryx stood outside the room of the General, Rannax and Bard either side of him.

The two warriors had given him a pep talk the previous night and again this morning. 'Stay close, listen to us and you will be fine,' were the reassuring words he'd received.

First assignment was to escort the General back down to the barracks, Fallax wanted to begin his training regime in preparation for battle against Karathal. There was no trouble, nice and simple journey as they strolled up to the lines of squads ready to go off on their morning run through the rocky terrain. Fallax ordered that he wanted formation training to be done immediately. Eryx admired the leadership qualities of Fallax, the way he commanded the entire army was impressive.

"Listen here men, you are now serving your king directly. This is the biggest honour of your lives. You will fight until you can't no more. Anyone who gives up or chooses to leaves these barracks will be seen as treasonous. I want to see all you men survive, so listen and follow my orders. You will be fine!" Fallax finished his speech and the men stood taller, posture straightened. He had already lifted the mood in the camp.

Eryx scanned the troops confused as there seemed to be an increase in numbers. Quite considerably as well. He turned and asked Rannax why and how the population of the barracks had increased. "Lad, we're off to war. Every capable man in Tydell has been summoned to fight for their country". The pace at which Fallax's group of captains had rallied all these men was inspiring. Apparently, this was happening all across the north of Thearon.

Ξ

Fallax stood at attention beside Urasmus, flanked by the rest of the captains and sergeants, each rigid in the formal formation dictated by the General's protocols. The organization of the barracks was sound, disciplined, but subtle tensions rippled beneath the surface. Rivalries between units, simmering competition, and the recent influx of an additional one hundred and fifty men all posed potential challenges—especially on a battlefield where cohesion could mean the difference between victory and disaster.

"How did the recruitment drive proceed?" Fallax asked, his tone clipped, betraying both curiosity and concern. The lines of his face hinted at frustration with the Tydellese resistance.

"We encountered significant refusals," Urasmus reported, voice steady but firm. "Approximately eighty recruits were persuaded to join; the rest enlisted voluntarily. There remain another three hundred able-bodied men in Tydell who meet the criteria for service."

Fallax nodded once, his gaze sweeping across the assembled officers. Each statistic and report were weighed not only for tactical value but also for political consequence. He understood the importance of restraint—forcing the citizens of Tydell into service risked unrest. Strategically, it was safer to offer a choice here, while in the northern borderlands, men would have no such option; there, conscription was unavoidable.

"Maintain pressure," Fallax instructed, his voice low but commanding. "Document every refusal, every willing recruit. Ensure the battalions understand the hierarchy and their obligations. Morale is as critical as manpower. Any sign of disunity, any hesitation, will be noted."

Urasmus inclined his head. "Understood, General. Orders will be executed. Reports will follow."

Fallax allowed a moment to survey the assembled officers. Discipline, training, loyalty—these were the pillars that would hold the army together. Yet he could feel the undercurrent of friction, a reminder that men could be broken as easily by politics and pride as by swords and spears. He would have to navigate both to maintain control.

Ξ

As training began, Eryx's eyes darted across the field, scanning the disciplined chaos of soldiers moving in tight formations. And then he saw him—Eroge. His best friend was struggling to keep pace with the seasoned soldiers, legs pumping and arms flailing just slightly behind the rhythm. Sweat gleamed on his brow, and his uniform clung to him from exertion, but he didn't give up. Eryx's chest tightened with a mix of worry and excitement.

He wanted to rush over, call out to him, tell him everything that had happened over the last whirlwind of days—the victories, the fears, the dizzying intensity of weapons training—but rules and orders pinned him in place like a soldier frozen in inspection.

Eryx shifted his weight from foot to foot, unable to still the frantic beating of his heart. "Rannax, him there, the tall, large one... we need him on this team," he thought, every muscle in his body buzzing with urgency. His mind raced: if he could convince Rannax and Bard, if he could get them to see Eroge's potential, then maybe— just maybe—he could keep his friend safe amid the chaos.

The sounds of clashing wooden weapons and shouted commands filled his ears, but Eroge's determined movements stood out like a beacon. Eryx's stomach twisted, equal parts anticipation and dread. Could he really pull this off? Could he navigate the rigid structure of the barracks and somehow mould the team to protect someone he cared for? The thought sent a shiver down his spine, mingling fear and exhilaration into a single, overwhelming pulse.

Ξ

Alicius wasn't annoyed with Gremallax. She understood he had no authority over the situation—her worry for Eryx was hers alone—but still, seeing him gave her a quiet comfort. "Morning, Sir," she said as she stepped into the Captain's home, the words slightly warmer than necessary. Over the past few days, she'd begun to look forward to these brief encounters. Gremallax had a way of commanding the room without ever demanding it, and slowly, he was growing on her.

"How are you holding up?" His voice carried a subtle hint of guilt, soft enough that only she could hear it.

"Listen, I'll try again today, but…" he began, hesitating as if the weight of his own failures lingered on his tongue.

Alicius cut him off gently, a small, reassuring smile tugging at her lips. "Honestly, it's okay. A mother worries at the best of times—I'm sure he'll be fine." Their eyes met, a flicker of unspoken disagreement passing between them, a silent acknowledgment neither wanted to voice aloud.

For a brief moment, the world seemed to shrink to just the two of them in the quiet of the room. Gremallax's gaze lingered on her longer than necessary, and Alicius felt a flutter she hadn't felt in years. When he finally straightened, offering a polite bow and a small smile, she felt her pulse quicken. "Anyway, I best be off. If you need anything, just let me know."

Their eyes met again as he departed, a lingering tension hanging between them—charged, intimate, unspoken. She caught herself watching his back until he disappeared from view, and a small, almost guilty smile crept onto her face. Was she really beginning to like this man?

Her mind raced. She knew the implications—a woman of her standing pursuing a man like Gremallax would invite scandal, ridicule, and countless whispered judgments. And yet, a small defiant spark whispered that it didn't matter. For the first time in years, she felt something raw and unexpected—a warmth that reached beyond worry, beyond duty.

CHAPTER 9- BUILDING A TEAM

Everyone had surprisingly agreed to let Eroge join Fallax's personal guard. Rannax thought it was a sensible move to strengthen the squad, and Fallax trusted his instincts. Eryx, meanwhile, held deep respect for the General—his discipline, his calm authority, and the way he balanced strategy with intuition. That was the man he wanted to emulate.

Eroge staggered out of the General's office, shoulders slumped, clearly exhausted. Eryx couldn't tell if it was the walk to the office or the morning's relentless training that weighed him down. Without warning, the large man grabbed Eryx and practically crushed him in a bear hug.

"What on earth is going on? My dad made me join the army, then I'm running around clueless for hours. Now I'm part of some elite personal guard for the highest-ranking officer in the whole country. Rabuga save me!"

Eryx blinked, momentarily startled by the invocation. Rabuga—the titan said to slumber along the Karathal Peninsula—was considered a relic of superstition in Thearon. Openly worshipping the titan marked someone as an outsider, someone who dared flout the dominant religious traditions of the land. The priests of Thearon frowned upon such beliefs, and many citizens quietly mocked it.

Eroge, however, didn't seem to notice—or care—about the subtle cultural condemnation. His faith was raw and unashamed, a connection to something older and larger than any officer, any order, any law. Eryx found himself grinning despite the chaos.

"Join the club! At least you haven't had to do desert runs like I had to," Eroge's eyed widened with the fear of running, "Thank you, thank you, thank you!" the red-haired behemoth gratefully responded, crushing Eryx with a hug again.

"You two lovers going to stop tickling each other long enough to come train?" Bard interrupted the reunion with the snide remark. The two young men followed their seniors off to the armory.

Rannax requested his usual weapon, the spherical mallet. Bard just grabbed his shield from behind the counter leaving the girl attending the armory in disbelief. Eroge went next and just asked for a bow and arrow. A man of his size should be carrying a long sword according to Bard but Eroge was too nervous for such a big weapon, even if he did make them every day of his life. Finally, Eryx stepped forward. "What would you like?" asked the attendant, her voice calm but warm.

Eryx's stomach lurched. He stared at the ground, fumbling with his words, suddenly shy in a way he had never felt before. "Can I… uh… have the bow staff and the throwing knives, please?" he mumbled, eyes fixed stubbornly on the stone floor.

She nodded and began to turn away, but Eryx couldn't stop himself from sneaking another glance. Her golden hair shimmered in the morning light, cascading past her shoulders down to the middle of her back. The curve of her figure was subtle but undeniably graceful, moving with a natural confidence that made his chest tighten.

Then, as if sensing his gaze, she met his eyes—deep, swirling green, like the forest after a storm—and for a brief heartbeat, the world seemed to shrink. Eryx felt heat creep into his face, his pulse skipping in a way that startled him. Something in the way she held her gaze made him aware, almost painfully, of the fluttering in his chest.

For the first time, Eryx realized that this wasn't just admiration for a skilled attendant—it was something sharper, something that made him nervous and excited all at once. And, just perhaps, the subtle lift of her brow and the faint curve of her lips suggested that the feeling might be… mutual.

He was locked into her gaze and his smile grew matching hers, their hands touched as she passed him the items he had requested. He began to walk away, repeatedly turning back to check if she was still looking. Unfortunately, other soldiers had occupied her attention.

They entered the combat pavilion. A covered space with padded flooring where the men could fight with less risk of injury. Rannax dragged Eroge onto the slightly raised area and began to talk him through some defense techniques. Eryx couldn't hear the exact details as Bard was muttering on about how his shield was too big and his back was too old to carry it anymore. The two giants then began sparring. Rannax was the aggressor, moving Eroge around the contest area, the large black smith did well to use his thick limbs to block the attacks. Rannax was obviously holding back but he was still forceful, throwing calculated punches to the body and head. A swing right hook caught Eroge sweetly on the jaw, the whole pavilion stopped at the sickening sound. Even Rannax was shocked at the purity of his shot. Eroge just brushed it off and continued to shift his feet and hold his defensive stance against his squad leader.

They finished up and stepped down from the square platform. "That, big fella, is some chin you've got there." said Bard to Eroge as he sat on a bench almost inhaling the water from his canteen. "Are you even dazed?" Rannax asked. "No, I don't think so. It didn't feel that bad really." Everyone was impressed with him.

Eryx was next up, facing the smaller but definitely heavier and more experienced Bard.

The raised square in the centre of the barracks was padded with thick mats, absorbing every impact, every grunt, every thud of a body meeting the floor. Sunlight streamed through high windows, casting harsh lines across the training area. Eryx stood opposite Bard, barefoot and unarmed, feeling the nervous tension coiling tight in his stomach.

Bard grinned, cracking his knuckles. "Ready to learn, kid?" His tone was playful but carrying an unmistakable edge.

Eryx swallowed hard. "I… I'll try."

The spar began with Bard pressing forward immediately, his movements fluid and precise. He aimed to test Eryx's defence, jabbing, sweeping, and trying to use his superior reach to keep Eryx off balance. Eryx stumbled, ducking too late, taking a light blow to the shoulder, barely catching Bard's next strike as it grazed him.

Every time Eryx tried to counter, Bard's experience dominated—he was faster, smarter, and far more coordinated. Sweat beaded along Eryx's brow as he absorbed another shove, another grapple attempt, and another expertly timed sweep that nearly sent him sprawling. The world seemed to narrow to the pounding of his heart, the scrape of feet on the padded floor, the sound of Bard's heavy breathing.

And then something strange happened. A surge, sudden and unexplainable, flowed through him. Where before his strikes had lacked weight, now they carried force he hadn't realized he possessed. His arms moved faster than he expected, his legs steadier. Bard lunged for a takedown, confident he had Eryx's rhythm figured out— but Eryx twisted, pivoting with raw, surprising strength, and shoved Bard back with a force that rattled the older soldier.

Bard blinked, taken aback. "What—?"

Eryx seized the moment. With a flurry of instinctive movements, he sidestepped a grab, spun low, and slammed a solid hip check into Bard's midsection, sending the larger man stumbling across the mats. He didn't pause. Channelling the sudden surge of power coursing through him, Eryx grappled Bard's arm, twisted sharply, and leveraged his own weight to pin him down.

For a breathless moment, time froze. Bard's eyes widened, not with anger, but genuine shock. Eryx's own chest heaved, disbelief mingling with triumph. Somehow, against every expectation, he had bested the veteran.

Bard finally exhaled, a slow, amused grin spreading across his face as he pushed himself up. "Well... I'll be damned. Didn't think you had it in you, kid."

Eryx staggered to his feet, legs trembling, but the rush of exhilaration made him dizzy with adrenaline. He could hardly believe it himself—but as Bard clapped a hand on his shoulder, the warmth and respect in the gesture confirmed it.

Ξ

A couple days had passed since Eroge had joined and things had been running rather smoothly. They got up, followed their superior around all day then went back to the inn way up in the second tier. That was the only difficult part, climbing the steps. Rannax and Bard discussed the secret meetings Fallax had frequently, they were a highly suspicious duo. Eryx understood the confidentiality those meetings must require.

CHAPTER 10- THE MOMENT

It had become their ritual. Every morning, she would drop Oliax off with her friend, then climb the first tier of the north mountain, giving herself enough time to catch Gremallax before he left for the day. Each step upward was a mixture of excitement and nervous anticipation, a thrill she hadn't felt in years.

Their mornings together were growing longer, laughter spilling between them over the steam of shared tea. Walls she had spent three years meticulously building were crumbling, piece by piece. The past—painful, heavy, isolating—seemed to drift further away with every smile, every teasing remark, every shared glance.

"Well, if it isn't little Miss Eager!" Gremallax greeted, eyes twinkling, as she entered. He was rising earlier these days too, clearly making the effort to see her. The casualness of the greeting made her pulse quicken. She sank into her chair as the sun rose over the mountains, painting gold across the landscape and through the expansive window. Time seemed suspended as they talked, their conversation light and effortless.

When the moment of parting came, her chest tightened. How had she fallen for him so completely, so unexpectedly? He left with that same joyous grin that had first captured her attention—the one she found impossible to resist. She sat back, cheeks warm, heart fluttering like a teenager's, and realized just how far her carefully constructed defences had fallen.

Suddenly, the door burst open, and Gremallax's voice rang out, almost breathless: "Alicius, have dinner with me tomorrow night!"

He froze, awareness dawning on him, and quickly corrected himself. "I mean—please, will you have dinner with me tomorrow night? I'm sorry—I'm just... nervous. You're... you're such a remarkable woman."

Alicius's heart skipped a beat. Her answer tumbled out in a rush, eager and genuine: "Yes! Yes, of course, I will!"

Relief and something warmer crossed Gremallax's face. He stepped closer, hugging her gently, and pressed a brief, tender kiss to her cheek before turning to leave, still glowing with that irrepressible energy.

Alicius sank into her chair, heart racing, cheeks flushed. She knew this was only the beginning. She had to tell Oliax—she had to prepare herself. And somewhere in the back of her mind, she realized the thrill of anticipation was just as intoxicating as the man himself. Tomorrow night would change everything.

CHAPTER 11- HEIGL

Arriving in Heigl in the early hours, Romius moved like a shadow through the narrow back streets encircling the town square. Days of travel had left his legs sore, but the town—a mid-sized settlement in Thearon's midlands—was worth the effort. Tonight, rest was secondary; his target, a man of influence whose name was irrelevant but whose status mattered, awaited in the manor at the square's edge.

Romius pressed himself against a wall of rough stone, eyes fixed on the manor. The square slept under a blanket of mist, the benches and statues silent witnesses to the approaching storm. From his hooded jacket, he pulled a coin and rolled it across his calloused knuckles, letting it spin, hover, then hover higher, as if resisting gravity itself.

A faint smile tugged at his lips. Steelmancy. The manipulation of Thearon steel was a rare art, mastered only through destiny and discipline. His father, Romiax, had begun teaching him as a child before leaving him to forge his own path. Steelmancy allowed him to bend metal to his will, augment his strength, speed, and resilience beyond normal human limits.

Romius' gaze swept the manor windows. Offices on the left, living quarters to the far left—there, the target slept.

The red bandana over his nose and mouth hid his features, leaving only his eyes, sharp and predatory. He leapt across the square with fluid grace, every muscle coiled, every step silent.

The door to the manor loomed ahead. Romius' fingers brushed the steel handle, and it trembled beneath his command. The lock gave way with a whisper of warping metal, and he slipped inside, ghost-like, into the dim corridor.

Then the alarms rang. A single torch-lit guard rounded the corner, eyes widening. Steel bent at Romius' command, a shroud of force enveloping him as he struck. Metal met metal with a sharp, ringing impact, and the guard was thrown backward, skidding across the stone. Romius' heart hammered, not from fear, but anticipation. This was the dance he had trained for.

More guards surged into the hall. Steel surged through him, strengthening his limbs, his reflexes doubling, tripling beyond human capacity. A sword met his shoulder; his arm shifted like liquid steel, the blade snapping harmlessly into the wall. He countered, sending the nearest soldier flying across the corridor with a whip of metallic energy, the sound echoing like thunder.

Romius moved like a storm incarnate, every strike precise, every motion bending metal and momentum to his will. His target's bedroom was in sight now. The door shuddered under his approach, and he pressed a hand against the frame. Steel whispered through his veins, fortifying his body, sharpening his senses. He could almost taste the tension in the air, the fear of those who would dare oppose him.

Ξ

The deed was done. He dipped Domir in the fountain to wash the blood from his trusty axe. No one would find the Mayor until morning, and by then the sirens would wail and word would reach Poltan. Romius would be long gone, though his bounty would only grow. The death of a small town's mayor might normally be a local concern—but this man had once been an advisor to King Leax. Suddenly, the stakes were far higher.

Romius moved through the shadows, his mind flickering back to the reason he had become Thearon's most wanted man. Eighteen years had passed since the king's betrayal, when Romius had been set up as the fall guy in a political scheme far above his station. Loyalty had been repaid with treachery, and the man he had once served with faith had cast him out, leaving him hunted and reviled. That wound had never healed—it had only sharpened his resolve.

Keeping to the back streets, he headed north toward Tydell. Horses and carts were too obvious, too tempting for spies to track. Foot travel, winding through the woodlands that dotted the heart of Thearon, was slow but safe. Every step reminded him why he moved in the shadows now, why trust was a weapon sharper than any steel.

CHAPTER 12- MOVING ON

"Mother, you look amazing!" Oliax's smile was shy but radiant, her honest eyes lighting up as she looked at Alicius.

Alicius felt a flutter of warmth. "Thank you, darling," she said softly, smoothing the hem of her hand-sewn green dress. The fabric clung to her curves, the result of days of careful labour—scrubbed, pressed, and stitched with painstaking care. Yet in her mind, it wasn't enough. Not good enough for Gremallax.

Oliax's small hand found hers, and Alicius squeezed it gently. The girl's excitement was contagious, but it also deepened her own apprehension. How much change could she put her children through? The past few weeks had been full of upheaval, with Eryx gone and the barracks taking over so much of their lives. Could Oliax handle her mother stepping out, trusting someone else to care for her even for one night?

"Your brother is off duty today," Alicius said, forcing a calmness into her voice. "He's going to come look after you tonight."

At that moment, Eryx arrived. Alicius' heart skipped. Seeing him again after weeks away, grown yet still her little boy, she felt both pride and a pang of worry. It was strange to imagine him and his sister being cared for without her, to think of leaving them while she went for a dinner with a man. For all her carefulness, she knew it was a necessary step—not just for her, but for them.

She leaned down, kissing Oliax lightly on the forehead, then Eryx. "Remember the rules," she said gently, her voice carrying a trace of a smile. "I'll be back before the moon reaches its peak. You both behave, and keep each other company."

Oliax hugged her tightly, the small gesture anchoring Alicius' heart. Letting go was always the hardest part. She paused, running a hand through Oliax's hair, feeling the bond between them strengthen with every shared heartbeat. "Be brave, little one," she whispered. "I'll be back soon."

With one last glance, Alicius left, climbing toward tier one, leaving her children in each other's care—and in the quiet hope that they would be safe, happy, and resilient even in her brief absence.

Ξ

Climbing the final few steps, Alicius' heart skipped. There he was—Gremallax, a grand figure in pristine blue and gold uniform, standing tall, commanding yet somehow warm. He offered his hand, helping her up the last step, and brushed a quick, polite kiss against her cheek. Butterflies erupted in her stomach. *Why am I so nervous? Does he feel the same way?*

"We're going to a place called the Cavern of Lights," he said, his deep voice smooth as velvet. "They have lovely fish, imported from Yelast." His eyes flicked over her, noting the slight hesitation, the flutter of nerves she couldn't hide. "Don't worry about the price," he added, his smile teasing yet sincere. "The owner personally invited me and a guest. I helped him with a tax issue not so long back. And before you say it, I know you don't need charity—it's just a gift."

Even in the brief time they'd known each other, he read her like an open scroll, sensing her fears, her restraint. Alicius brushed a strand of hair from her face, suddenly conscious of how small her gestures felt under his gaze. "Thank you," she whispered, her voice softer than she intended.

When they entered, the grandeur of the place threatened to overwhelm her: velvet drapes, softly glowing lanterns, the murmur of well-dressed patrons. But Gremallax's presence grounded her. They were treated like royalty—greeted at the door, cut through the queue, and escorted to a booth with plush seating and the finest silverware.

He leaned close as they settled in, and Alicius caught a faint scent of him—smoky, clean, intoxicating. She felt a thrill at the nearness, a pull in her chest she hadn't expected. As she shuffled into the booth, she instinctively corrected a misplaced soup spoon, and he chuckled quietly, a soft, warm sound that made her cheeks flush.

"You always notice the small things," he said, eyes twinkling. "Even here, surrounded by splendour, you notice the details. It's… remarkable."

Her pulse quickened. She dared a glance up, locking eyes with him. His gaze held her, steady and appreciative, sending heat through her veins. Every polite gesture, every careful word between them seemed charged now with a subtle intimacy, a promise unspoken but deeply felt. She realized, with a mixture of exhilaration and fear, that her walls—built so carefully over years—were crumbling in the gentle weight of his attention.

And for the first time in a long while, Alicius allowed herself to hope.

Ξ

They talked and drank late into the night, laughter spilling easily between them like a pair of old friends reuniting. Alicius couldn't believe how natural it felt, how effortless their conversation was, or how wonderful the night had become. Every glance, every smile from

Gremallax made her pulse quicken in a way she hadn't expected.

Eventually, the evening had to end. They left the Cavern of Lights, hands brushing, then intertwining. His boldness was palpable. "Would you like to come back to mine for a drink?" he asked, eyes locking with hers, a teasing spark dancing in their depths. His confidence, so unshakable, was now undeniably alluring to her.

Alicius hesitated, torn between her responsibilities and the magnetic pull of the moment. "I have to get back to my children, but thank you—for this night, for everything."

"It was my pleasure," he said, his voice low, smooth. He whistled to a passing cart. "Cart driver, Tenth Tier, please. I am sure this will suffice." He handed the begrudging man a generous collection of coins, then turned back to her, eyes lingering. "Take the cart—it will be much safer."

Alicius shook her head, smiling despite herself. "How am I ever going to pay you back for all this?"

Before she could think further, he closed the distance, capturing her lips with his. Shock coursed through her, followed by a warmth she couldn't resist. Her body responded almost instinctively, lips parting to meet his in a slow, tentative kiss. The world fell away, leaving only the two of them suspended in that fleeting, perfect moment.

When they finally parted, breath mingling, she stepped gracefully into the carriage. The door shut behind her, and she couldn't help but smile like a young girl experiencing first love. For the first time in years, she felt unburdened, free to simply enjoy the moment—and perhaps, let herself fall a little.

Ξ

Eryx and Oliax kicked the ball back and forth in the candlelit room, the warm glow flickering across their faces. They were breaking one of their mother's rules, but the quiet thrill made them laugh all the same. Eryx's shot rolled through the doorway—point for him.

As Oliax bent to retrieve the ball, a sudden, piercing screech ripped through the night, followed by a heavy crash from outside. Eryx's heart skipped. He lunged forward, shielding his sister instinctively. She was unharmed, but wide-eyed and trembling.

"Go to your room," he commanded, his voice low but urgent. "Bolt the lock Eroge fitted. Only open to three knocks—like this." He tapped out the pattern sharply; Oliax didn't hesitate, scurrying off with uncommon obedience.

Eryx crept to the door, easing it open just enough to peer into the shadowed street. Panic churned in the night air. Noise erupted at the far end of the street—screaming, pounding hooves. A frantic horse bolted straight past, heading toward the fields. Horses don't wander here unless someone important is present.

His pulse quickened. Normally, he would have locked up and prayed for his family's safety, but tonight was different. His mother was out—potentially with someone wealthy and influential. That horse could only mean one thing: danger. And if the passenger was his mother… he had to act, now.

Ξ

Lay on the floor of the overturned cart, Alicius' head throbbed fiercely, blood trickling down her temple and staining the fine fabric of her green dress. The world swayed with every heartbeat. The cart had tipped violently on its side—how, she didn't know—but the fear curling in her chest was immediate and sharp.

Outside, chaos reigned. The crack of a whip split the night air as the driver tried desperately to fend off the attackers. Shouts and the clatter of hooves and steel rang from the street beyond. Her pulse raced, her ears straining for every sound, trying to piece together what was happening.

With trembling hands, she pushed herself up just enough to peer out of the shattered window. Moonlight glinted off the edges of weapons, and shadowy figures darted across the cobblestones. Her stomach churned as she realized the bandits weren't intimidated—if anything, they advanced more aggressively.

The cart tilted again with a harsh groan, forcing her to brace against the side. Her head throbbed with each movement, vision swimming as adrenaline surged through her veins. She knew she couldn't stay pinned inside, trapped and helpless. She needed to see, to understand, and somehow, survive.

Ξ

Eryx began to speed up as he saw what seem to be his mother rising from the crashed carriages window. He pulled the throwing knife from its sheath attached to his belt. He was there before he had thought through his plan. Seven men, one of him and the driver. "Screw it!" he launched the knife straight into the back of the closest man, he dropped in pain. Eryx swiftly retrieved the knife and began his attack on a second man.

Rannax and Bard had been training him and Eroge intensely, working on a range of different fighting styles and building strength, speed and stamina. He was beginning to feel like it was working.

He blocked a swinging fist with his forearm and bestowed a lethal left jab to the bandit's ribcage. Cracks rippled through the man's body. *Two down, five to go.*

Eryx assessed his options three men were still being occupied be the manic driver who was flailing his whip around carelessly. The other two had begun to scale the carriage. That's where he needed to be.

With new found physical prowess, he dashed past the group attending to the driver and yanked the coat of one on the carriage. He came crashing to the ground. Without hesitation he climbed side of the vehicle and was met by one of the thieves on the top. His mother curled up inside, injured and afraid. He stared the man down, his response seemed to be fear. *Am I really that intimidating?*

The bandit dropped from the top, Eryx presumed to regroup. He didn't care he lifted his mother up and out the cart, "run around the back of the house and knock like this so Oliax will let you in" she nodded and sprinted off into the darkness.

He dropped down from the carriage, rolling to break his fall, and met five bandits charging toward him. For a moment, it seemed his improbable luck might carry him again. He ducked, swung, and rolled—landing a few lucky blows—but the bandits were relentless. One slammed his elbow into Eryx's back, another caught his leg, tripping him into the dirt. Dust and blood coated his face, stinging his eyes.

A punch to the jaw sent him sprawling, his vision blurring. He rose only to be kicked in the ribs, gasping for breath. His arms ached from blocking strikes, his legs wobbling as he stumbled over uneven cobbles. Every attack he landed seemed to cost him twice as much—his luck had run out.

The bandits surrounded him, relentless and precise. One knocked him down with a sweep of a boot, another slammed a fist into his side. Pain flared up his spine, his vision flickering between dark and light. He tried to strike back, but his movements were sloppy, desperate, failing.

Finally, they pushed him to the ground, kicking and hitting until he lay gasping, bruised, bloodied, and broken. One of the men raised a knife above him—an audible hiss of triumph.

Then, a strange, silvery mist began to seep across the courtyard, swirling unnaturally around Eryx. They shrieked and stumbled. Eryx's head lolled to the side, barely conscious. The last thing he saw before blacking out was the men staggering away in the mist.

.

Ξ

Beaten within an inch of his life, Eryx lay sprawled across the cobbled street, each stone pressing cruelly into his bruised body. The early morning mist clung to the uneven stones, curling around the wheel ruts and pooling in the depressions between them. Blood smeared the grey cobbles, mixing with the damp dew, leaving dark streaks that gleamed in the first hesitant rays of sunlight.

The narrow street was lined with aged buildings, their timbered frames sagging slightly, plaster cracked and worn from years of weather. Shutters hung crooked on windows, some rattling in the gentle morning breeze. A thin wisp of smoke curled lazily from a distant chimney, the scent of baked bread and wood smoke mingling with the metallic tang of blood and dust. Broken crates and discarded market debris littered the edges of the alleyways, remnants of the previous day's trade, now overlooked in the town's awakening.

Above, the early sun gilded the gables in a muted gold, casting long shadows that stretched across the street like silent witnesses to his defeat. A single lamp post, blackened with age, flickered weakly from the last vestiges of night, its glass catching droplets of dew. The faint clatter of carts on distant streets echoed through the alleyways, but here, in the narrow backstreets, silence pressed heavily, punctuated only by Eryx's ragged breaths.

A lamp attendant finally appeared, lantern in hand, the soft glow cutting through the mist. He knelt beside Eryx, brushing damp hair from the young man's bruised face. Turning him over carefully, the attendant checked for life—his fingers trembling slightly at the pale, bloodied skin. Against all odds, he was alive, barely. The faintest sign of a pulse flickered beneath the bruised collarbone, a fragile thread holding him to the waking world.

Ξ

"He'll recover... but it might take some time..." The voice was muffled, distant, as if it were coming from far away. Eryx's head throbbed with each heartbeat, and every sound felt warped and unreal. He couldn't make out the man's face—only the cadence of the words, a strange calmness in contrast to the chaos in his body.

Then—her voice. His mother's. Tight, trembling, breaking under the weight of fear. "Gremallax... what am I going to do?" The words were a whimper, raw and fragile.

"The doctor said he will recover," came another voice, firm and steady, though still edged with concern. "He needs rest! Come back to mine—both you and Oliax."

Eryx's chest heaved, each inhale sending sharp, shooting pains through his ribs. His eyelids felt impossibly heavy, as if weighted with lead. Every sense screamed to close, to escape the world—but through the fog, he forced his gaze open. One swollen eye cracked, letting in slivers of the room around him.

He saw movement—his family leaving. His mother's arm looped tightly with Oliax, guiding her down the hall. The sunlight from the doorway caught Oliax's hair as she glanced back, her green eyes wide, shimmering with worry. Eryx could only manage a faint flicker of recognition, a feeble attempt at reassurance.

The door clicked shut, muffling their voices and cutting him off from the warmth he so desperately needed. Alone, weak, and battered, Eryx felt the crushing weight of his vulnerability. His pulse slowed, but his mind raced—haunted by the memory of the fight, the pain in his chest, and the fear he had seen mirrored in Oliax's gaze.

Everything was quiet now, save for the ragged rhythm of his breathing. The world outside moved on, but here, in this dim, silent room, devastation pressed down like a living thing, and Eryx lay helpless beneath it.

Ξ

Alicius arrived at Gremallax's house with Oliax in tow, her heart heavy with worry. She felt a rare sense of safety here, but anxiety gnawed at her thoughts—what of her son? And how would her daughter cope with the aftermath of such violence?

"I think it's best if you stay here for now," Gremallax said firmly, his tone leaving no room for argument. "Use the guest rooms, just for a little while. The thought of you returning to those conditions frightens me." She nodded, relieved yet shaken, too afraid to face the reality they had fled.

When Eryx had pulled her free from the overturned carriage, she had sprinted straight to Oliax, scooping her up and refusing to stop until they had reached the front door of this sanctuary. Gremallax had acted immediately—no questions asked—arranging medical care and sending a patrol to track down the culprits. His calm efficiency was a balm to her frayed nerves.

"Thank you, Gremallax," Alicius said, her voice soft but resolute. "We'll gladly accept your generous offer." Poverty and circumstance had once dictated her path, forced her into corners where hope was scarce. But here, in this haven, she allowed herself to move forward, to breathe, and to imagine a life unshackled by fear.

CHAPTER 13- COMING BACK STRONGER

Oliax made it a point to see her brother every day since the accident. To her, he was a hero—her mother's saviour, a fighter against bad men, a real-life superhero.

She walked briskly down the corridor of the medical centre; every surface gleamed, every corner immaculate. In fact, every building in the ninth tier seemed to shine with the same precise care. Reaching the door to her brother's room, she was stopped by two imposing men.

"Move you potatoes!" she demanded, a mischievous smile tugging at her lips. Rannax and Bard chuckled, shaking their heads, and let her pass, ruffling her hair affectionately.

Inside, an aging man in crisp black military attire trimmed with forest green spoke quietly to her brother. Eroge stood on the other side of the bed, his finger pressed to his lips in a silent plea for quiet. Oliax mirrored the gesture instinctively, remembering how often her mother had done the same. *Probably because she likes to say what's on her mind... but she wants to control it,* Oliax thought, *just like me.*

"I'll let you rest now, boy," the general said, turning to leave. "I hope to have you back on your feet soon." The two guards at the door followed him out, leaving only Eroge.

"So, how's it going?" Eryx asked, his voice still tinged with exhaustion.

"Good," Eroge replied. "Rannax and Bard are teaching me more fighting techniques, and the fitness work is getting a little easier."

Eryx's face fell slightly, envy and admiration mixing in his expression. He loved learning, loved the thrill of new styles and skills.

"It'll be better when you're back," Eroge said with a knowing wink. "Then we can spar." Both knew that Eroge was much stronger—taller, wider, a living wall of muscle.

"It won't be long. Don't worry. I'll be back on my feet in no time," Eryx said, though a trace of doubt lingered in his tone.

"You two are boring me," Oliax piped up, instantly brightening the room. "Can I check your heartbeat again?"

With the practiced hands of someone who had watched doctors many times before, she grabbed the shiny equipment from the bedside and used it just as she had been shown—one end in her ears, the other pressed to Eryx's chest.

Joy spread across the room, warm and contagious. Laughter mingled with the rhythmic thump of his heart, and for a moment, the harshness of the outside world seemed miles away.

Ξ

Rannax led the way back to the barracks. Fallax had set up a makeshift office there, spending most of his time training the troops or holding meetings with senior officers. Yet Rannax's suspicion lingered—he was never allowed in those meetings, always forced to wait outside.

Bard, ever the optimist, tried to convince him otherwise. "We've worked hard to earn this post. Just enjoy it," he said. But Rannax couldn't. Not when a nagging hunch kept him on edge.

"Men, you may go train. I'll be leading barracks one through eight in today's exercises," Fallax called, striding toward the open fields without a backward glance.

Bard nudged Rannax sharply with his elbow. "Put a smile on your face, you miserable oaf," he teased, snapping Rannax out of his thoughts.

"Come on, let's do a bit of log running out in Exia," Bard said, striding over to the stack of sanded logs with handles. He lifted one over his shoulders and waited for Rannax to join.

"Listen, Bard… I need to find out what's going on with Fallax. Urgently," Rannax muttered, his voice tight with concern.

Bard's response was instant. He dropped the log to the sand with a resonant thud, shaking his head. "Leave the man alone, Ran. He's done nothing wrong since we've been with him. He's even paying for Eryx's medical bills now. Why can't you just move on?"

Rannax stared at him, momentarily speechless. Surprisingly, it was Bard—the stocky, easy-going soldier—who sounded like the voice of reason.

"Okay, okay," Rannax conceded, a faint smirk breaking through. "Come on then, porky. Pick that log up—we've got a run to survive."

With a grunt, the two hefted the dense logs onto their shoulders and began the run, sweat already soaking their shirts as the sweltering desert sun bore down on them. The air shimmered with heat, but neither man dared slow down, their footsteps pounding against the sand as their minds spun—one focused on physical endurance, the other on questions that still demanded answers.

Ξ

Eryx was all alone now. His family had stopped by, but they had to leave, and Eroge was called back to the barracks to assist General Fallax. He lay on his bed, eyes closed, staring at the ceiling, turning over the events in his mind. How had it all gone so wrong? And why hadn't the bandits he had injured been caught?

The door creaked open, and the captain stepped inside. "Ah, sorry—I thought you'd be asleep. I just came by to drop off these," he said, placing a neat pile of casual clothes on the chair in the corner. "Your mother insisted."

He paused, almost as if weighing his next words. "I would have come sooner, but I've been dealing with this debacle—and two of my sergeants were badly injured in some incident, so I've had to juggle their barracks training. Thankfully, the General stepped in…" His voice carried a subtle edge, a twinge of envy at the General's effortless authority.

Eryx didn't comment, only nodded. "Thank you very much, sir. And… thank you for taking in my mother and sister."

The captain's smile was slight, almost knowing, a shadow flickering in his eyes. "Don't worry about that, lad. Just focus on getting fit."

He left, and the door clicked shut. Eryx lay back down, closing his eyes again. Thoughts of the training ground and sparring with Eroge filled his mind. Warmth spread through his body, and a faint, bright light seemed to glow from within, easing the aches and pains that had plagued him. And somewhere in the quiet corners of his mind, he felt the subtle, calculating gaze of Gremallax, as if the man were always a step ahead—watching, waiting.

CHAPTER 14- FIRST DAY BACK

It was like nothing the doctors had ever seen. Bones that should have taken months to mend knitted themselves together in days. Severe internal bleeding, the kind that would have left most on the brink of death, seemed to vanish almost overnight. They checked and rechecked their notes, convinced they must have misjudged the extent of Eryx's injuries.

Yet even as his strength returned at an alarming rate, a quiet unease settled over the hospital. Staff whispered among themselves, exchanging furtive glances. Some spoke of the impossible speed of his recovery, others of fleeting shadows glimpsed near his room, as if unseen eyes were always watching.

Eryx himself felt it, in moments between sleep and wakefulness—a faint pulse of energy, subtle but insistent, threading through his veins. He didn't understand it, couldn't name it, but it made his body warm, his aches recede, and his strength surge beyond reason. The doctors were mystified, the nurses cautious, and somewhere beyond the white walls, forces unseen seemed to take note of each heartbeat, each breath, every step he took toward full recovery.

It was as if the world itself—or something within it—had chosen to intervene. And while Eryx remained unaware

of the full scope, the air around him had changed:
charged, expectant, and quietly dangerous.

Ξ

Eryx arrived at the barracks, the dry, dusty air filling his
nose and scratching the back of his throat. The heat
clung to his skin, but he welcomed it—it reminded him
of every gruelling run, every strike of the training staff,
every moment that had forged him from a street thief
into a soldier. This place wasn't just where he trained; it
was where he'd proven to himself that he was worth
more than the gutters of Tydell.

The courtyard was alive with activity. Soldiers lifted
logs, practiced their strikes, and shouted commands
across the dust-choked air. Each movement, each grunt
and scrape of boots against the cobblestones, seemed to
reverberate through Eryx's chest, reminding him of the
rhythm he'd fought so hard to master.

He spotted her then, arranging weapons in the corner of
the armoury. She moved with a precise grace, the way
her fingers traced the hilts and checked the edges of
blades making him pause for just a moment longer than
he intended. The sunlight caught the copper highlights in
her hair, and for a fraction of a second, the heat of the
desert and the sting of dust faded.

"You're late," she said, not looking up. The words were casual, but the faint lift of her brow betrayed her amusement.

Eryx grinned, leaning casually against the doorway. "Blame the bandits." His voice held that familiar mixture of teasing and challenge.

Finally, she looked up, and their eyes met. "I'm Charliax," she said, as though introducing herself formally to someone he already should have known.

"Eryx," he replied, letting his eyes linger a moment too long on hers. Her smile deepened, almost imperceptibly flirtatious, and she shook her head.

And for the first time in weeks, Eryx felt a spark of something beyond exhaustion —a dangerous, thrilling curiosity that made the barracks feel a little less like a place of training, and a little more like the start of something unexpected.

Ξ

Urasmus was waiting at the entrance, his arms crossed, boots planted firmly in the dirt. But the Sergeant's face… it was wrong. The usual gruff warmth was gone, replaced with a heaviness that pulled at his features. Behind him, Eroge stood in the shadow of the barracks, head bowed, eyes refusing to meet Eryx's. Bard and

Rannax lingered nearby, their usual banter absent, their silence heavier than the heat.

Eryx slowed his steps, his pulse beginning to thud in his ears. *Why are they looking at me like this?*

"Boy," Urasmus said finally, his voice low, almost reluctant. "It's good to see you on your feet again." He hesitated, shifting his weight. "Unfortunately, you can't be here."

Confusion flashed hot in Eryx's chest. "The doctors have cleared me—it's fine," he interrupted, desperate to dismiss whatever this was.

"No," Urasmus said, shaking his head, "that's not why." His eyes darted briefly to the others, as if searching for support he knew he wouldn't get. "Listen lad… this isn't my choice. The higher-ups have decided it would be bad publicity for the City Lord to allow you back. The story going around… it doesn't paint you in a good light."

Eryx blinked, trying to make sense of the words. *Bad publicity?* His mouth went dry. "What story?"

Urasmus didn't answer.

The silence was worse than any explanation.

It hit him like a blow. His knees buckled, and the hard ground rose to meet him. The dirt bit into his skin, but he barely felt it. His mind churned with unanswered questions—anger clawing at confusion, confusion drowning in disbelief.

Two figures stepped into view—armoured men, crests of the City Lord glinting in the sun. They emerged from Urasmus's cabin like shadows given form. Without a word, they seized him by the arms, their grip cold and unyielding.

"Tydell no longer requires your service," one of them intoned, voice flat with rehearsed authority, "and you are banished from this territory for your crimes against the City Lord."

Crimes. The word lodged in his chest like a splinter.

"Goodbye, Eryx," Urasmus said quietly, before turning and walking back into his cabin, not once looking over his shoulder.

Eroge had already gone, his broad frame retreating into the fields, urged away by Bard and Rannax. None of them could meet his eyes.

The guards didn't loosen their grip until they reached the edge of the wilderness beyond Tydell's mountain gates. There, they released him without ceremony.

He stumbled forward, the dust swirling at his feet.

The gates closed behind him with a hollow *thud*.

Silence.

Eryx turned to face the endless expanse beyond—the jagged peaks of the great mountains at his back, and the wild, untamed lands ahead. His pulse steadied, his breath slow and deliberate.

They'd taken his place. His honour. His future.

But not his will.

Not yet.

Ξ

The sun had spent the last three hours hammering him with its relentless heat, each ray like a burning spike against his skin as he trudged across the endless plains. The ground was cracked and pale, dust rising with every step, swirling around his boots in ghostly clouds. Sparse tufts of dry grass struggled against the arid soil, bowing and snapping beneath the wind that carried a faint taste of sand and stone.

Small settlements might exist somewhere in the distance, but the horizon offered little more than wavering heat and mirages. The South was forbidden, a path his mother had warned him against. East bled into the edge of the desert, where the sun's fury would only intensify. West was his only option, and even that promised only uncertainty. A lone abandoned shack had flashed past his eye hours earlier, its wooden boards warped and sealed, a silent reminder that refuge was not guaranteed.

The mountains of Tydell, once towering and imposing, now seemed distant and ghostly behind him, their sharp peaks softened by the haze rising from the plains. The sky above was a solid sheet of blue, unbroken by cloud or shadow, amplifying the solitude of the land. The wind whispered past him, carrying the faint echo of some unseen creature, but offered little relief from the oppressive heat.

Hours blurred together, the sun climbing higher and the air shimmering with its intensity. Each step weighed heavier than the last, dragging him forward not just across the land, but through the swirling haze of exhaustion, worry, and determination. And then, in the distance, a faint glimmer of life appeared—a cluster of structures, small but unmistakably human. A settlement. A sign that perhaps, after hours of walking under the sun's merciless glare, he was not completely alone.

Ξ

Exiled. The word looped in his mind like a cruel echo. Exiled. By the city guard. Him. Eryx. *Why?* He ran it over and over, dissecting every memory of the past week, the past month, searching for the slightest misstep, the tiniest spark that might have justified this. But there was nothing. He hadn't stolen, hadn't harmed anyone, hadn't betrayed the city—or had he?

The sun beat down on him as though mocking his uncertainty, the dust sticking to the sweat on his skin. What crime could a man like him have committed to deserve this? Was it a mistake? A misunderstanding? Or something more sinister, a deliberate act of someone with influence who wanted him gone? The thought made his stomach knot. Tydell had been home. Not the cramped rooms, the narrow streets, the cold stone, or even the familiar market smells, but the rhythm of life there—the camaraderie, the small victories, the routines he knew by heart. And now it was all torn away.

He ran through every conversation he'd had with the guards, every interaction that might have sparked their ire. Nothing. Just empty, stone-faced men delivering judgment with no explanation. *No trial, no chance to defend myself, nothing.* It didn't make sense. The city he had sworn to protect, that he had scraped, fought, and bled for, had spat him out like a broken tool.

The plains stretched before him, empty and unyielding. And yet, the emptiness mirrored the hollow pit in his chest. He had no allies here, no guideposts, no plan. Was this the city testing him? Or was it abandoning him? Every instinct he had screamed at him to run, to fight, to prove them wrong, but to what end? How could he fight a city he could no longer enter, a law he didn't understand, against enemies he couldn't see?

And still, beneath the frustration, beneath the confusion and betrayal, there was something else—an ember of resolve, faint but persistent. *If they think they can cast me aside, they're wrong. They haven't seen what I'm capable of yet.*

Exiled, yes. But not defeated. Not yet.

CHAPTER 15 – MEETING THE BOY

A well stood about a hundred and fifty feet outside the town, its wooden pavilion offering shelter from the brutal sun. The shade was scant, but enough to give a fugitive a brief reprieve until evening fell.

Romius had pushed himself through the nights to arrive within a day's journey of Tydell. He now found himself in Tockston, a small, dusty mining town few had reason to visit—unless, of course, one knew where to look. Beneath these lands lay veins of Thearon Steel, formed from the extreme heat beneath the surface, where iron and carbon fused into something both rare and deadly. Exactly what he needed.

A figure moving like a ghost caught his eye. Once a proud soldier, the young man now appeared hollowed out, a shadow drifting through the scorching daylight, searching for refuge. Romius shaded his eyes, studying him. Beneath the grime, the wear, and the scars, he could see resilience. Potential. Grit. He adjusted the bandana over his mouth and stepped closer.

"Need a hand?" Romius called.

Eryx's cracked lips managed a hoarse reply: "Please."

Romius noticed the wary calculation in the boy's eyes, the way he shifted weight from foot to foot, every movement betraying the training of Rannax and Bard.

"What kind of help you offering?" Eryx asked, voice rough and cautious.

"The kind that stops you from shrivelling up and being eaten," Romius said, shrugging with an air of careless confidence. "You don't have to take it."

Eryx weighed the offer. He had nowhere else to go, no money, no allies—and the man standing before him radiated quiet authority. Saying no wasn't an option. He followed Romius to the well, lapping greedily at the wooden bucket's water, his body parched and trembling with hunger.

"Listen," Romius said, leading him along a narrow dirt path toward the town, "I can sort you out with food and a place to stay. But I need a favour first. Lost my key… need some things from my workshop."

Eryx considered the proposition. He had no other choice. He nodded.

The path led them to a small work shed, the air thick with smoke and the scent of hot metal. Inside, two blacksmiths hammered away at their anvils, sparks leaping like fireflies. Eryx's chest tightened at the memory of his best friend back in Tydell, gone before he could even say goodbye. He swallowed the pang and focused.

Romius approached the blacksmiths. "You sell chisels?" he asked casually.

The men shook their heads, curtly pointing to the market, and ushered him out. Romius spun on his heel and motioned for Eryx to follow him around the back.

"Listen carefully," he said. "Grab a small silver cube with a bluish glow. Back-left corner."

Eryx peered at the shed. "How do I just… grab it with two people still working?"

"Leave that to me." Romius disappeared around the corner. Moments later, a cacophony erupted—screams, the clash of metal, the shriek of wood against steel. Eryx's heart raced as he edged closer, peeking around the corner.

Romius moved like a phantom, unarmed yet untouchable, every swing narrowly missing the blacksmiths as if the universe itself guided his strikes. Eryx's eyes found the blue glow, exactly where he'd been told. He crept along, skirting workbenches, heart pounding.

A blade shot past him, embedding in the back wall. The glow flared brighter. Eryx leapt over the last bench, gripping the cube in his hands. The metal was cool, humming faintly, alive with energy.

Romius gave a quick nod, the faintest smile beneath his bandana, and Eryx felt an odd mixture of awe—and unease. He had no idea what he'd just stepped into.

Ξ

Alicius stormed into Gremallax's study, her hands trembling with barely contained fury. "Where is he?" she demanded, her voice sharp, echoing against the polished wood and leather-bound ledgers. "How could the City Guard exile my son without explanation? I *need* to know!"

Gremallax rose from behind his desk, stepping closer. His voice was low, soft, almost soothing. "Alicius… please, calm yourself." He reached out, brushing a loose strand of hair from her face. "I know your heart is heavy with worry. I would feel the same if it were me."

Alicius pulled back slightly, but the warmth in his chest betrayed her anger. "You… you *do* know something. Don't lie to me, Gremallax. My boy has fought for this city, bled for it, and now he's cast out like a common criminal!"

Gremallax's eyes softened, his hand lingering near hers, just short of touching. "I would never lie to you, not truly. But you must understand, Alicius, some matters are… delicate. I assure you, he is not without protection. Not entirely. Trust me."

She swallowed, fighting both fear and the fluttering warmth that always came when he spoke to her like this. "Trust… I don't even know where to begin. I feel as if the world has shifted beneath my feet."

He took a step closer, lowering his voice. "Then lean on me for a moment. Let me be your anchor. I cannot change what the Guard has done, but I can promise you, I will watch over him… and over you."

Alicius's anger faltered under his gaze. There was a tenderness there, a comfort she hadn't allowed herself in weeks. "You… you really mean that?"

"I do," he whispered. He gently cupped her cheek. "You are stronger than you know, but even the strongest need someone at their side."

After a beat, he turned away, a calculating edge returning to his posture as he opened the secondary door. Amalric, the young officer, stepped inside. "Amalric… we need a revised account of the bandit incident," Gremallax whispered, voice now calm and authoritative. "Make it appear Eryx acted recklessly, attacking City Guards without provocation. It must be flawless."

"Yes, sir," Amalric replied, eyes flicking nervously to him.

Gremallax paused at the door, glancing back at Alicius, giving her a small, reassuring smile. "Rest now, my love. Worrying will not bring him back to you. Let me handle this… quietly."

As he stepped into the hallway, his expression sharpened into the cool, commanding presence he always displayed. Yet the warmth of his promise lingered in the room, a silent comfort to Alicius even as he orchestrated the deception that would soon shape Eryx's fate.

Ξ

Romius's eyes caught the shorter of the two workers turning toward Eryx. With a swift, fluid motion, he deflected the taller man's swinging blade into the shorter one, who yelped in surprise and staggered backward, clutching his injured arm. The distraction gave Romius the upper hand, and he seized control of the chaotic scene.

Eryx's heart hammered in his chest as he sprinted toward the glowing cube. Heat radiated from it, tingling against his fingertips as he snatched it up. The object vibrated subtly, almost as if it were alive. He didn't dare linger.

Tucking it carefully into the inner pocket of his worn jacket, he spun toward the door.

"Move!" Romius barked, his voice slicing through the clamour.

Without hesitation, Eryx rolled to his left, using a workbench as cover before weaving through scattered tools and shards of metal littering the floor. Behind him, Romius disarmed the taller worker with a deft strike, sending him crashing into a heap of scrap. A low groan escaped the man as he struggled to rise. Romius seized a nearby chain and bound both workers to a central support beam with swift efficiency, ensuring they couldn't pursue.

"Faster!" Romius urged, gripping Eryx's arm as they darted out into the narrow alleys of the small town. Shadows stretched long as the sun began its slow descent, the air thick with dust and tension.

At a safe distance, Romius halted, studying Eryx with sharp, assessing eyes. Panic and confusion swirled on the boy's face. "Let me see it," he demanded.

Eryx hesitated, then reluctantly pulled the cube from his jacket. Romius's gaze lingered on the glowing object, a slow smile tugging at the corners of his mouth. "This," he murmured, almost reverently, "is exactly what I needed."

"What… what is it?" Eryx asked, curiosity and caution mingling in his voice.

Romius slipped the cube into his own pocket with a casual flick, then started walking toward Tydell, the sound of his boots crunching over the dry dirt. "You've done well, kid. Better than I expected," he said over his shoulder. "Come on—we'll get you fed. There's more work ahead, and you'll need your strength."

Eryx's mind raced with questions, but before he could voice any, he fell into step beside Romius. The sun dipped lower, casting the alleys in molten gold and deepening shadows. He knew, with a chilling certainty, that the danger was far from over—and that whatever path he had chosen, there was no turning back now.

CHAPTER 16- BARRACK THIRTEEN

Complete silence. The barracks felt emptier than it had in months. The bunk opposite Rannax's was stripped bare, its blanket folded neatly in the corner as if the owner had only stepped out for the day. But they all knew better.

Bard sat on the edge of his bed, head down, elbows on his knees, chewing on a strip of dried meat he clearly wasn't tasting. Eroge stood near the window slit, staring at the mountains as if they might somehow give him answers.

"He's gone," Bard muttered. "Just like that. No trial. No chance to speak for himself."

"They didn't want him to speak," Rannax replied from his bunk. His tone was flat, but his eyes were hard. "They wanted him gone before anyone could ask questions."

Eroge finally turned, his voice low but steady. "We're not leaving it like this. I've known Eryx since we were kids. He's my brother in all but blood. If he's out there, we find him and bring him back."

Bard gave a short, bitter laugh. "And how do you plan on doing that? March right through the City Lord's guard and ask politely for his return?"

"No," Rannax said, leaning forward. "We don't ask anyone. We do it ourselves. Quietly. No reports. No orders. Just us."

Eroge nodded. "I can guess where he'll head. I know how he thinks. If we move fast, we can reach him before the wilderness or Tydell's patrols do."

Before Bard could argue further, heavy boots sounded in the corridor. The three men exchanged a look—conversation over.

Ξ

The door swung open without warning.

Captain Gremallax stepped inside, blue-and-gold uniform crisp as a parade banner, the gold trim catching the lamplight. His presence filled the room — not loud, but heavy, commanding. His gaze moved slowly over them, as though he could read their thoughts if he stared long enough.

"Gentlemen," he began, his tone clipped but smooth, "we need to discuss your former squad mate… and his rather *unusual* feats during his time here."

Bard's jaw tightened. "Unusual?"

Gremallax's lips curved, just enough to look like politeness without ever touching his eyes. "Strength beyond his training. Speed that outstrips seasoned soldiers. Recovery from injuries that should have kept him down for days. All of it… abnormal. I want to know exactly what you saw, and I expect the truth."

Silence.

He took a step forward, voice dropping, silk over steel. "This isn't just about the Guard. I know his mother… cares for him. I'd like to think I'm looking out for her interests as well." He let the suggestion linger, knowing they'd hear what he wasn't saying: that he had his own connection to Alicius.

Still, no one spoke.

The Captain's eyes narrowed, the faint charm draining from his voice. "If you know something and keep it from me, you will regret it. Consider this your only opportunity to speak freely."

The silence held.

Finally, Gremallax straightened, his expression settling into cool detachment. "Very well. But understand this — Eryx is not coming back. If you value your positions here, you'll stay out of it."

He turned sharply and strode out, the door shutting behind him with a quiet, deliberate *click*.

For a moment, the only sound in the barracks was Bard's slow exhale.

Rannax looked at the others, voice low. "Looks like we're doing this without him."

Eroge's reply was almost a vow. "Barrack Thirteen takes care of its own."

Ξ

The midday sun burned overhead as Fallax strode across the training grounds, his long coat trailing behind him. The clatter of weapons and the shouted commands of officers barely registered—his mind was elsewhere. The message had reached him that morning, delivered in the hurried, nervous tone of a junior officer: *Eryx had been exiled from Tydell.*

Fallax's jaw tightened. Exiled. The boy had fought bravely, proven himself on the training grounds, and yet now he was cast out, as though the city itself sought to erase him. He couldn't shake the feeling that something darker was at work.

Urasmus, appeared beside him without a sound. "You've heard, I take it," Urasmus said evenly, eyes narrowing.

"I have," Fallax replied, keeping his voice low, controlled. "Eryx. Exiled. By the City Lord himself… and the guards. Do you know what has become of him?"

Urasmus hesitated, carefully choosing his words. "The reports are… incomplete. All we know is that he was accused of attacking guards. The details are… murky."

Fallax's hand clenched at his side. "Murky? The boy has never been violent beyond training exercises. I've watched him myself. Something isn't right, Urasmus. I need to know what the City Lord is planning, and why he would turn on one of our own so suddenly."

A shadow passed over Urasmus's face. "It is… dangerous to question him too closely, Fallax. But you're right. Something feels off. If the boy's exile is a pretence, then we are dealing with more than a simple misjudgement. Someone is pulling strings."

Fallax nodded, his decision made. "Then I need eyes and ears where it matters most. Barrack Thirteen. My personal guard. I want them prepped. Quietly, Urasmus. I don't want the City Lord knowing what I am about to do."

Urasmus inclined his head. "As you wish."

Ξ

The night was quiet over the barracks, a rare silence broken only by the distant calls of desert birds and the whisper of wind through the stone walls. Fallax crouched beside a small metal cage in the corner of his private chamber. Inside, a craekee—its plumage dark as midnight and eyes glinting with intelligence—ruffled its feathers nervously.

Fallax gently unlatched the door. "It's time," he murmured. The bird hopped onto his gloved hand, its claws gripping tightly. "You'll carry this directly to the King. No detours, no mistakes. Can you do that?"

The craekee tilted its head, a soft cooing acknowledgment. Fallax had trained these birds for years; their loyalty was unmatched.

He unfolded a thin sheet of parchment, careful not to crease it. In neat, deliberate handwriting, he wrote:

Your Majesty, I write to you with urgency. The City Lord of Tydell has taken actions that defy reason and threaten the stability of the realm. The exile of Eryx, a loyal and capable soldier, is only the beginning. I suspect manipulation of reports and deliberate misrepresentation of events. I fear the safety of those who serve faithfully under him is at risk. Further investigation is needed, discreetly and swiftly.

Fallax rolled the parchment into a slender cylinder, securing it with a wax seal bearing his personal mark. He pressed it gently into the craekee's talons.

"Go," he whispered. The bird leapt into the air, wings beating with powerful precision. It vanished into the night, a dark silhouette against the moonlit sky.

Fallax watched until it disappeared completely, his jaw tight. The message was sent, but that was only the first step. If the King heeded it, perhaps he could begin to untangle the web of corruption in Tydell before it spread further.

A shadow stirred in the doorway behind him. Urasmus stepped silently into the chamber, his expression cautious. "You trust the craekee with the King?"

Fallax straightened, eyes still following the bird's path. "I trust the bird more than the City Lord." A faint smile touched his lips, but his eyes remained sharp, calculating. "If Tydell burns, I intend to be ready."

The room settled into tense silence, the only sound the soft rustle of the curtains as the desert wind whispered through the open window.

CHAPTER 17- THE KING

The royal war room was dim, lit only by the muted glow of the craekee stone sitting atop a table carved from a single block of obsidian. Its surface rippled like disturbed water as the voice of General Fallax echoed faintly in the chamber. The King stood with his hands behind his back, dressed not in ceremonial robes but in the black lacquered armour of his youth—battle-worn yet still imposing.

When Fallax's message ended, the King's lips pressed into a thin line. Without looking at his advisors, he began talking, the scribes began to write.

"General Fallax," the King's voice rolled like distant thunder. "Your concerns are… noted. But your *task* remains unchanged. Karathal sharpens its blades, and I will not have my generals distracted by whispers from Tydell."

The rippling surface stilled, and the King leaned closer. "You are to ready Barracks One through Thirteen for full mobilization. I expect supply lines in order, siege equipment primed, and every soldier blooded in the yard before the month's turn. If the City Lord is playing games, let him. It is Karathal that will test our gates, not his politics. Fulfil your orders. The crown expects victory."

With that, the craekee shivered its neck and flew through the stained-glass window. The King turned to his war advisors.

"Double the smiths. And have the quartermasters prepare rations for a long campaign. When Karathal falls, perhaps then we will deal with Tydell's little... eccentricities."

Ξ

The Craekee landed on the City lord's desk clicked and chirred in the dead of night, its glassy surface shimmering faintly.

In the dim study of Tydell's manor, the City Lord broke the gold-wax seal of the message cylinder. The parchment inside bore the royal crest at the header, the script sharp and deliberate—King Leax's own hand.

The words were wrapped in politeness but lined with steel. The King praised his stewardship of Tydell, then slid swiftly to the heart of the matter: *discretion.* The incidents with the guards, the street fights, the quiet disappearances... they had begun to attract the wrong kind of attention. The King urged him to tread lightly. War with Karathal was coming, and the Crown could not afford "noise" from its key cities.

The Elderly leader leaned back in his chair, the candlelight flickering over his sharp features. A slow, humourless smile curled his lips. He reached for his own quill.

When the Craekee carried his reply back toward the royal capital, it bore the black-wax seal of Tydell's lordship. In his letter, the tone was measured—respectful on the surface, but beneath, there was an unmistakable pressure. He reminded the King of *certain matters* from his earliest days on the throne—scandals that could unravel more than the King's dignity. Matters that *the City Lord's own house had handled* in shadow and silence.

He made it clear: his loyalty was not in question, but neither would he temper his hand without revisiting "old agreements." Discretion, as he put it, was a *mutual responsibility*.

By the time the letter reached the palace, the King's jaw was already tight before he even broke the seal. Whatever else was brewing in Tydell, The Lord had just made one thing clear—he wasn't the kind of subordinate you could simply order into obedience.

CHAPTER 18- FALLAX'S FALL OUT

Fallax sat at the small, creaking desk in his rented chamber at the *Copper Hawk Inn*, the faint smell of stale ale and desert dust hanging in the air. The Craekee on the table was still twitching following its long flight from the south, as he unrolled the parchment it had just produced.

At first, his eyes moved slowly over the King's seal and careful script. Then faster. His jaw clenched. The words struck like hammer blows—dismissal, condescension, the casual command to *focus on preparing for war* and leave Tydell's affairs untouched.

Get on with the task at hand.
As if the King didn't understand the stench of rot spreading through the city.

Fallax's fingers tightened around the parchment until it crumpled in his grip. "He doesn't see it," he growled under his breath. "Or worse… he *does*."

The chair screeched against the floor as he shot to his feet. The desk went next, overturned in a burst of violence, ink splattering across the wall and pooling on the rug. A clay mug of water shattered, droplets scattering like flecks of blood.

Outside the chamber, the sudden crash made Rannax, Bard, and Eroge turn sharply toward the door. They

Daniel Berrisford © 2021

exchanged glances—none of them had heard that tone from their General before.

More thuds, the sound of wood splintering. Then silence.

The door opened a crack, Fallax's shadow cutting across the lamplight in the hall. "Rannax," his voice was low but sharp, the kind that left no room for hesitation, "inside. Alone."

Bard raised an eyebrow but didn't move. Eroge frowned, glancing between them. Rannax stepped forward without a word, the heavy tread of his boots muffled by the carpet. The door shut behind him, leaving the others in the hall with nothing but the muffled sound of their own breathing—and the quiet, electric sense that something inside had just shifted.

Ξ

The *Silver Vellum* was the kind of place where the tables gleamed with polished oak, where gold-trimmed curtains muted the sunlight into a warm amber glow, and where the faint hum of a harp from the back room made even silence seem intentional.

It was also entirely empty.

Gremallax stepped through the door, his boots clicking softly on the marble floor. He paused, scanning the room. The only movement came from a booth in the far corner, where the City Lord sat with his back to the wall, leisurely spooning a rich, velvety soup from a porcelain bowl. The aroma of truffle cream and saffron hung thick in the air.

A bottle of deep red wine sat open beside him—imported from the Western vineyards, no doubt, the kind that cost more than a soldier's yearly wage.

"You're late," the City Lord murmured without looking up, his tone far too calm for the venom underneath. "I trust you have a *good* reason for making me eat alone."

Gremallax slid into the booth opposite, unflinching. "I was ensuring the reports were… persuasive."

The City Lord's eyes finally lifted—cold, calculating, with the faintest glint of amusement. "Persuasive? They'll have to be *more* than that, Captain. The attempt on the boy was sloppy. Public. And then—" he set his spoon down with deliberate care, "—you salvage it with exile? I told you to make it final, not theatrical."

Gremallax leaned forward, his voice low. "The exile will hold. And if it doesn't—" he reached into his coat and produced a slim folder, sliding it across the table, "—this will."

The City Lord's long fingers opened the folder. Inside, a series of neatly written witness statements, each one carefully damning Eryx. All agreed: the young soldier had *attacked high-ranking members of the Guard without provocation.*

A slow smile crept across the City Lord's lips as he read. "Yes… this will do nicely. Truth, after all, is whatever people agree to believe." He closed the folder and set it beside his untouched wine glass.

He poured himself another measure, swirling the dark liquid lazily before taking a sip. "Now, Captain… there is a more pressing matter."

Gremallax said nothing, but the faint shift in his posture showed he was listening.

"General Fallax." The City Lord's tone hardened, though his voice never rose above a conversational murmur. "He's beginning to sniff around things best left undisturbed. I want him… removed."

Gremallax's brow furrowed, though only for a heartbeat. "An accident?"

The City Lord's smile widened, sharp as a blade. "Make it convincing. Discreet. Not like last time."

Outside, the city's hum continued, unaware that inside this quiet, expensive booth, the fate of another man had just been sealed.

Ξ

The air in Fallax's sleeping chamber was still heavy with the scent of spilled ink and the faint tang of rage. The overturned desk lay against the far wall, one of its drawers split open like a cracked ribcage.

Rannax stepped inside at Fallax's word, closing the door quietly behind him. The General stood by the window, back to him, silhouetted against the lantern-light.

"Tell me, Rannax," Fallax began without turning, "how much do you trust this squad? Bard, Eroge… you."

Rannax didn't hesitate. "Enough to walk into a storm without a shield."

Fallax finally faced him, eyes narrowing, studying him like a man weighing a blade in his hand. "Even if the storm comes from our own gates?"

Rannax's jaw tightened. "Especially then. We do the job, no matter the source of the order."

The General stepped forward, his boots crunching on fragments of broken glass. "Good. Because I'm about to put you three in the teeth of one. I trust the City Lord about as far as I can throw him, and the King…" His voice dropped into a bitter rasp. "…the King is starting to sound more like a man guarding his own shadow than his people."

Rannax remained still, letting the weight of the words hang.

"I want you, Bard, and Eroge to work quietly—elusively. Ask no one, answer to no one but me. I want to know what's moving in this city when no one's watching. Who's pulling strings. Who's hiding the knife."

Rannax gave a single, sharp nod. "We can do that." He paused, then tilted his head slightly, a hint of calculation in his eyes. "But I want something in return."

Fallax's brow rose. "Go on."

"Information. About Eryx." Rannax's tone was steady, but there was an edge beneath it. "Why he was exiled. Where he is now."

Fallax's expression didn't shift, though his gaze sharpened. "You have an interest in him."

"I have a reason," Rannax replied simply.

The silence stretched between them for a moment before Fallax nodded once. "You'll have it. But only after I have what I need from you."

"Then we have a deal," Rannax said.

They clasped forearms, the quiet gesture sealing their pact.

Outside, everything carried on as though nothing had changed—yet between these two men, an agreement had just been struck that could turn the city inside out.

Ξ

The heavy oak door to Gremallax's home closed behind him with a soft creak. The silence of the house felt heavier than the armour on his shoulders. His meeting with the City Lord replayed in fragments—the reprimand, the thinly veiled threats, the assignment to get rid of Fallax. The weight of it all pressed against like a mule carrying supplies.

He found Alicius anxiously waiting in the sitting room, perched on the edge of a cushioned chair, her hands wringing together. Her eyes lit up briefly at his arrival, but the hope in them quickly turned sharp.

"Gremallax," she began, voice trembling with urgency, "you promised you'd help me find out where my son is. Days have passed, and you've said nothing. Tell me you've heard something—anything—"

"I've been busy," he snapped before he could stop himself, the words sharper than intended. "Do you think the world stops for your personal troubles?"

Alicius flinched, the hurt plain in her face. "He's my son," she said, her voice cracking. "I have a right to know if he's alive."

Gremallax's stomach twisted with guilt. The anger wasn't meant for her—it was for himself, for the choices he'd made, for the lies that had to follow. He exhaled slowly, setting his gauntlets aside on the table, and stepped toward her.

"I'm sorry," he murmured, his tone softening. "I shouldn't have spoken to you like that." He lowered himself to the chair opposite her, leaning forward. "Alicius… I know what it's like to lose the people you love. My wife and daughter…" His voice faltered, and he looked away, waiting for the lump in his throat to dissipate. "…They died while I was stationed at the barracks. A fire. I wasn't there to save them."

Her expression shifted, the anger giving way to sympathy. "I didn't know…" she whispered.

"I don't talk about it," he said, his voice low, tinged with practiced pain. "But I understand your fear. And I promise you—" He reached for her hands, his calloused fingers warm against her trembling ones. "—I will find out what happened to Eryx. You have my word."

Alicius's breath caught, the tension between them no longer just grief and frustration. The space seemed to draw them closer. Gremallax's thumb brushed over her knuckles, and for a moment, neither of them spoke.

When he leaned in, it was slow, deliberate, as though giving her the choice to pull away. She didn't. Their lips met, the kiss carrying the weight of shared pain and the fragile thread of trust he was weaving around her.

When they parted, Gremallax rested his forehead against hers. "We'll get through this," he murmured, knowing full well the lie buried in his promise.

Ξ

The low murmur of voices in the inn masked their conversation well enough, but Rannax had still chosen the farthest booth in the shadowed corner, where the flickering light of the hearth barely reached. A half-empty tankard sat untouched in front of him, his sharp eyes scanning the room before settling on his two companions.

"We can't move too openly," Rannax began, his voice low but commanding. "Fallax wants information, not a bloody spectacle. We dig too deep in the wrong places, and the City Lord will smell it before we're close."

Bard leaned back in his chair, smirking, his boot propped casually against the table leg. "You're overthinking it. We break into the City Lord's private quarters, rifle through his desk, maybe… persuade a few guards to loosen their tongues." He tilted his head with mock innocence. "By persuade, I mean break their fingers until they talk."

Rannax shot him a flat look. "And you think *that's* subtle?"

"Subtle is overrated," Bard said with a shrug.

Eroge, who had been quietly nursing his drink, leaned forward. "I know people down in the tenth tier," he said, his voice hushed but confident. "People who survive by knowing things they're not meant to. They can slip into places, hear things, and no one up here will even remember they were there. If the City Lord's dealings touch the lower tiers, and they will, I can have word back within a week."

"That's better," Rannax said, nodding. "The tenth tier's a rat's nest. No one looks too close at what crawls in and out of it. You think your people can keep their mouths shut?"

Eroge's lips curled into a faint grin. "They don't live long otherwise."

Bard rolled his eyes. "Fine. Use your street ghosts. But if we get nothing, we do it my way."

Rannax tapped the table once, decisive. "We'll start with Eroge's contacts. If they can lead us to something concrete, we'll decide the next move from there. The

Daniel Berrisford © 2021

City Lord's hiding something big, and we'll find it…
quietly."

The three men exchanged a brief, silent understanding
before leaning back into the shadows, their voices
dropping further, already discussing the names of those
who could be trusted—and those who couldn't.

CHAPTER 19- GATHERING SUPPLIES.

Romius, upon meeting Eryx, quickly decided the boy could be more than just company—he could be a tool. Another set of hands to gather resources, and, if the job soured, a convenient body to toss under the carriage.

Instead of heading toward Tydell, Romius steered them north—a far riskier route. The closer they came to the border, the greater the chance of crossing paths with Thearon scout posts. Not the kind of company the nation's most wanted man should keep. But the prize waiting ahead made the risk worth it.

Their destination was Garraw, the last northern settlement before the sands of the Exia Desert swallowed the world. Few even knew Garraw existed. Romius knew—because he had once helped the King hide it from the maps.

They approached the town's crude spiked wooden palisade, the heat shimmering off the dry earth. A portly guard, red-faced and sweating, reluctantly pushed himself out of a sagging chair. His expression was a mix of annoyance and confusion.

"You're lost," the man grunted, waving them away. "Head south—you'll find where you're meant to be."

His tone carried the weight of someone used to being obeyed.

Romius didn't slow. In one sudden movement, he seized the man's shoulder, and with blistering speed, hurled him thirty feet across the sand. The guard's rotund frame bounced twice, each impact sending up a spray of grit, before he landed flat and still.

Romius glanced at Eryx, a crooked smile tugging at his lips.
"We're in."

Ξ

Poise and delicacy were virtues Bard had little patience for. Yet the task required a steady hand—if only to extract the information without causing a scene. Words and subtlety, however, were foreign to him.

He dragged the Tenth-tier urchin into a makeshift stall they had erected, the flaps of cloth barely hiding them from the dim lantern light of the alley. Bard pressed his thick thumb into the man's collarbone, hard enough to make him yelp, his body twisting in panic. The boy squirmed, thrashing in Bard's grip, pleading incoherently.

Bard loosened his grip slightly, watching the sweat bead along the man's temple. "I have Flax for you," he said, his voice low and tempting, "if you can give me some information."

The boy's eyes widened, desperation overtaking defiance. His tongue darted over cracked lips, licking them nervously, as if testing whether he could even speak. Bard could smell the fear radiating off him—the sweet, pungent tang of someone pushed to the edge.

"This… this is serious," the boy stammered. "I-I don't know much, I swear!"

Bard leaned closer, his voice dropping to a near whisper, yet carrying a weight that made the urchin flinch. "I don't care if it's a little, or a lot. You tell me what you know, or you get nothing. Your choice."

The boy swallowed hard, eyes darting between Bard and the shadows beyond the stall. The tension crackled, thick and heavy, like the air before a storm. It was only a matter of seconds before the first words slipped out, the secrets of the Tenth-tier beginning to unravel.

The boy's voice trembled as he spoke, each word forced from his lips. "A… a few days ago… in the early hours… I saw them. Generals, all in blackened armour… carrying wounded men… up through the tiers. They were moving fast, like they didn't want anyone to see."

Bard's eyes narrowed. "Generals? How many?"

"Three… no, four… maybe five," the boy stammered, his hands shaking as he tried to steady himself. "They had… they had someone tied to a stretcher. Couldn't see his face, but… but he wasn't moving much. They went past the Fourth and Third tiers, and then… I lost sight of them."

Eroge, leaning against the edge of the stall, muttered under his breath, "High-ranking, and moving injured soldiers at night… that's not routine."

Rannax stepped closer, voice calm but laced with authority. "You saw this clearly. Do you know which way they went after the Third tier?"

The boy nodded, terrified. "Towards the upper tiers… towards the city lord's old quarters. I think… I think they're hiding him there, or… or somewhere he can't be found."

Bard's lips curled into a thin, satisfied smirk. "Good. That's what I wanted to hear." He let go of the boy, who slumped to the ground, gasping for air and shaking like a leaf in the wind.

Rannax turned to Bard and Eroge, his expression grim. "This confirms what we suspected. The City Lord isn't just playing politics—he's hiding something, and whatever it is, it's tied directly to Eryx's exile."

Eroge cracked his knuckles. "Then it's time we start digging deeper. Quietly."

Bard spat to the side. "Quietly is for amateurs. But fine… we work shadows tonight."

The three exchanged a nod, the tension in the air replaced with resolve. They had a lead—and it was dangerous, but it was the closest they'd been to the truth.

Ξ

The war table in the Officers Tent was covered in parchment maps, wooden markers shaped like cavalry, archers, and shield wielding soldiers. The scent of oiled steel and old parchment hung heavy in the air. Fallax stood at the head of the table, leaning forward, a finger pressing into a cluster of markers that represented supply lines threading through the Exia desert.

"This," Fallax said, voice steady but edged with command, "is where we break or win the campaign. The Karathi know the desert. They can move faster than we can imagine. If our supply chain falters for even a day, we lose more men to thirst than to their blades."

Across from him, Gremallax leaned back in his chair, arms crossed, helmet resting on the table beside him. "And you think my men should be mules," he said flatly. "Hauling water skins and grain carts while others fight?"

Fallax met his eyes without flinching. "I think your men—your *undisciplined* men—don't yet have the formations, or the tactical understanding, for open desert warfare against a mounted enemy. They would break under the first Karathi charge."

Gremallax's jaw tightened, his voice sharp. "They've trained for years under me. They can hold a line as well as any in Thearon. You put them on the front, they'll fight like men with misted eyes."

Fallax tapped the edge of the map with a calloused finger. "Holding a *desert* line is not the same as holding a city street, Captain. The Karathi will not meet you face to face. They will surround you. Pick you apart. Cut your water, and wait for the sun to finish the job."

A tense silence settled over the room. The two men stared each other down while the junior scribes pretended to be busy with their ledgers.

Finally, Gremallax leaned forward, lowering his voice but not his defiance. "The other sergeants have been talking, General. They wonder if you've lost the fire for the front. Too cautious. Too… detached."

Fallax's gaze sharpened, his tone calm but lethal. "Caution is why we've won every engagement I've commanded. I will not throw away lives to satisfy your pride, Captain. If you disagree with my orders, you can take it up with the King himself."

For a moment, Gremallax seemed ready to push further, but he settled for a stiff nod. "Very well. My men will guard your precious wagons, General. But don't forget—when the fighting starts, it's *soldiers* who win wars, not supply trains."

Fallax's lips curled into the faintest, knowing smile. "And soldiers are nothing without what those supply chains bring."

The two returned to the map, their silence heavy with unspoken rivalry.

Ξ

The streets of Garraw twisted like a knot of narrow lanes and low, crooked buildings, their stonework scarred by years of heat and wind from the Exia desert. The air here was thicker than the surrounding plains—tinged with the metallic tang of ore dust, faintly glowing flecks drifting in the gloom like fireflies. Romius moved through it with practiced ease, his bulky frame somehow slipping between shadows as if he'd been born in them. Eryx followed close, mirroring his movements, every step careful to avoid loose gravel that might betray them to the guards.

The central mine shaft dominated the heart of Garraw like a great wound in the earth. A jagged maw rimmed with wooden scaffolding and rusting chains, it breathed out a constant haze of heat and ore-laden steam. Guard towers surrounded it, each manned by soldiers in mismatched armour that glinted under the faint glow from below. Their eyes scanned the streets lazily, but their crossbows were loaded and ready.

"Keep your head low," Romius muttered without looking back. "These bastards have orders to shoot first and sort the bodies later."

Eryx caught sight of movement down in the shaft— figures hunched and skeletal, faces smeared with grime, their wrists shackled to heavy picks and sledges. They worked without pause, their bodies swaying under the rhythm of the overseers' whips.

"They're slaves?" Eryx whispered.

Romius' voice was low, almost a growl. "Criminals. Or at least, that's what the King calls them. Petty thieves, deserters, debt-dodgers—anyone who crossed the wrong noble. Once you get sent here, you don't leave."

He pointed subtly toward a cluster of ore carts being hauled up by a creaking pulley system. Each cart carried a different kind of prize from the depths. One load shimmered with shards of blueish-silver, the glow almost liquid in its intensity, similar to the cube they had retrieved from the previous town. Another was filled with coarse, golden-brown chunks that seemed to hum faintly in the air. The last cart bore jagged lumps of deep green stone, each piece swallowing the torchlight around it like it drank the dark.

Romius gave a knowing smirk. "Three types. The blue-silver's Thearonite—stronger than steel, lighter than bone. The golden's Auracite—burns hotter than any coal when refined. And the green…" His voice dropped into something almost reverent. "That's Verdacryl. Nobody outside the King's Circle knows what it's for, but people kill over it."

They ducked into a narrow passage between two storage sheds, sidestepping a patrolling guard. Romius moved with a predator's timing, waiting until the clank of armour was swallowed by the churns of the mine before slipping out into the next street. Eryx matched him, his pulse quickening as they edged closer to the shaft's perimeter.

The deeper they went, the stronger the colours from the ores seemed to pulse, casting strange, shifting lights across the grime-caked faces of the slaves. Down here, even the shadows seemed alive.

Eryx barely knew this man. He had so quickly returned to his old ways of thievery and deception. As Romius scanned and assessed from their hidden position, Eryx stopped to reflect on how he got into this situation.

Ξ

His mind wasn't on the guards or the glowing ore anymore—it was on himself. On how far he'd fallen in such a short time.

Exiled. Thrown from Tydell like a scrap of rotten meat, and for what? He still didn't understand. One day he'd been a soldier—trained, disciplined, wearing the crest with pride—and the next he was nothing more than a name whispered in accusation. A criminal. An exile.

Now here he was again, slipping through shadows, pockets lighter than his pride, following a man he barely knew into trouble. And worse—he'd agreed to it without much thought. Was it desperation? Or just instinct?

The truth pressed against him like the heat from the mine: stealing was all he knew. The skills he'd learned on the streets of the tenth tier—before the barracks, before the uniform—had kept him alive when no one else cared if he lived or died. In the gutters, kindness was a rare currency, and Eryx had been poor his whole life.

Romius… well, Romius had shown him something that felt close enough. A kind of rough respect, a recognition in his eyes that Eryx mattered—if only as a tool. Maybe that was all it took for him to follow. After all, Eryx had grown up without a father, without a steady voice to tell him where the line was, or why it was worth not crossing. The people who did notice him back then had only ever wanted something from him.

And maybe that's why trusting Romius felt so... familiar. Because it was the same game he'd been playing since he was a boy: find the strongest player in the room, stick close, and hope the shadow you're standing in keeps you alive a little longer.

He didn't like the way that truth tasted. But in Garraw, under the weight of the King's mines and the stink of forced labour, Eryx knew one thing for certain—if he wanted to survive, he'd have to keep playing.

Ξ

Romius stopped abruptly, placing a heavy hand on Eryx's chest. "Don't look too long," he warned. "You start staring at the glow, and you'll forget why you're here. Seen it happen."

They pressed on, keeping to the blind spots in the guards' rotations, every step bringing them closer to whatever it was Romius had come to take.

Ξ

The low murmur of the barracks mess hall was a distant hum beyond the closed door. Fallax sat opposite Urasmus in the small side chamber, the table between them bare save for a half-empty jug of water and two untouched cups. The air smelled faintly of oiled leather and the silt of the forge outside.

"You've served with him longer than anyone," Fallax began, leaning forward, voice low. "How did Gremallax make captain? Men don't rise that fast without leaving a trail."

Urasmus exhaled slowly, leaning back in his chair. The years showed in the deep lines carved into his face, but his eyes were sharp, still tracking every twitch of Fallax's expression.
"I knew him when he was a new recruit," Urasmus said. "You wouldn't believe it now, but back then, he was… something else. A force of nature. The kind of man you'd want on your flank when the Karathi came screaming out of the dunes. He wasn't just strong—he made the rest of us stronger. Fierce in the fight, tireless on the march. And he had this way of making the feeblest of lads think they could take on the world."

He paused, eyes narrowing slightly. "That's what caught the officers' attention. He won skirmishes that should've broken us, pushed through wounds that would've put other men on their backs. His rise was… inevitable."

Fallax tilted his head. "And yet, here we are, talking about him like a problem instead of an asset."

Urasmus's jaw tightened. "Because somewhere along the way, his eyes shifted from the men beside him to the ladder above him. He started chasing ranks instead of victories. Family suffered for it—hardly saw his wife or daughter. Then… the fire."

Fallax didn't move, but the word seemed to darken the room.

"That night changed him," Urasmus went on, voice low. "He came back colder. More ruthless. Less… human. Still effective, mind you—maybe even more so—but his way of fighting changed. Less about protecting, more about controlling. And whatever he's doing now for the City Lord?" He shook his head. "That's not the man I knew."

Fallax studied him for a long moment, then said, "I need men I can trust, Urasmus. Men who still fight for the right reasons. I'm working to find out what the City Lord is playing at, and I need you in this—quietly. No word to anyone, not even the men you command."

Urasmus's gaze lingered on Fallax, weighing the risk. Then he gave a slow, deliberate nod.
"You'll have me. But if Gremallax's changed sides, you'd better be ready to face what that means."

Fallax allowed himself the faintest smirk. "I already am."

Ξ

The air was thick with pipe smoke and viscous ale. The underground *chips* hall was larger than Bard, Rannax, or Eroge expected—its low stone ceiling arched overhead, strung with blazing lanterns casting amber light over the crowd. The place had the aroma of something both illicit and strangely polite; laughter and the clatter of glassware mingled with the sharp *clack* of weighted chips striking lacquered wood.

Six long, oval tables sat in a loose circle, each topped with a painted board marked into concentric rings. The goal was simple enough: flick your coloured chip from the far end and land it in the highest-scoring circle without bouncing off. Easy to learn, almost impossible to master. The coloured disks gleamed in the lamplight— bright reds, deep blues, pale ivory—each worth different points. Coin satchels hung from the belts of eager participants, looking to spend frivolously or win big.

The clientele was a bizarre mix. Mid-ranking officers in unbuttoned uniforms, their belts hanging loose, shoulders relaxed for the first time all month. Politicians without their ceremonial robes, pretending not to notice their wives three tables away, gossiping and sipping rich wine as they laid down bets of their own. A sprinkling of street-level regulars—dockhands, smiths, errand boys— kept to themselves, eyes flicking up at the higher-class crowd in disbelief that they'd stoop to share the same tables.

Bard, Rannax, and Eroge stepped inside like they belonged there, though Bard's swagger was the most convincing. He twirled a spare chip between his thick fingers, grinning at the nearest table as if sizing up prey rather than competition. Rannax's eyes scanned the room, not for the best game but for the best target— someone with loose lips and an expensive drink in hand. Eroge kept to the shadows a step behind them, already noticing which servants and attendants moved between the tables unnoticed.

"This is where we start," Rannax murmured, leaning toward the other two without breaking his stride. "Someone here knows about the night of the carriage attack. And about those high-ranking bastards climbing through the tiers before sunrise."

Bard smirked. "So, we play. Win a few rounds. Make 'em trust us enough to talk."

Eroge's voice was low, almost lost in the chatter and soft music echoing from the band. "Or we just find the drunkest one and ask."

The three drifted toward a half-empty table by the bar, where the laughter was looser, the piles of coin higher, and the rules of conversation far less guarded.

Ξ

"All we need," Romius said, eyes glittering under the furious sun, "is as much Thearonite as we can carry." His voice was low, each word clipped with urgency. He unfastened a leather strap on his pack and produced two satchels, one for each of them. "Move fast. Move quiet. Different directions."

Eryx felt the weight of the satchel in his hands—it wasn't heavy yet, but the promise of what would fill it gave it a strange gravity. Romius had already vanished into the shadowed street before Eryx could answer, his hulking silhouette slipping between buildings like a predator with intent.

Eryx moved in the opposite direction, hugging the line of buildings until he reached a squat, weather-worn structure wedged between a miner's barrack and a storage shed. A narrow window sat open near the roofline, barely large enough for a grown man to squeeze through. He gripped the sill, pulled himself up with practiced ease, and wriggled inside.

The small room he landed in was empty—dust and stale air greeting him like an unwelcome host. No furniture, no crates, nothing but the faint scent of ore dust and old timber. A single door stood opposite him.

He eased it open and stepped into a far larger chamber.

The space was lined with crates, barrels, and wooden racks. The metallic scent pierced the air, unmistakable. At the far end, two men in patched leather aprons were sorting through ore on a broad table glad to be indoors as the heat raged on outside. The stacks were neatly separated.

Eryx spotted a pre-organised stack of the silvery-blue ore—Thearonite—piled in the corner nearest him. His pulse quickened.

Keeping low, he weaved between the crates, boots silent on the packed dirt floor. Every step was calculated, every breath measured. Reaching the stack, he crouched and began loading his satchel. The faint warmth of the ore seeped through the leather, the glow casting strange shadows across his hands, twirling up him arm and disappearing as if being absorbed by his skin.

A dry cough broke the silence.

Eryx froze.

One of the sorters, a lanky man with a crooked nose and a permanent scowl, had turned from the table. His gaze locked on Eryx immediately, disbelief flashing into anger. The man stepped forward, slow at first, then quicker, a calloused hand reaching toward the hammer looped at his side.

The man did not speak, he simply just came closer and closer.

Ξ

Rannax kept his movements deliberate, flicking a crimson chip into one of the circular sections carved into the smooth table, leading to celebrations across the table, his eyes less on the game and more on the room.

A few seats down, a Tier Five councillor was red-faced with arrogance, berating a young serving girl for not refilling his wine quickly enough. His words dripped venom, sharp enough to cut the fragile dignity she tried to maintain, even gripping her arm as she passed.

Before Rannax or the others could even exchange a glance, a drunken City Guard staff sergeant—broad-shouldered and glassy-eyed—lurched up from his seat. He seized the councillor's arm in a tight grip, yanking him back before his words turned uglier.

"Enough," the sergeant slurred, though his tone was still heavy with authority.

The councillor stiffened, his powdered face flushed with indignation. "Unhand me," he spat, his voice carrying across the Chips table. "Or I'll tell everyone in this room exactly what you were up to the other night."

The sergeant's drunken bravado faltered. His grip slackened almost instantly, and he released the councillor with a sheepish grunt, retreating to the betting table like a dog with its tail between its legs.

The councillor, still seething, attempted to rally his dignity, but the tavern's security had already moved in. Two large men in dark uniforms escorted him out, ignoring his blustering protests as they pushed him toward the doors.

At their own end of the table, the three remained silent, watching the exchange with interest. Eroge stacked his chips methodically, his keen eyes following the sergeant's every move. Bard, meanwhile, rolled a chip across his knuckles, his grin wolfish as if sensing opportunity.

Rannax leaned forward slightly, his tone calm but commanding. "Bard," he said under his breath, "restroom. Wait for the sergeant, we will follow."

Bard's grin widened. He pushed back from the table, rising with practiced nonchalance, as though he were simply stretching his legs. "Don't lose my pile while I'm gone," he muttered before disappearing into the back corridors of the tavern.

Rannax and Eroge exchanged a brief look, both understanding what was to come. Neither said a word. They simply placed their next bets, the flick of their chips blending seamlessly into the hum of the tavern as they waited for the trap to spring.

Ξ

The sorter's eyes darted nervously between Eryx's crouched frame and the silent stacks of ore. Then, in a voice barely louder than a whisper, he blurted:

"Help me… please. Get me out of here."

Eryx froze, his gaze falling to the man's ankles. Shackles, blackened and ashen with years of wear, bit deep into scrawny skin. The iron chain led down into the stone floor itself, anchored like the roots of a tree. For a moment, hesitation clawed at him. But the man's sunken face—half hope, half desperation—cut through him.

Eryx dropped his sack and gripped the chain. Cold metal tingling in his palms, but as he pulled, a strange shimmer rose from the stacked Thearonite ores. Wisps of silver-blue smoke drifted into the air, twining around his fingers, coiling up his arms. His breath wavered.

The harder he pulled, the more the smoke thickened, seeping into his skin, clouding his mind with strange pulses of energy. The chain groaned and warped under his grip, as though bending not just to muscle but to his very intent. His vision blurred, the world sharpening and twisting at once. The link embedded in the floor stretched like softened wax.

What is happening to me…?

With a snap like a thunderclap, the steel fractured. The shackle split wide.

And then the room splintered.

An enormous crash split the air as the roof above caved in. Shards of timber and dust showered the floor. A guard screamed as he plummeted through, his armoured bulk smashing down on the sorter's table, scattering ores in every direction.

Before Eryx could react, another figure tore through the opening—Romius, landing with predatory grace, his boots slamming onto the wrecked station. His eyes glowed fiercely, his skin shimmering, wreathed in a silvery-blue mist that bled off him like smoke from a forge.

He extended a hand, voice sharp and commanding: "Now, boy!"

Eryx snatched up his half-filled sack and grabbed Romius's hand without thinking. A surge of force yanked him off his feet as Romius propelled them out. They tore through the gaping roof and burst into the open square, the light of Garraw's central pit burning before them.

Around them, the heart of the town lay exposed—a great yawning chasm where miners toiled like ants in the shadows. And ringing its edge, dozens of guards were already converging, weapons drawn, voices rising.

The alarm had been sounded. They were surrounded.

Ξ

Bard leaned against the cracked marble sink, arms folded, his broad shoulders blocking half the lamplight in the cramped restroom. The stench of pipe smoke and cheap spirits hung heavy in the air. He waited, patient as a wolf by the den.

The door creaked open. The guard stumbled in, his uniform stained, his eyes glazed with drink. When he noticed Bard, his steps faltered. Then he tried to backpedal.

Too late.

Rannax was already there, a silent shadow at the door, barring the way.

Bard smirked. "The kid getting in on the action?"

"Hot streak," Rannax muttered. "Leave him to it."

The guard's throat bobbed as he swallowed hard. "I… I'm not the man you want," he stammered, hands raised clumsily. "You've got the wrong—"

His excuse was cut off as Bard swatted aside a sloppy attempt at resistance and seized the man's hand. With deliberate cruelty, he bent it back, using the might strength from his thick forearm. The guard howled, a high, ragged sound—until Rannax clamped a hand over his mouth, muffling it into a whimper.

Bard leaned close, voice low, controlled. "What happened the night of the carriage attack in Tier Ten?"

The guard shook his head violently, refusing. But his eyes… his eyes betrayed him. They darted, flickered, the fear in them screaming truths he didn't dare speak. Bard squeezed harder. Bone grated under his grip. The guard's knuckles crumpled like twigs.

"Talk."

At last, the words came spilling out between muffled groans. "We… we were told it was a flax shipment. That anyone defending it… they were the mastermind. Orders came down—no arrests. Just… just make a statement. That's why… that's why we left him for dead."

Rannax's gaze hardened. "Who gave the orders?"

The guard's jaw tightened, teeth grinding as he shook his head. Silence.

Bard's patience snapped. With a sudden twist he released the hand, then drove a short, brutal right hook into the man's jaw. The crack echoed in the tiled room. The guard's body went limp, slumping into a heap on the grimy floor.

Bard dusted his knuckles, breathing steady. Rannax let out a quiet breath, pushing open the door.

Together, they stepped back into the haze of the gambling hall. Eroge was still at the table, grinning as he raked in another pile of chips. They collected him— along with their winnings—and left the underground game without a word, fading into the night.

Ξ

Eryx's chest thundered like a war drum. His breath tore through his throat as the silvery-blue haze writhed around his arms, bleeding off his skin in wisps. It pulsed in rhythm with his heartbeat, each thud sending another shock through his veins. He stumbled, half in awe, half terrified—yet Romius smiled as if proven right to a theory only he knew of.

The first guard lunged, spear levelled. Instinct—not training, not thought—drove Eryx's hand forward. The wooden shaft splintered on impact, shards spraying across the square. The soldier was hurled backward as though struck by a hammer, his body crumpling against the stone steps. Eryx studied his hand as it return to normal, the steel retreating from his skin.

Romius barked a laugh, weaving between two attackers with predatory ease. His hand, glowing the same eerie silver, carved through the air. Both men dropped as though strings had been cut, clutching their chests, choking on invisible weight.

"Don't think—move!" Romius snapped, twisting to catch a sword with his bare hand. The steel bent like softened clay before he shoved the stunned guard into two others.

Eryx obeyed. His legs carried him, slipping through the clash of steel and shouts. A mace swung low; he ducked, heat searing his scalp. The energy surged down his arm. He struck out at the legs of the soldiers around him. They fell screams of agony piercing the air. The impact ruptured ligaments, the man dropping in a spray of dust.

More came. Shields locked, spears jabbing, boots pounding the dirt. The gate was only a dozen yards away, but it might as well have been a mile.

Romius barrelled through them like a beast unleashed, his movements a blur, precise and merciless. This pathetic force was no match for a man with the experience he had. Eryx mirrored him in flashes—awkward, raw, but devastating with every hit. He smashed a shield aside with a forearm, his body trembling from the recoil yet the guard collapsing under the blow. Another tried to grab him from behind, only to be flipped over his shoulder with far too much ease for a man Eryx's size.

The ground shook with the clash. Screams and shouts echoed against the wooden structures.

Finally, the gates loomed ahead—two vast planks bound with iron. The same guard Romius had hurled earlier still lay in the arid sand outside, groaning faintly, too broken to rise.

"Together!" Romius shouted.

They pressed shoulder to shoulder, hands glowing like molten silver as they shoved. The doors groaned, iron bolts snapping under their grip, dust showering down. With a final roar, the gates burst outward.

Romius didn't pause, sprinting into the open expanse. Eryx followed, lungs burning, the haze around his body flickering but refusing to fade. Behind them, chaos erupted—horns blaring, guards yelling, the mine-town of Garraw thrown into bedlam. A desperate Craekee darted to the skies, Help was being summoned.

Ξ

The shutters rattled as a blur of wings cut through the night. A Craekee burst through Fallax's window, feathers scattering across the chamber. The creature's chest heaved as if it had flown for days without rest. A thin scroll, sealed in crimson wax, dangled from its leg.

Fallax snatched it with a grunt, breaking the seal with his thumb. His eyes scoured the words, and each line drove his jaw tighter.

Two men with skin of steel. Blue-silver mist. Dozens of guards left broken. The gates of Garraw forced open.

His hand trembled—not with fear, but with fury. He slammed the parchment down against his desk so hard the wood cracked. The Craekee startled, screeching, before scuttling back to the sill.

"Damn him," Fallax growled, pacing the length of the chamber. His fists clenched white. "Damn him to the pit."

The door burst open. Urasmus rushed in, blade half-drawn at the noise. "What's happened?"

Fallax whipped around, his eyes burning. "I've found him." His voice was a snarl, heavy with both triumph and loathing. "Romius. The man with the steel skin."

Silence fell heavy. Urasmus froze mid-step, the colour draining from his face. His hand slipped from the hilt of his sword.

The look said it all.

Recognition. Fear. And something darker, buried deep.

Fallax leaned across the desk, his knuckles pressing into the cracked wood. He was glad to have finally pinned him down to an area but the message claimed there was two. Who was the second?

CHAPTER 20 - HISTORY

The room was quiet, the sort of quiet that only came after the lamps were lit and the bustle of the barracks wound down to nothing but distant boots echoing in stone corridors. Alicius sat curled in a worn armchair, her knees tucked beneath her as she traced each line of text with her finger. Across from her, Gremallax reclined heavily, the broad frame of a man who could wrestle an ox yet seemed oddly at peace with a book in his hands.

He glanced up from the page, studying her in the lamplight. "You read well," he said simply, his voice more curious than complimenting. "How'd you come by it, if you don't mind me asking? Poverty doesn't usually afford such a luxury."

Alicius froze for a moment, her eyes flicking instinctively toward the adjoining room where Oliax slept. Only when she was certain her daughter wasn't within earshot did she lower the book to her lap and exhale slowly.

"I haven't been… entirely open with you," she admitted, her voice fragile. "I've struggled with that since—since their father left us."

Gremallax leaned forward, elbows on his knees, his heavy brow softened by patience. "Then be open now," he urged quietly. "With me."

Her hands tightened on the spine of the book before she began.

"I wasn't born in the gutters of Tydell," she confessed. "I grew up by the Southern sea, on the outskirts of Poltan, in a house overlooking ships that belonged to my family. My father owned vessels—trading ships, and even a harbour along the southern coast. We were wealthy. Comfortable. I was expected to marry into another merchant house, to strengthen the family name."

Gremallax's brows rose, but he didn't interrupt.

"But I… I chose otherwise. When I was nineteen, I began courting a man. Kind, stubborn, and… Karathi." Her lips quivered at the memory. "My father hated them. He never forgave them for the war. When he found out, his rage was—" she swallowed, "—unforgiving. I was cast out. No inheritance. No protection. No family."

Gremallax's jaw tightened, a flicker of recognition in his eyes. "And this man… he was Eryx's father?"

Alicius nodded, tears brimming though her voice remained steady. "Yes. Though Eryx never met him. The town was quick to drive him out once word spread of his heritage. The hatred ran too deep. I never saw him again."

She drew in a sharp breath, bracing herself before continuing. "Later, I met Oliax's father. A good man in many ways, though married more to his career than to us. He helped raise Eryx as his own, but… we were poor. And worse, word of Eryx's bloodline followed us. A drunken man once tried to hurt him—just for who he was. I couldn't stand by. I struck back. Harder than I should have."

Her voice trembled now, her shoulders shaking with the weight of old choices. "That's why we left the coast. North, where tolerance was kinder for those with Karathi blood."

For a long moment, silence filled the room.

Then Gremallax rose and crossed to her, lowering himself into the chair beside hers. His calloused hand brushed hers, grounding her trembling fingers. "I understand," he said, voice low, steady. "More than you know. You fought to protect your son. You did what you had to. There's no shame in that."

Alicius turned her eyes toward him, uncertain, vulnerable. His gaze didn't waver. In that moment, sympathy bound them tighter than any words could.

Ξ

The desert night was colder than Eryx expected. A thin chill clung to the dunes, hissing with every breath of wind. The silver mist still pulsed faintly beneath his skin, bleeding through his pores in ghostlike wisps that shimmered under the pale moonlight. He could feel his heart hammering in his chest, his body aching from exhaustion, but the energy wouldn't die down—it coursed and churned like a storm looking for ground to strike.

Romius's hut appeared like a shadow out of the shifting sands, a crooked wooden frame held together more by stubbornness than by craft. The older man led the way, his broad steps unhurried, as though the night's chaos hadn't touched him at all.

Eryx stumbled onto the porch and leaned against a post, his chest heaving. "Enough," he rasped. His voice cracked with both fatigue and fury. "I want answers, Romius. Now."

The man didn't turn immediately. Instead, he pushed the door open, hinges creaking as he stepped inside, and began stacking kindling in a dented iron stove. "Sit," he said calmly, like a father correcting a child's tantrum.

"I said I want answers!" Eryx's shout tore through the stillness of the desert. His fists clenched, silver mist curling in furious coils around his knuckles. "Who the hell are you? Why are we stealing and killing? Why were there slaves in Garraw?!"

Romius glanced over his shoulder, eyes glinting pale in the lamplight. For a moment, he looked almost amused. Then he struck a flint, sparks leaping, and the small fire caught. He set a kettle over the flames and exhaled.

"You'll have them," he said at last, voice low, deliberate. "But first—" he pointed toward the porch with a heavy hand, "—you will sit. Outside. Let the night air cool your head. Let the mist inside you settle, or it will burn you hollow before dawn."

Eryx's chest rose and fell in ragged bursts, anger warring with the pulse in his veins. He looked at Romius, at the steady way he moved, at the complete lack of fear. For a moment, he thought about storming out, about walking into the dunes and never looking back. But the thought of the chains, the slaves, the glowing ores—all of it— gnawed at him. He needed to know.

With a growl, he shoved the door open wider and dropped onto the porch steps, the old wood groaning beneath his weight. The desert stretched endless before him, moonlight painting the sands in silver streaks that mirrored the glow in his skin.

Behind him, Romius busied himself with the kettle, the clink of metal and the soft crackle of fire filling the silence. Then came his voice, measured, heavy with something ancient.

"You want to know who I am? Why Garraw hides slaves in the dirt, why kings covet their chains, and why you feel the way you do now?" He paused, letting the desert itself hold its breath. "Then listen. And do not interrupt."

Ξ

The inn was dim, its lamps burning low, the last of the day's smoke curling in lazy trails across the rafters. Fallax pushed the door open, boots dragging a faint line of dust across the wooden floorboards. He had not rested, not truly, since the King's summons—his shoulders hung low beneath the weight of command, but his eyes were sharp as ever.

Bard and Eroge looked up from where they sat, half-drunk mugs of ale before them. Rannax, ever composed, sat straight-backed, as if he'd been waiting all night for Fallax's return.

"Rannax. With me." Fallax's voice was clipped, allowing no room for question. "The rest of you—bed."

Bard grunted but rose, his chair scraping. "Aye, Captain." Eroge followed with only a glance at Rannax, his youthful curiosity thinly veiled beneath exhaustion. The two disappeared up the narrow stairwell, their steps fading until only silence and the crackle of the hearth remained.

Fallax gestured toward his chamber and Rannax followed. Inside, the shutters were half-drawn, moonlight cutting silver lines across the desk and the worn map of the tiers laid upon it. The hour was deep, and both men wore the lines of fatigue like scars.

"Report," Fallax said, sinking heavily into the chair by the desk.

Rannax stood, hands folded behind his back. "We entered the underground Chips game tonight. The place was thick with all sorts—politicians, middle-rank officers, even the City Guard. It didn't take long before a Tier Five councillor and a drunk sergeant lost their tongues. The sergeant cracked under pressure."

Fallax's gaze sharpened. "And?"

Rannax's jaw flexed. "He admitted the attack on the carriage wasn't about flax at all. That their orders were to make a statement—no arrests, no witnesses. Whoever tried to protect that carriage… he was marked as the mastermind. They left Eryx for dead. A boy, not a drug lord. This isn't one- or two-men pocketing coin. This is infestation. An infestation of rats gnawing through the City's walls."

Silence pressed between them. Fallax leaned back, the chair groaning under his weight. He rubbed his temple, a grim shadow falling over his expression.

"I've seen this before," he muttered, more to himself than to Rannax. "Poltan. The same disease spreading through the ranks. First whispers, then bribes, then the Guard itself rots from the inside. By the time the King acted, half the city was under the thumb of traitors, and the other half starving in the streets. Worst of all, vigilantes thinking they can take the law into their own hands."

His fist tightened against the desk, the map crumpling beneath his palm.

Rannax tilted his head. "And how did Poltan end, Captain?"

Fallax's eyes flicked up, dark and burning. "With fire. With the streets awash in blood, both guilty and innocent. The King did his absolute best to keep it all under lock and key. But I saw it all. And I'll be damned if I watch it happen here."

Ξ

The porch creaked beneath their weight, the wooden slats cool under bare feet. Beyond, the Exian night stretched endlessly—an ocean of black sand and silver starlight. The moon hung swollen and pale, veiling the desert in a sheen of ghostly light.

Romius set the kettle on small table that separated them, steam curling faintly into the air as it hissed. His hands, still faintly shimmering with the blue-silver haze of the earlier battle, rested calm on his knees. Eryx sat opposite him, shoulders tense, sack of stolen ore beside him.

"You owe me answers," Eryx demanded, his voice low, cracked with exhaustion yet edged by a strange fire. "Who are you really? What are we doing stealing and killing? And those men—those slaves in Garraw. Why?"

Romius didn't meet his gaze at first. Instead, he looked upward, as if weighing the right to speak under the judgment of the stars themselves.

"Long before kings and banners, before the cities reached the tiers you know, there was only the land," Romius began, his tone softened, almost reverent. "Warrah. The living earth. The old ones believed she was more than soil and stone. She was pulse, hunger, gift and grief alike."

Eryx frowned but listened.

"There is a legend," Romius continued, eyes still fixed on the desert horizon, "of three siblings who wandered this very wasteland millennia ago. Starved, parched, their rations gone, they stumbled upon a disturbance in the rock—glowing, alive. From it spilled mist, silver and wild, wrapping them in Warrah's embrace."

Romius's hand rose, gesturing faintly as if painting the image in the night air. "The eldest, Heaphius, was the first to step forward. He reached into the crack and the Thearonite within answered him. His hunger, his thirst— gone. In their place, strength, endurance. Steel skin, unbreakable will."

Eryx shifted, his breath caught.

"Then his sister, Rabuga. She followed, her fingers brushing a green glow that danced like shadows on leaves. Verdacryl. It gave her vitality, the power to mend and to twist the living world to her will."

Romius's voice dropped lower, as though speaking Psamallax's name carried its own weight. "Last came the youngest. Desperation drove him into the light, golden and fierce. Auracite. Its beacon filled him with clarity, with the ability to guide, to inspire… but also to burn with the fury of the sun."

The kettle hissed louder, steam swirling into the desert air like a reflection of the tale itself. Romius finally turned to Eryx, his eyes burning faintly with silver mist.

"Each sibling was touched by Warrah's wonder. Each passed down fragments of their gifts. In secret, in bloodlines." He leaned closer, his voice hardening now with conviction. "And I… just as Heaphius before me, am a Steelmancer."

Eryx swallowed hard, staring at Romius's faintly glimmering skin, remembering his own arms wreathed in silver smoke as chains bent beneath his grip. His chest tightened—not only from awe, but from fear.

"What does that make me?" he whispered, almost to himself.

Romius didn't answer.

Ξ

The voices still echoed in his skull long after the chamber had emptied. Hours of councillors bickering— North Mountain against South Mountain, Tier against Tier, each member shouting over the other, drowning him in their petty demands. His temples throbbed with the rhythm of their endless questions. Taxes. Rations. Guard deployment. Trade routes. All of it pouring down like stones in a landslide.

The amphitheatre of politics was no place for rest. It was a battlefield without blades, and tonight he felt every bit of his age. His joints ached as he descended the stone steps, each footfall hollow against the grand chamber's expanse. At the bottom, the curved wooden desk waited—reserved for Tydell's highest officials. A place built for power, not for comfort.

He lowered himself into the chair, letting the weight of it embrace him. And then, as if on cue, Gremallax appeared—broad shoulders filling the entranceway, his stride deliberate. The City Lord straightened, exasperation lifting like fog. Gremallax brought news, and news was currency.

The captain leaned across the desk, voice clipped and heavy. "I can tie the boy—Eryx—to Karathi blood. His mother courted one of them. But I don't know how clean the tie will look if it's traced back. A Karathi spy in Tydell could justify his exile, yes… but it could also shatter the public confidence in our guards. They'd start questioning our vigilance. Our control."

The City Lord clasped his fingers together, eyes narrowing. He had taken this job not for service, nor duty, but because power bought wealth, and wealth bought freedom. He had clawed his way here through secrets—knowing things no man ought to know, and trading them like coin.

But scheming wore on a man. And though he was tired—too old, perhaps, for the endless games—it was still the only way to survive at the top.

"Exile alone will not hold," he muttered. "The city thrives on confidence. On fear. We can't afford doubt among the ranks. Ruthlessness is the only currency that lasts."

He tapped the desk, already shaping the lie in his mind, already weaving the narrative. "We'll lay this not at our own doorstep, but elsewhere. The general of Poltan will bear the weight. Fallax." His lips curled into something between a smile and a sneer. "A convenient scapegoat. The boy's bloodline, the attack on the carriage, all of it— let it be painted as Poltan's corruption bleeding north. The King will have no choice but to bow to the allegations. To deny them would be to risk his seat at the throne."

The chamber fell silent, but in the City Lord's mind the play was already moving, pieces shifting on the board. Ruthlessness was the only truth left in this world. And he was still ruthless enough to win.

Ξ

Rannax leaned back in his chair, hands folded tightly. It felt rude—dangerous, even—to press a general for answers, but the more he saw, the more necessary it became. If they were to peel back the layers of corruption strangling Tydell, then Poltan's history couldn't remain half-shrouded.

Fallax seemed to sense his thought. His expression hardened, eyes fixed on some point far beyond the inn's timber walls. "You should know," he said at last, voice low, deliberate. "You and I are in this together now. And if you're to understand what we're up against, you need to hear it all."

The general's words carried a gravity that demanded silence. Rannax listened.

"Crime in Poltan has always been a tide—you can hold it back for a while, but it rises all the same. Bandit groups running smuggling rings, Flax dealers hiding behind legitimate shops… by the time I was a boy, they held more sway than the Guard itself. Captain Leax was drowning in it. And yet…" Fallax's eyes narrowed. "Somehow, he began pulling at the right threads. One by one. And at the centre of it all…" he paused, letting the weight hang, "was King Renaesius himself."

Rannax shifted in his seat. "The old King?"

Word of this struggled to escape the grand stone walls of Poltan.

Fallax nodded grimly. "Bribes. Investments. Entire rings of criminals tied directly to his treasury. The king and his noblemen grew fatter while poverty rotted the streets. And Leax—Leax had the proof. Contracts, ledgers, payments… years' worth of filth. He gathered a force, turned on the King, and imprisoned him. The city cried out—some in fury, some in relief. But the documents were undeniable."

Fallax rubbed his jaw, as if trying to massage the memories loose. "I was just a boy then. Barely sixteen. A common soldier in the Guard. But word spread like wildfire in Poltan but no further. Problems in the capital, stay in the capital. The king was finished, and Poltan… Poltan was reborn in fire and fury. Leax became more than captain. He became the iron hand that strangled corruption from the streets."

He drew a slow breath. "In the years after, Leax hunted them all. Bandits, syndicates, shadow-dealers—he broke them. And when the officials questioned how such rot had been exposed so easily, Leax produced a name. A ledger, supposedly written by a mercenary in service to the old king's crimes. One name, scrawled like a curse across every page."

He looked directly at Rannax.

"Romius."

Rannax's eyes flickered, unsettled.

Fallax's tone grew heavier, more personal. "Romius was no name to me then. He was my friend. My closest. A boy I grew up with. We fought together, bled together. But when the King's men demanded his capture, I was ordered to lead the search along the waterfront. And what I found…"

His words faltered, as if even years later the memory refused to sit cleanly.

"He wasn't the man I knew. His eyes bled silver mist. His skin glimmered like poisoned steel. He fought like some beast torn from the earth's belly. Tore through men with savagery I'd never seen before. Ruthless. Cornered. Not Romius, not the boy I remembered—just a demon clothed in his skin."

The fire in the hearth popped. Neither man moved.

Fallax's voice dropped to a whisper. "He had been missing for years, escaped at my hand. And now…" He clenched a fist. "Now he's back again, just as Tydell is drowning in corruption of its own."

Rannax sat in silence, the pieces rattling through his mind like scattered dice. Crime, kings, betrayal, a boyhood friend twisted into something unnatural… It was a web far more tangled than he had imagined.

Ξ

"Elemancy has all but died out," Romius said. "What once was wonder has become myth, and myth has become fear. The world punishes what it doesn't understand. It destroys what it envies. That is why… I am the last Steelmancer."

The silver mist that clung faintly to his skin seemed to shimmer with the weight of those words.

Eryx frowned, his brows furrowed. "But what about me? What happened back there, in Garraw? The chains, the guards—I did things I didn't even understand. That wasn't just luck."

Romius studied him for a long moment, his dark eyes reflecting the moonlight. Then he spoke, slowly, deliberately. "When I first met you, I thought of Heaphius—the eldest of the siblings who first stepped into Warrah's embrace. There was something in you. The way you survived from Tydell to where you met me... You covered a distance in hours that would have killed a seasoned traveller in days. That isn't chance, Eryx. That is Warrah whispering to you."

Eryx blinked. His mind leapt backward, combing through his memories like rifling through old parchment. He thought of the times he had climbed too high on crumbling stone and landed without a scratch. Of fights where older, stronger boys had struck him down only for him to rise, stubborn, as though his body simply refused to quit. Of narrow escapes where the odds had seemed impossibly tilted, yet he had somehow stumbled through.

It had always felt like survival. Now... it felt like something more.

Romius leaned back in his chair, the timber creaking under his weight. "In Garraw, the sheer volume of Thearonite acted as a catalyst. It awakened the truth in you. What you did there, you did not do by accident. But mastery is not a gift—it is practice, patience, will. Without them, power is nothing but chaos. With them…" He lifted one hand, turning it palm-up, and a fine wisp of silver smoke curled into the air, dancing like a flame.

Eryx's breath caught. The porch fell into silence again, save for the occasional night insect in the brush.

Romius had been open—so open, more than any man had ever been with him. His words felt steady, comforting, even fatherly. And yet the unease dug at Eryx's chest.

Am I clinging to this? he wondered. *Am I so desperate for guidance, for the father I never had, that I'll trust a stranger who steals and kills? Am I filling hollow void that was never meant to be filled?*

He looked at Romius, at the calm certainty in his face. A man claiming to be the last of his kind, reaching out to him not as an enemy or rival, but almost as a teacher.

Eryx left the man to rest under the descending moon and took refuge indoors. The dissipating Thearonite in his blood stream leading to a tiredness worse than any desert run he had faced.

Ξ

Gremallax had long since departed, leaving the chambers quiet, but the City Lord lingered. The hour was late, far later than any man should still be in uniform, yet duty—or perhaps ambition—kept him rooted.

From beneath his desk, he drew out a worn leather folder, its cover scarred by age, etched faintly with the letters *LX*. Leax. An old friend. A usurper turned king. Within the folder lay the original parchments that had elevated him: forged evidence of Renaesius' corruption, contracts inked with bribes, ledgers of blood money that had widened the gulf between wealth and poverty. The City Lord leafed through them with a dry smile. Leax had been the weasel in the kingdom, but he had been ruthless enough to seize what the weak old king could not defend. He respected that.

The smile faded. Ruthlessness alone was never enough to hold power. You needed shadows—men who could twist the truth, bend records, shape the past until it suited the present. He himself had been such a man, For Leax. And tonight, he would be again.

He slid the folder shut and pulled a fresh sheet of parchment to the desk. No ink, no quill. Instead, he reached for the small drawer where a cube of *Verdacryl* pulsed faintly with its mossy-green glow. The light spilled over the desk as he hovered his hand above the parchment. Letters began to appear, clean and deliberate, as if scribed by the finest hand in Tydell. A forged lineage, crafted with care—Eryx's bloodline rewritten, tethered to the most heinous of Karathi, scandal wrapped in official seals.

A final flourish: the forged signature of Poltan's chief scribe, indistinguishable from the real. He leaned back, studying the work. Perfect. Tomorrow the tiers would be buzzing, truth drowned by rumour, rumour legitimised by proof no one would dare to question.

The City Lord blew out the candle. In the darkness, he thought briefly of old King Renaesius, a man he once condemned to spend the rest of his life in prison. All to help cover up Leax's sloppy criminal enterprises.

CHAPTER 21- THE RISE AND FALL

It still felt wrong to Alicius, this slow descent through the tiers. Life was always a climb—upward, toward light, toward safety. Now she descended into those shadows she used to call home.

Her anxiety over Eryx had not lessened. Gremallax, despite his claims and constant assurances, had learned nothing of her son's fate. That silence gnawed at her. Still, the days required her labour. She scrubbed floors, polished dishes, and now—having been "promoted"— cooked for Gremallax. It was clear what he thought of her role in his household: a convenient housewife, bound by gratitude and coin. She was letting their relationship grow but the dynamics were becoming ever more complicated.

That morning she carried a small satchel, intending to fetch cleaning supplies. Her path wound through Tier Eight's merchant street, crowded and loud, the air thick with a variety of trades and vocations. At the corner, she passed a news stand, its racks of parchment fluttering faintly in the mountain breeze. Curiosity tugged at her— news here moved faster than it ever reached the gutters of Tier Ten. She stepped inside.

One headline caught her eye. The words struck like a fist to the stomach. Her breath fled. The satchel fell from her shoulder with a dull thud as her hands flew to her mouth.

A Karathi spy uncovered—mission squandered, heritage confirmed.

Her son's name. Eryx. Printed there for all the tiers to see, smeared with accusations she knew would follow him forever. The article painted him as a traitor, his supposed infiltration undone before it began. And worse: Fallax, the proud general, dragged into the mud, accused of harbouring treason in his own personal guard.

The words blurred through her tears. Rage burned away her breathlessness, replaced by a fire so fierce she thought it might consume her whole. She ran—faster than she had in years—her legs hammering against the stone steps, her lungs searing. Anger, fear, devastation, all of it propelling her forward with one thought only: Find Gremallax.

Ξ

Eroge wandered Tier Four with wide eyes and an eager stomach, letting himself drift through the early bustle of merchants and craftsmen. Everything here felt sharper, brighter, richer than the tiers below. The sandwich in his hands was proof enough—the meat tender and dripping with flavour, the salad leaves crisp, the spices burning and fragrant on his tongue. Even food seemed to thrive in the higher air.

But it wasn't just the food that caught him. The forges here sang with precision. Tools gleamed on racks outside workshops, their edges honed, their steel unmarred by overuse. The hammer strokes of the smiths rang in perfect rhythm, their bellows pushing heat with effortless strength. Every weapon, every plate of armour, every tiny chisel looked born of mastery.

His chest tightened. He missed it—standing shoulder to shoulder with his father at the forge, working until sweat blinded him, the fire scorching his arms. He could almost smell the coal and hear his father's steady hum as he stoked the flames.

He paused at a ledge that overlooked the great sprawl of Tier Ten below. The forge would be alive by now, his father bent over the coals, his mother shaping metal with practiced care. Closing his eyes, he whispered to Rabuga, the Verdant Mother—offering a blessing for their health and strength, for their craft to honour Warrah as it always had. He asked for protection, for prosperity, for the quiet pride that came from honest work.

The moment passed, but the ache remained. He pushed on, wandering until a gleaming façade caught his attention—an immaculate building, its walls polished stone, its doors flanked by the crisp robes of scribes.

Inside, desks stretched in rows, quills scratching endlessly. Fresh sheets were posted at the front for passers-by.

Curiosity drew him closer. He pulled one free.

His eyes skimmed the words—and his pulse exploded. The parchment trembled in his hands.

Eryx. Accused of treachery. Of being a Karathi spy. Fallax named.

The blood drained from his face. Without thinking, he bolted. His legs pumped furiously, weaving through the morning crowd, parchment clutched to his chest.

Rannax. Bard. They needed to see this—now.

Ξ

A shock of cold tore Eryx from sleep. He coughed, sputtering as water soaked his hair and shirt, thrashing to get free of the blanket tangled around his legs. Romius loomed above him, a battered wooden pail dangling from his hand, his expression carved from stone.

"Up," Romius said flatly. "We don't have time. They'll come hunting, and you'll be nothing but prey if you're not ready."

Eryx pushed himself upright, groggy and furious. "What in Warrah's name—"

"Outside." Romius's tone left no room for debate.

Still scowling, Eryx dragged himself into the morning air. The sun had barely crested the trees, and the clearing around the hut was damp with mist. Romius walked to the centre, planted his feet, and gestured to a pile of silver ore glittering faintly in the light.

"Thearonite," Romius said. "This is where you begin. You've already taken it in before, instinctively, when the fear was loud enough. Now you need to learn to do it with intention. Fear may light the spark, but discipline keeps it burning."

He held his hand over the ore. A faint shimmer lifted, twisting like smoke, and curled into his skin. His flesh hardened, gleaming silver, the faint haze of steel-mist rising from his arms.

"Close your eyes. Feel it. The ore breathes. You draw it in."

Eryx tried. He stood over the stone, shutting out the world, searching for whatever Romius had tapped. He reached... but nothing came. Sweat gathered at his brow. His lungs tightened with the silence of failure.

Romius sighed. Then, without warning, he snatched up *Domir*—the great battle axe—and swung.

Eryx's eyes flew wide. He stumbled back, heart slamming against his ribs, certain the blade would split him in two. Instinct roared—his skin flared silver, mist swirling as the axe struck. The metal rang against his hardened body like steel on steel.

Panting, Eryx staggered, staring at his shimmering arms in disbelief.

"Better," Romius said, lowering *Domir*. "But you only reacted. That won't save you next time."

Eryx clenched his fists, his chest still hammering. "How am I supposed to *choose* that? I don't—"

"Fear," Romius cut in. "Let it drive you. Not the momentary kind. The kind that gnaws at your bones."

Eryx swallowed hard. He closed his eyes again, forcing himself to feel the weight buried in him: the thought of never seeing his mother again, of Oliax walking the path of thieves because he wasn't there to stop her, of Eroge fading from his life like every other good thing had.

The ache sharpened. His chest tightened. He drew breath—and the ore answered. Wisps of silver rose, flowing into his skin, his body hardening, the mist pouring from his shoulders. This time, it didn't feel like chance. It felt like choice.

Romius watched, eyes narrowing with something between pride and warning. "Good. Hold on to that. Fear isn't your enemy, boy. It's the chain that ties you to Warrah. Learn to pull on it."

Ξ

Alicius burst through the front door, her skirt tangled around her legs, her breath ragged from the sprint up through the tiers. She barely noticed the warmth of Gremallax's home, the scent of parchment and polished oak—her eyes locked only on the office door.

She shoved it open.

Gremallax sat hunched over his desk, the morning light slanting across the parchment spread before him. The bold ink of the headline still fresh. Her son's name screamed up at her from the page.

"What did you do?" Her voice cracked, raw and piercing.

He looked up, and for a fleeting moment his face was a mask of sorrow. A sorrow so deep it seemed older than either of them. He rose slowly, arms open. She resisted—then collapsed into him, her body giving way, tears strangling her breath. He held her, heavy arms closing tight around her shoulders.

His grief was real, but not for Eryx. Not for Fallax.

It was the old, festering wound of guilt. The guilt of a husband and father who had failed to protect his family—his wife and daughter buried years ago, their shadows still haunting every quiet moment. And now, a fresh layer pressed upon it, sharper, crueller: the guilt of betraying this woman and her son, the woman he had begun to care for, the son whose name now stood condemned.

He wished he had a choice. But choice was for free men. The City Lord's hand gripped him like reins on a bridled horse, pulling him where he didn't want to go, promising punishment if he strayed.

Alicius pulled back, her face streaked with tears. "How?" Her voice trembled. "How did they know? I told you… I told *you* about his father only days ago—"

His eyes fell, and the lie came smoother than he expected. "Mission notes. Found in his barracks. Written in Karathi."

She shook her head violently, disbelief flooding her. "No. No, he would never. Eryx—he steals, yes, he makes mistakes, but he would *never* betray his country. He wouldn't betray me. Or Oliax."

Her hands trembled as she snatched the parchment from his desk. She scanned it again, her eyes catching on another name buried in the accusations: *Fallax.*

The general of the Thearon National Guard.

Something shifted in her expression. Beneath the tears, beneath the devastation, there was a flicker of steel. She folded the parchment with trembling fingers, hiding it against her chest.

If she was to learn the truth, it wouldn't be from Gremallax. Not anymore.

She would seek out General Fallax herself. Quietly. Away from Gremallax's gaze.

Ξ

Eroge shoved through the door of the Copper Hawk Inn, the morning bustle of the dining room briefly falling quiet at the sound. Bard and Rannax sat at their usual corner table, chewing through breakfast. Fallax's seat was empty.

Without a word, Eroge slammed the parchment down so hard the bowls rattled. Bard raised a brow, pushed the sheet toward himself, and frowned. He could make out a few of the words but gave up quickly, sliding it across to Rannax.

Rannax scanned it once, then again, his jaw tightening as the ink bled its poison into his thoughts. The infestation of rats was no longer rumour—it was fact. And Eryx…

He wasn't some schemer. He was a boy, reckless, headstrong, but obedient. A victim of circumstance.

Rannax's gut twisted. He remembered the boy who slept in the bunk beside him, full of questions, full of mischief but not malice. He looked up at the others, eyes sharp. "This isn't him. Not like this."

Bard didn't argue. Eroge didn't need convincing. Both rose the instant Rannax did, the three of them moving as one toward Fallax's chamber.

The door swung open to chaos. The room looked like a battlefield—papers torn, a chair overturned, the table split in two. The General stood amid the wreckage, his chest heaving, his face twisted with barely leashed fury.

Fallax turned, his voice a thunderclap. "We go to the barracks—NOW!"

The walls themselves seemed to shudder at the force of his command.

Ξ

Romius did not relent. Every moment was a trial, every breath a test. He barked orders, his voice carrying across the barren stretch of desert.

Eryx tore through the sand, each stride faster than the last, grit spraying at his heels. His lungs burned, his chest heaved, but the silver pulse of Thearonite in his pocket drove him forward. The ore's energy thrummed in his veins, keeping his body moving when his will begged him to stop.

"Again!" Romius roared.

Eryx wheeled back toward him, sweat dripping down his steel-tinged skin. Romius pointed to a boulder squatting in the sand, its bulk the weight of ten men.

"Move it!"

With a snarl, Eryx pressed his hands against the rock. Muscles trembled, sinews screamed, but he heaved— veins glowing faintly as the power surged. The boulder toppled, slamming into the earth with a dull quake. Before he could even breathe, Romius sent him sprinting back into the desert.

Back and forth. Run until the world blurred, lift until his arms shook, then run again. Over and over. The sand sucked at his legs, the sun bit his skin, but he did not stop. He *couldn't.*

Romius watched, arms crossed, expression hard but eyes alight. "Good," he muttered to himself. "Break him down. Build him back stronger."

And still, Eryx kept going—driven by the fear of failure, by the image of his mother, by the thought of losing everything.

Romius pushed. Eryx endured.

Ξ

Gremallax stormed past the soldiers at the City Lord's office door, fury written into every step. The guards made to seize him, but a lazy flick of the City Lord's hand sent them back to their posts.

"Why the boy?" Gremallax thundered, slamming his fists against the curved wooden desk. "What does he have to do with anything? I've bled for you. I've done your filthy work. But this—this has gone too far. I won't do it anymore."

The Captain loomed, every inch the soldier, jaw set and muscles coiled. Yet the City Lord, seated in calm repose, looked upon him with the serenity of a man who already knew he had won.

"You forget yourself, Captain," the City Lord murmured. His voice was quiet, but it landed like a blade point-first. "You sold me your soul long ago. Do not pretend otherwise."

He leaned forward, eyes glinting.
"You were nothing. Scum in the gutters of this great city. Flax using, drowning in debts. And when your debtors came to collect, they burned your wife and daughter alive. *Your fault.*"

The words ripped into Gremallax like steel. He stiffened, but said nothing.

"I cleaned it up," the City Lord went on, smooth and merciless. "I gave you a hero's name. A tragic story to gild your reputation. I let you bathe in the adoration of this city while I buried the truth. Even your vengeance, I gave you that. Without me, you are nothing but a broken man with blood on his hands and ashes in his home."

Gremallax's rage trembled into silence. His fists clenched. His teeth ground. But behind the fury, shame and grief gnawed at his heart. He wanted to scream. He wanted to strike. Instead, he turned sharply on his heel, the faint glimmer of a tear betraying him as he strode out the door. He needed to find a way out before the chains strangled him completely.

From the shadows of the chamber, the air shimmered. A tall, elegant woman stepped forward with the poise of a serpent gliding into the light. She had been there the entire time, unseen.

The City Lord's mask softened. "Caelius," he said warmly, "my jewel."

She inclined her head. "You were right, father. The boy carries the gift. He is an ellomancer. The fugitive has already found him. He's begun the boy's training."

The City Lord sat back, fingers steepled, his expression unreadable. For years he had searched the tiers, rooting out even the faintest hint of Warrah's cursed touch. Ellomancers were rot to the world—poison. Even in his own veins the gift festered, a reminder of the blight he meant to extinguish.

"Good," he said at last, his tone colder than stone. "Continue to watch him. I want to know how deep his potential runs—before we cut the line at the root."

Caelius' crimson lips curved into a knowing smile. "As you wish, father."

Ξ

Fallax, Rannax, Bard, and Eroge pushed through the heavy gates of the barracks. The camp fell silent. Soldiers and scribes froze mid-task, eyes following the group with unspoken judgment. Whispers rippled in their wake, but no one dared speak aloud.

They cut through the weight of the stares and slipped into the officers' tent. Empty—save for Urasmus, hunched over a pile of unfinished reports. He looked up, startled, until Fallax gestured sharply.

"Stay. We'll need you."

Eroge pulled the flap down and tied it shut, muting the mutters outside. The tent was dim, thick with the smell of ink and oil. The five men circled the central table.

Fallax placed both hands flat on the wood. His voice was low, urgent, heavy with a soldier's finality.
"We're under threat—from the very top. The Elite have marked us. No one will come to our aid. We stand alone. So, we need a solution."

The words hung in the air, and silence settled like a shroud. Rannax stared at the maps scattered on the table, mind racing for a plan. Bard drummed nervous fingers on the hilt of his knife. Eroge's jaw clenched, sweat pricking at his temples.

Then the canvas above them split with a shriek of tearing cloth. Talons punched through. A black-feathered shape clawed its way into the tent, scattering parchment and ink. The men staggered back, hands darting to blades.

A Craekee. Its eyes were like molten copper, unblinking, wild with command. With a deliberate motion it dropped onto the table, claws gouging the wood. In its beak it bore a letter, sealed in crimson wax, pressed with the royal emblem of the King.

The bird released it with a final rasping caw, then fixed them with a stare so sharp it felt more message than the parchment itself.

Fallax reached for the letter, but his hand lingered, as if he already knew its words.

Fallax broke the wax seal with a thumb that trembled despite his effort to hide it. The men leaned closer as he unfolded the parchment. His eyes flicked over the words, narrowing with each line. Finally, he let the letter fall flat on the table, his jaw set.

"It's from the King," he said, voice sharp, clipped. "Effective immediately, I'm suspended. The Thearon National Guard stationed here in the north… is no longer ours. Tydell now commands it. The City Lord holds our leash."

The words sucked the air from the tent. Bard cursed under his breath. Eroge slammed a fist against the table hard enough to rattle the ink pots. Rannax just stared, the weight of betrayal sinking in.

"They've stripped us clean," Bard muttered.

"They've taken more than that," Fallax said. His tone stern. "They've taken control."

Rannax straightened, his voice calm but edged. "Then we take something back. Romius. He knows things— truths that cut deeper than forged parchments. If we get him to talk, we have leverage. Proof."

Fallax hesitated, running a hand across his beard. He thought of Romius: friend, fugitive, weapon. Every step toward him was a step toward chaos. But Rannax was right—without something undeniable, they'd all be crushed under the City Lord's lies.

At last he gave a sharp nod. "We find Romius."

Urasmus rose from his chair, squaring his shoulders. "Then go. All of you. I'll cover your tracks, stall anyone who comes sniffing. You'll need a head start."

The four clasped his forearm in turn, gratitude unspoken but understood. Then they moved swiftly, gathering bags and weapons.

Eroge made for the armoury. The cool metallic scent of steel greeted him as he stepped inside. Charliax stood polishing a breastplate, her sharp eyes flicking to him.

"You're leaving." It wasn't a question.

Eroge strapped a sword to his hip. "We have to. And before you ask—I don't know where Eryx is. But I'm going to find him."

Charliax studied him for a long moment, then reached behind a rack of weapons. She drew out a long, polished bow staff, its wood veined with faint streaks of silver. She held it out.

"Then take this. For him. He'll need it more than you will."

Eroge hesitated, then accepted the staff with a solemn nod. The weight of it was comforting in his hands, like an unspoken promise.

He slung it across his back and turned toward the door. "Thank you."

When he returned to the others, Fallax, Bard, and Rannax were already waiting, packs strapped, weapons ready. The silence between them was heavy, but their purpose was sharp. They were no longer soldiers under a banner—they were out casts chasing the truth.

Ξ

Romius let Eryx collapse against a rock, a water skin clutched in his hands. The boy drank with such desperation that half of it spilled down his chin, but Romius didn't stop him. He had earned it.

Eryx wiped his mouth with the back of his sleeve, chest heaving. "You've told me about… the steel, about drawing from Thearonite. But what about you? Who are you really?"

Romius's eyes narrowed, the weight of memory pressing into his jaw before he finally spoke. "My story is not one I share freely. But perhaps you've earned a piece of it."

He crouched across from Eryx, his tone low, deliberate.

"When I was your age, I joined the Poltan Guard. Not out of loyalty to crown or coin—but because my closest friend joined, and I couldn't leave him to it alone. At first, I was just another boy with a sword. But I excelled in training. Too much, perhaps. The old king, Renaesius, took notice. He needed men who could operate outside the laws he himself was bound to. Men invisible, unknown. I became one of them."

Eryx frowned. "You mean… assassinations? Spying?"

Romius's mouth curled, humourless. "Infiltrations. Bandit gangs, smuggling rings, crime dens. I tore them apart from the inside, brought their leaders to ruin. It was bloody work. But it gave me access to the royal archives, the Poltan library. That is where I found the old writings on ellomancy—its histories, its methods. I trained in secret, built strength in the shadows. But I never used my gifts openly. Not until Poltan fell."

His voice grew darker. "Renaesius suspected betrayal from his captain, Leax. He sent me to uncover proof. I did more than that—I haunted the man, dug into the filth he kept buried. I found enough to topple him twice over. But Leax was clever. He twisted the government, turned the people against the very king who'd once lifted them. And me? I became the scapegoat. A phantom assassin, branded traitor."

Eryx leaned forward, caught between disbelief and fascination.

"That was when I used my powers for the first time," Romius said, his eyes glinting like steel catching sunlight. "When the noose closed, I shattered it. I escaped the city and vanished into exile. Since then, I've worked alone. Hunting. Every corrupt official, every snake in politics or the Guard who fattened themselves off Leax's lies. I strip them down, piece by piece. Not for vengeance. For truth. For proof. Enough to clear my name. Enough to release the old king."

He stood, looking out over the empty desert as if the horizon itself carried the weight of his vendetta.

"My last target," he said after a long silence, "is Sallomannax. The City Lord of Tydell. Leax's most trusted advisor. A man whose hands are soaked in more blood than mine. When he falls, the truth rises."

Romius turned back to Eryx, his stare unblinking. "That is why I live. And why you must learn quickly. Because they will come for you, boy—just as they came for me."

Ξ

Alicius spotted them just as they emerged from the barracks—Fallax leading, the others flanking him with their packs slung and weapons readied. She rushed forward, catching the general by the arm before he could disappear into the bustle of the street.

"Please," she begged, breathless. "Tell me what's happened to my son."

Fallax turned to face her. For once, the man who usually barked orders like hammer blows seemed to weigh his words with care. His jaw tightened, and he lowered his voice.

"Listen to me. This city is poisoned. Every stone, every parchment, every whisper drips with lies. If you value your life, and your daughter's, you must leave Gremallax's house. Now."

Alicius shook her head, clutching at his arm tighter. "But Eryx—"

"I'll find him," Fallax cut across, a promise in his words. "But you must protect what remains. Hide. Keep your daughter safe. Do not trust the walls you live in, and do not trust the man you share them with." His gaze flicked past her, toward the towers of Tydell rising above them. "The City Lord has his hand in this, I can feel it. And I'll dig out the rot at the heart of it, no matter how deep it goes. Your boy is tangled in it—but he will not be left behind."

Tears burned her eyes, but the conviction in his voice gave her something she hadn't felt since the news broke: hope. She released his arm, her hands trembling.

"Go," Fallax commanded, already moving. "Survive this."

She stood rooted as the four men vanished into the crowd, their figures swallowed by the morning haze. Then she turned on her heel, urgency snapping through her limbs. She had no time to waste. She would find Oliax, pack what they could carry, and vanish before the city crushed them too.

She had survived ruin once. She would survive it again.

CHAPTER 22- ESCAPE

King Leax sat slouched upon his throne, the golden crest of Thearon gleaming dimly in the torchlight. His crown felt heavier than ever, not as a symbol of glory but of suffocating burden. Behind the mask of composure, his mind churned with dread.

So much pressure. So many lies.

On the surface, he was the protector of the realm — a ruler defending his people from Karathal's relentless pressure on the borders. But beneath that surface? A man drowning in secrets.

His corruption in his youth had festered into something monstrous, now bound to the town of Garraw. Only he and Sallomannax knew the truth: Karathal's interest in Thearon was not for conquest, nor for trade, but for the pit. That cursed pit hidden in Garraw's depths — a secret so ancient and volatile that even Leax barely understood its true nature.

Very few souls in Thearon knew what lay beyond their borders. Even fewer dared to ask. Leax himself had shrouded the kingdom in austerity, tightening its walls until Thearon became a cage. Ships patrolled the coast, their orders absolute: no one in, no one out. Exploration was forbidden. Discovery, punishable by death.

But Karathal knew. Somehow, they had learned what slept in Garraw. And if they broke through his defences, if they reached the pit, everything he had built would unravel in an instant.

Leax gripped the armrests of his throne, knuckles white. His entire reign balanced on a knife's edge — a kingdom fed on lies and silence. If the veil fell, if the truth surfaced… outrage would consume the streets. Civil war would ignite. Thearon would burn, and with it, every soul who had believed in him.

Even the throne beneath him felt unsteady.

Ξ

The City Lord had grown tired of waiting.

Every day wasted in Leax's hesitation was another stone pried loose from Thearon's crumbling defences. The Karathi threat pressed harder at the borders, and yet the King sat idle, a man too weak of stomach and spirit to command the fate of a nation.

Sallomannax sneered at the thought. Power demanded action, not endless worry.

He seized the opportunity. With a single decree, the order went out across the northern territories: the recruitment drive was to end immediately, and every new sword and shield was to reconvene in Tydell. There, under his banner, the might of Thearon would be reforged into an army worthy of victory.

Not Leax's army. His army.

He paced his chamber, the echo of his boots sharp against polished stone, already envisioning the ranks of soldiers marching at his word. If Karathal broke through, the world itself would become an open door — the pit in Garraw no longer Thearon's secret, but everyone's curse.

No. He would not allow it.

If the King would not rise to the challenge, Sallomannax would. And when Thearon survived, it would be his name sung in the streets, his rule whispered of in reverence and fear.

The crown was already rotting on Leax's brow. Soon, it would fall.

Ξ

Alicius kept Oliax close, her hand pressed firmly against her daughter's back as they moved through Gremallax's expansive home. To the guards and servants drifting between corridors, she was just another maid with a rag and bucket, cleaning as duty required. But in truth, every movement was carefully measured — a mask to hide the storm inside.

She had studied the office for weeks, watching where Gremallax set down his keys, where he lingered, which drawer he guarded with unnecessary attention. That was the one. That was where her way out lay.

The moment arrived when the hall fell quiet, no footsteps or clinking armour in earshot. She nudged Oliax toward a corner seat with whispered instruction to stay put, then slipped into the office.

The room smelled faintly of oil and parchment. Sunlight cut through the shutters, painting thin lines across the desk. Her pulse thundered as she crossed the rug, her hand trembling as she slid the drawer open.

There they were. Coins, polished until they gleamed. Symbols of power, of freedom. Alicius hesitated for a fraction of a breath — the enormity of the theft sinking in — then scooped a careful handful, tucking them into her skirt pocket. Not too much. Not enough to raise immediate alarm. Just enough to survive.

She pressed the drawer closed, soft as breath, and slipped back out. The old hinges gave a faint creak that felt like a shout in the silence. Alicius froze, heart stuttering, but no one came. She motioned quickly to Oliax and headed for the front door, every step measured, every glance casual.

Ξ

Gremallax's financial aid, a tall, thin woman with sharp features and sharper habits, entered the office only moments later. She carried a ledger under one arm, prepared as always to cross-check coin against expenditure. Her eyes, trained to notice the smallest detail, fell instinctively to the desk drawer.

Something was wrong.

She opened it, hands moving with the precision of ritual. Her fingers hovered over the coins, counting by weight and instinct. The amount was wrong. Short. Not carelessly short — *deliberately*.

Her jaw tightened. She had been trained to see patterns others missed, and this was no accident.

She straightened, scanning the room, the way the rug was angled, the subtle shift in how the drawer sat. And then — the faint sound of a door easing shut further down the corridor.

The aide strode from the office, skirts brushing the marble floor, eyes narrowing on the far end of the hall. Just vanishing around the corner, she caught a glimpse of a trailing hem.

The maid.

Alicius.

The aide's lips pursed, her thoughts calculating. Should she raise the alarm immediately? Or keep this knowledge to herself for the moment, to see what game the Captain's woman was playing? Reporting theft might bring Gremallax's wrath down on Alicius — but reporting too soon meant revealing that the aide herself had failed in vigilance.

She stood silently in the hallway, ledger clasped tightly against her chest, eyes narrowing as she watched Alicius disappear from view.

Ξ

Meanwhile, Alicius gripped Oliax's hand tighter, her pace quickening as they slipped lower through the tiers. Every step away from Gremallax's home felt like air returning to her lungs. But she could not shake the sensation that eyes followed her — sharp, calculating, patient.

She swallowed hard, whispering to her daughter.

"Keep walking. Don't look back."

But deep inside, Alicius knew: she had not escaped cleanly.

Ξ

The sun beat down like a hammer, unrelenting in its fury. Sand stretched out in every direction, rippling dunes and jagged black stone cutting the horizon. The heat shimmered, twisting the air into cruel mirages.

Fallax and his company trudged onward, boots sinking into the scorched earth, every breath pulling in dust and fire. Sweat streamed down his neck, his cloak offering little relief, his personal guard were sweating but unfazed. They were accustomed. Garraw was still days away and already the desert seemed eager to strip them to bone.

Bard grumbled first, wiping his brow with the back of his hand. "If the rats don't kill us, this cursed sun will."

"Keep moving," Fallax barked without slowing, his eyes fixed dead ahead. "You stop, you bake. You complain, you waste air."

Rannax shifted the strap of his pack and glanced toward Eroge. The blacksmith's son bore the march in silence, though his lips were cracked, and his eyes glowed with a stubborn flame. The past few weeks had seen the boy trim the fat and build in muscle. He was still large but his figure more hulking than bulging. He had carried the staff for Eryx this far without once letting it slip from his grasp.

The wind picked up suddenly, stinging their faces with sharp grains of sand. The desert howled as if alive, forcing them to shield their eyes and press onward with lowered heads.

When the gusts finally relented, Rannax spotted shapes in the distance—carved stone markers jutting out from the sands, weathered and half-buried.

"Old waypoints," he muttered. "Caravan trails."

"Caravan trails mean bandits," Fallax replied, scanning the horizon with a soldier's suspicion. "Eyes sharp. This wasteland isn't empty. But it means we're close to a settlement."

They pushed forward, the silence between them heavy. Every footstep was a test of will, every mile a battle against the land itself.

Somewhere ahead, Garraw waited. But so, did Romius— and whatever truth he held that was worth killing for.

Ξ

Gremallax sat hunched in his office, the aide's words echoing in his skull.

She's gone.

The accusation lingered heavier than the theft itself. He didn't care about the coins — pocket change compared to the wealth he handled daily. What seared through him was the thought that, despite all his efforts to bury the truth of his past, to rebuild himself into something more than the wreckage he once was, he had still managed to lose another woman he had begun to care for.

His gaze drifted to the corner of the desk, to a drawer few even knew existed. An intricate wooden slot, hand-carved, hidden by design. He hesitated. The key weighed against his chest on its chain, cold as guilt.

His fingers trembled as he slipped it into the lock, turning until the mechanism clicked. The drawer slid open with a whisper.

Inside lay a single vial. Small, unassuming. White powder pressed tight within glass. A demon he thought he had locked away forever. His breath caught as temptation washed over him.

The door creaked. Gremallax snapped the drawer shut, shoving the key back beneath his breastplate. His jaw clenched as heavy boots crossed the threshold.

No one refused the City Lord entry.

Sallomannax didn't knock, didn't wait. He simply glided in, an easy confidence in every step, and lowered himself into the chair opposite. He leaned back, resting one arm across the desk as though it were his own.

Neither man spoke. The air thickened, a silent duel of patience and pride.

Finally, Sallomannax broke the quiet. His voice was silk lined with poison.

"I know she stole from you, Captain. The ones closest to us… they always cut the deepest."

Gremallax's eyes narrowed, but he said nothing.

Sallomannax leaned forward, his smile thin, insincere. "I have a proposition. How would you like to lead the Thearon army into battle? Drive back those Karathi scum with your own hands. Prove your loyalty — once and for all."

The words hung like a noose. Gremallax gave no reply. His mind was already elsewhere — haunted by the sound of Oliax's laughter echoing through the halls, so much like his daughter's had once been. By the image of Alicius curled in the armchair, soft and tired, the same way his wife had before.

How could a man lose the same life twice?

Sallomannax read the silence, then rose smoothly, brushing invisible dust from his robes. "An answer by morning," he said, as though it were already decided. And then he was gone, leaving the office heavy with shadows.

Hours passed. The house emptied. The world outside sank into sleep. Still Gremallax sat in that chair, alone with his ghosts.

At last, the drawer slid open again. His hands shook as he twisted the vial's cap free. He poured the powder into a glass of water, stirring until the liquid clouded white.

He stared at it for a long, trembling moment. Then he lifted the glass, drained it in one desperate swallow.

The burn hit his throat, then his veins.

The pain — that deep-rooted, suffocating pain he had carried since the night his family died — began to lift, leaving him hollow.

Years of sobriety, abandoned in a single night.

Ξ

Training had been going well. Romius had pushed Eryx to the edge of exhaustion and dragged him back again, shaping his raw strength into something sharper, more controlled. Now it was time to test whether the boy's instincts matched his potential.

They trekked south, covering a surprising distance in a short space of time. Eryx barely felt the weight of his pack — the Thearonite in his pocket humming faintly, fuelling his endurance like a second heartbeat.

By morning, they crested a ridge and looked down upon a town nestled in the basin below. Unlike the dust-choked villages they'd passed, this place thrived.

Beautiful stone buildings lined clean, cobbled streets. Merchants called from brightly painted stalls. Flower boxes spilled colour from every window. The air smelled of a beautiful cuisine. This was no struggling desert settlement — the leader here had money, influence, and the will to keep appearances polished.

Romius's eyes narrowed. "Yes. This will do."

Eryx glanced at him, uncertain. "For what?"

Instead of answering, Romius crouched in the sand and drew a rough shield shape with his finger. Its centre was marked with a jagged rune.

"A Thearonite shield. Find it. Take it. Bring it back to me."

Eryx blinked. "In daylight? You want me to just… walk into town and steal from them?"

Romius's expression was unreadable. "You've had training. You have instincts. Now you must prove them. A soldier only survives by seizing what others say cannot be taken."

Eryx's mouth went dry, but he nodded. "And you?"

Romius's gaze swept toward the southern edge of the town, where the largest stone building towered above the rest, its banners bright with crimson and gold. His jaw tightened.

"I have another task. One that doesn't concern you."

That was all he offered.

Romius adjusted his cloak, already stepping away, vanishing into the flow of the crowd like a shadow swallowed by sunlight.

Eryx stood for a moment at the ridge, staring down at the thriving town with its neat streets and suspicious order. His stomach twisted with nerves. Daylight theft. He had done it before in the alleys of Tydell, slipping purses or swiping bread. But this — a shield of Thearonite — this was different. Dangerous.

Still, he inhaled deeply, feeling the ore pulse faintly in his pocket, reminding him of what he carried inside.

Then he started down the slope toward the town, each step carrying him deeper into the test Romius had set.

Ξ

King Leax sat hunched upon his throne, the weight of his crown heavier than ever. His chamberlain's words still echoed in his ears: *Sallomannax has seized command of the Northern troops.*

His old ally had turned the blade. Not only had Sallomannax undermined his authority, he had done so with elegance and venom — removing Fallax from his station with a forged suspension, wrapped in such convincing authority that even loyal officers had accepted it without question.

Leax's fingers dug into the gilded armrests of his throne. He had always known Sallomannax was dangerous, but he had believed distance would keep him contained. By gifting him the city of Tydell, he thought the man's hunger would remain tethered to the desert gates. Clearly, that had been a fool's gamble.

Now the court stirred like a nest of hornets. Council members whispered in corners, questioning his grip on the kingdom. Even those most loyal were beginning to ask how their king could allow a provincial lord to take such liberties.

To confront Sallomannax openly would be to risk war with Tydell's army — now bolstered by control of the North. Yet to do nothing would erode his authority until it crumbled beneath him.

When the council gathered, Leax forced a calm mask across his face.

"The City Lord of Tydell is now overseeing the Northern army," he told them, voice measured, deliberate. "It was my decision. He has the proximity and knowledge of the terrain that no other commander could hope to match. This is no usurpation — it is strategy."

There was muttering. Uneasy nods. After a tense pause, the council accepted the explanation. At least, outwardly.

But Leax could see it in their eyes: doubt. Doubt that spread like a sickness, eating away at the image of a king who commanded unchallenged.

He dismissed the court with a steady hand. But when the doors closed, when the echo of their steps faded, the mask broke. His jaw trembled with rage, his breath shallow.

He needed help. Real help. Someone beyond the council. Someone beyond the kingdom's borders.

At his desk, he pulled a scrap of parchment and dipped his quill. Not a long letter. Not one that could be intercepted and dissected. Just a phrase — short, sharp, written in a code known only to one.

He tied the parchment to the leg of a waiting Craekee and opened the window. The great bird launched into the sky, wings glinting as it soared northward — past Tydell, past the Exian Desert, into lands no common citizen of Thearon even dreamed of.

The king watched it vanish into the distance.

This was desperation. A gamble on an old bond. If the message reached its intended hands, there might yet be hope to save his throne.

If not — then the kingdom of Thearon was already lost.

CHAPTER 23- TWISTS AND TURNS

Alicius paid the market stall attendant for the food—food that would last. She needed to find a place to stay while she gathered her thoughts and planned. She didn't know what lay ahead, but she knew it could only bring danger. Tucking the change into her pouch, she squeezed through the bustling crowds of the Tenth Tier.

Though the poorest lived here, everyone came for the fresh fruit and vegetables grown in the fields along the river Tyde. Alicius knew the market well and made her way to the blacksmith: Horoge & Sons. After a few twists and turns, she arrived at the pop-up stall. The forge blazed, heat rippling through the air, as a variety of customers browsed weapons, cooking utensils, and tools.

Alicius stepped inside and waited patiently. Once Horoge's wife had attended to the customers ahead of her, Alicius approached, her voice urgent. She pleaded for help, asking her to shelter Oliax and herself.

Glorius recognized Alicius as Eryx's mother and nodded, stepping aside to allow her through to the back, where Horoge worked at the anvil, sparks flying with each strike.

Alicius leaned against the edge of the forge, letting the heat wash over her, the rhythmic clang of hammer on metal a comforting pulse. She watched Horoge's hands move with practiced precision, shaping the glowing metal as if it were an extension of himself.

"You worry about him," Horoge said gently, glancing at her. His eyes were soft but lined with concern.

"I do," Alicius admitted. "Eryx… in exile. I can't know if he's safe, or where he'll go next. It feels endless." She hugged herself, drawing in the warmth of the forge.

Horoge nodded knowingly, wiping sweat from his brow. "I worry about Eroge too. The army… he's strong, yes, but a craftsman at heart. I always imagined him here, hammer in hand, shaping iron instead of swinging a sword." He let out a small, rueful laugh. "Do you remember when he tried to make that cutting blade for you? Ended up bending every nail in the block instead."

Alicius smiled at the memory, a soft laugh escaping her. "Yes! And Eryx laughed so hard he nearly fell into the well trying to help him straighten it. They were so young… so fearless. And yet… look at them now." Her voice grew quiet, tinged with longing.

Horoge placed the iron aside and leaned back, his gaze distant. "Even then, you could see it—the fire in them. Eryx, always daring. Eroge, steady, careful. But both with hearts bigger than we could have imagined. I suppose it's natural we worry. We've given them roots… now they are learning to walk in storms."

Alicius sighed, her gaze drifting to the glowing metal. "I want to protect them, Horoge. But I feel so powerless."

Horoge put a hand on her shoulder, firm and warm. "I know. I feel it too. But perhaps what they need most is not our protection… but our trust. Trust that they carry a piece of us, and Rabuga will guide them even when we're not there."

Alicius nodded slowly, letting the thought settle. "Trust… yes. That doesn't make the fear go away, but… it makes it lighter, somehow."

Horoge smiled, the corners of his eyes crinkling. "And you're not alone in that. We carry each other's worry too. That makes it easier to bear."

For a while, they stood in quiet camaraderie, memories dancing in the heat and sparks of the forge. Then a small voice broke the reverie.

"Mother! What's this?"

Oliax crouched near a pile of tools, holding up a twisted piece of iron with wide, curious eyes.

Horoge chuckled, wiping his hands. "That, little one, is a work in progress. Metal doesn't tell its story all at once—it takes patience, care, and a steady hand."

Oliax's eyes sparkled. "Can I touch it?"

"Carefully," Alicius said, kneeling beside him. "We can watch Horoge quietly."

As Oliax explored the workshop under their gentle guidance, Alicius felt a profound sense of connection. The worry for her son lingered, but the warmth of shared memory, of friendship, and of life continuing around her reminded her she was not alone. Here, in the heat of the forge and the rhythm of hammer and anvil, she found a small sanctuary. For now.

Ξ

Karathal was a country that seemed to hum with life and invention. Jaimius had always been drawn here, wandering through streets lined with gleaming stone and steel towers that pierced the sky. The southern City of Bermańs had buildings curved and twisted with architectural daring, their surfaces embedded with shimmering panels that captured sunlight and reflected it in dancing patterns. Bridges of polished metal arched above bustling avenues, carrying pedestrians, sleek carriages in a steady stream. In comparison, Thearon felt rooted in a different era, its timbered houses and uneven streets clinging to tradition while Karathal surged forward, a country built on innovation and ambition. Jaimius' work led to information of countries even further beyond Karathal. It was fairy tales to a boy of Thearon.

The air itself seemed sharper here, scents bursting from street-side cafés. Humming mechanisms and soft chimes accompanied the footsteps of the city's inhabitants, each sound a note in a symphony of modern life.

Jaimius moved with practiced ease, blending among the Karathi, his eyes scanning for faces, listening for information. That was the work of a historian, yes, but also of a spy. Once Leax had recognised his talents beyond scholarship, he had been stationed in Tydell, close enough to the border to slip in and out of Karathal at will. Six years had passed in careful observation, in building relationships and collecting secrets.

Ahead, his destination came into view: a restaurant tucked at the foot of a towering inn, a grand building where travellers from across the nation sought temporary lodging. Unlike the inns of Thearon, this place was sleek and modern, its design blending comfort with elegance. The restaurant's wide glass walls allowed sunlight to flood the interior, lighting polished floors that reflected the soft glow of suspended lanterns. Tables of dark, flawless wood were arranged with deliberate spacing, each set with gleaming silverware and fine porcelain dishes. Servers moved fluidly among the diners, balancing trays heavy with exotic fare—smoked meats, colourful vegetables, and pastries that sent waves of scent across the room. The faint hiss of steaming drinks, clinking cutlery, and subdued conversation created a lively yet refined soundtrack.

Jaimius found his Karathi acquaintances seated at the centre, a small crowd gathered near them, their animated discussion a potential source of valuable intelligence. Plenty of patrons could hear, but it mattered little. He could work in plain sight. Every measured step, every casual glance, every deliberate sip of wine was part of the act. He was not merely observing; he was performing, weaving seamlessly into their world while keeping his true purpose hidden.

Even here, amidst the elegance and chatter, a tension prickled at his senses. The city's splendour, the refined aroma of food, the warmth of sunlight on glass—all of it was a mask, a dazzling distraction. Jaimius reminded himself to watch, to listen, to remember. Every detail could be a clue, every smile a test, every whisper a secret waiting to be uncovered.

Ξ

Eryx shifted through the pristine streets of the town, moving like a shadow. His eyes darted constantly, searching for the object he had come to claim—a Thearonite shield, clearly of immense value and protected by layers of security.

Near a beautifully gardened square, a cluster of scribes busied themselves outside a grand building. Eryx approached with careful poise, his calm demeanour belying the urgency in his chest. Above the entrance, a sign read *Museum* in crisp Thearonite script, rather than Tydellese—a detail he noted with quiet satisfaction. His mother had taught him both languages, and the lesson now proved invaluable.

He skirted around the side of the building, eyes scanning for a gap or an unlocked window. Along the second story ran a terrace that wrapped around the front and sides. With precise timing and measured strength, Eryx scaled a stone pillar, fingers piercing their own tiny grooves in the weathered stone to anchor himself. Each movement was deliberate, controlled, a test of balance and power.

At last, he reached the terrace. Fortune favoured him— the doors were ajar, letting a gentle breeze drift into the museum. He slipped inside, stepping into the cool shadow of the grand hall, his presence barely more than a whisper.

High above, hidden among the rooftops, a shadowy figure watched him, motionless. Eryx, unaware, continued his mission, every step bringing him closer to the prize and, unknowingly, deeper into danger.

The museum's interior was vast, its high ceilings supported by polished columns, and sunlight streamed through tall windows, illuminating exhibits in a soft golden glow. Eryx's eyes adjusted quickly to the light, scanning the room. Display cases lined the halls, holding artefacts of silver, bronze, and carved stone, each labelled in meticulous Thearonite script. The air smelled faintly of polished wood and aged parchment.

At the far end of the hall, on a raised pedestal beneath a protective glass dome, rested the Thearonite shield. Its polished surface gleamed even in the filtered light, intricate runes etched along its rim hinting at both artistry and power. The shield's aura of importance was unmistakable; it was the centrepiece of the museum, drawing Eryx like a magnet.

Yet the hall was not empty. Guards swarmed the place like bees protecting their queen. Eryx crouched low, moving with practiced stealth, each step deliberate. His mind raced, calculating the pattern of the guards' patrols and the layout of the defences.

From above, the shadowy figure shifted slightly, tilting their head as if weighing the boy's skill.

Ξ

Gremallax awoke in his bed, head pounding, the bitter weight of regret pressing down on him. The decision to use Flax clung to him like a curse, guilt and nausea twisting in his stomach as sharply as the ache in his skull. He forced down a sip of water from the tray his maid had brought and, with a rasping voice, ordered her to send a messenger to the City Lord. His words felt heavy, foreign, as he confirmed he would take command of the Northern army.

He didn't want it. In truth, he wanted nothing more than to curl into himself and disappear, to let the pain smother him until he was no more. Death, he thought, would be a gift he had not earned. And so, the torment remained— his punishment.

The reply came swiftly: *Have the forces ready to march north by dawn. You will face the Karathi at first light.*

There was no time for weakness. Gremallax bathed, the cold-water biting at his skin, forcing him awake. He dressed in the stiff layers of command, each piece of clothing feeling heavier than armour, and set out for the barracks. The carriage wheels clattered against the mountain road as his mind circled endlessly over the events of the past few days, memories he could not silence. He would not return home for months—perhaps longer—but it made no difference. He owned nothing of worth anymore. He had already lost everything that mattered.

Before the road crested toward the barracks, Gremallax ordered the carriage to stop. He stepped out, the chill air biting against his cheeks, and there, waiting in the shadow of a boulder, stood Damiax—the debt collector and Flax dealer.

The exchange was quick, discreet: coin for powder, poison for guilt. Gremallax's hand trembled as he pocketed the small parcel, shame rising like bile in his throat. Without a word, he returned to the carriage. As it rumbled onward toward the barracks, the weight in his chest grew heavier, not lighter.

He was a commander now, burdened with the lives of men, yet he carried into battle not just orders and steel—but the gnawing rot of his own weakness.

Ξ

Romius stalked toward the building, its façade polished and proud, owned by yet another of Leax's cronies. His steps were measured, deliberate, like the pacing of a predator. He had not set out to become a monster, but circumstance had carved him into one. Now he sought vengeance. He sought justice.

His king—his friend—Renaesius languished in a cell, reputation tarnished, name dragged through the mud. Romius would not rest while corruption thrived.

The guards at the door barely slowed him. They were no match for his prowess—too slow, too unprepared. By the time they raised their blades, he was already past them, striking with precision and silence. Not a single alarm sounded.

He reached the office at the heart of the estate. With a single kick, his boot shattered the thick wooden door, sending splinters scattering across the floor. Inside sat the local leader, a weaselly figure lounging in a plush chair, expression half smug, half expectant.

Romius's eyes glowed silver as he extended a hand. *Domir,* his weapon, answered the call, its presence surging toward him.

But the official did not beg, did not cower. Instead, with a grimace of effort, he yanked hard on a lever hidden beside his chair. The floor beneath Romius gave way, collapsing into blackness.

The fall carried him thirty feet before he struck the ground. He landed in a crouch, the force of his impact rippling outward in a shockwave that cracked the stone beneath his boots. Overhead, he glimpsed the door slam shut, the last sliver of light vanishing as iron shutters sealed him in.

Darkness swallowed the chamber whole. Then, with a whistle through the air, Domir streaked down through the closing gap to meet his master's hand.

Romius stood tall in the pitch black, silver eyes burning brighter.

Ξ

Jaimius greeted Roulea with his usual charm. She was a striking woman who ran a hired carriage service business, her riders spread throughout the city like a web of eyes and ears. Information flowed to her as naturally as traffic through the streets, and she wielded it with subtlety and discretion. Alongside her sat Florain, a portly woman in her early forties with quick wit and shrewd eyes. She owned a cleaning service contracted to the finest inns of Karathal, and it was through her connections that they had secured reservations in the restaurant that evening.

These women were highly successful, yet far removed from the corrupt and arrogant elite that often polluted Karathi society. That was why Jaimius trusted them—why he could draw upon their insights without fear of betrayal. Over plates of delicately spiced fish and wine poured into slender crystal glasses, they spoke of politics. Inevitably, the conversation turned to the border disputes with Thearon.

Roulea and Florain, like many Karathi, knew little of Thearon beyond rumour and assumption. To them, it was a land locked in the primitive days of hunters and gatherers, a nation fumbling in the dark while Karathal strode forward in brilliance. They spoke of Thearon almost with pity, as if it were Karathal's burden—and destiny—to guide their neighbours into civilization.

Jaimius nodded politely, masking his thoughts, though deep down he could not deny an element of truth in their words. Thearon lagged behind. Compared to Karathal's stone towers and radiant avenues, his homeland felt like a relic of a bygone age.

The conversation carried on well into the meal, laughter and speculation filling the space between sips of wine. When at last the gathering dispersed, Jaimius took his leave and returned to his accommodations: a chamber in one of Karathal's grand residential buildings, fitted with every necessity—bedroom, kitchen, bathing room. Luxuries Thearon's nobility might envy.

Later, he sat upon the stone balcony, gazing out at the lamp-lit streets below. The soft glow of the city's lights painted the night in hues of gold and silver. Karathal never truly slept; even at this hour, carriages rattled through the avenues, and the hum of distant conversation rose with the breeze.

Then came an unusual sound, a sharp flutter of wings. A craekee—a rare messenger bird—alighted beside him, its dark eyes gleaming. Tied to its leg was a letter sealed with the royal crest of Thearon.

Jaimius' heart tightened. He broke the seal and unfolded the parchment. The orders were clear: he was to return immediately, bringing with him all of his reports. Six years of painstaking research—Karathal's history, its culture, its technology, everything he had gathered in meticulous secrecy—was to be carried back across the border.

He had known this summons would come one day. Yet this time felt different. Final. Permanent.

He thought of his brief journeys home in years past, excursions only to retrieve Auracite before vanishing back into the city that had become his second skin. But this letter spoke of more than another errand. It carried the weight of inevitability, of something vast and irreversible.

Jaimius folded the letter slowly, his gaze drifting back to the glowing streets of Karathal. He could feel it in the air—a shift, a storm waiting on the horizon. Something that could change the whole of Warrah was on its way.

Ξ

It was rare for a news parchment to be released in the afternoon. When it was, it meant urgency.

This one carried two stories. The first announced the City Lord's new command of the Northern army, a bold declaration of his intent to halt the Karathi invasion. The second was more troubling—a plea for information regarding the theft committed on Captain Gremallax.

Alicius's chest tightened as she read. Fear gnawed at her. She had been welcomed with kindness into the home of Horoge and Glorius, and now she worried she might have placed them in danger simply by being there. The decision weighed heavily, but it had to be made: she would stay the night for Oliax's sake, then leave Tydell at dawn.

Her thoughts turned to Eryx, her son wandering alone somewhere beyond her reach. The ache of not knowing pressed on her, but she forced herself to breathe. She still had Oliax to care for—she needed her here and now. Eryx had made his choices, reckless though they were, and she would honour them by protecting the child still at her side.

Someday, she promised herself, she would find Eryx again. But tonight, she had to endure. And in the morning, she would run.

Ξ

Eryx bolted forward, every muscle coiled and released with flawless precision. His feet barely kissed the marble floor as he propelled himself through the first line of defenders. A guard thrust a halberd across his path— Eryx twisted his body sideways mid-sprint, the blade whistling past his ribs as his hand snapped out to shove the man's shoulder, sending him stumbling into his comrade.

Another swung a short sword down at him. Eryx ducked low, rolling across the floor, his palms grazing the polished stone before he sprang back to his feet. A spear jabbed toward his chest—he seized the shaft, spun, and let the guard's own momentum carry him into a display case that shattered in a burst of glass and dust.

Every step was calculation, every motion deliberate. His speed wasn't reckless—it was controlled, honed. A second guard lunged from his blind side. Without breaking stride, Eryx vaulted onto the man's shoulder, kicking off to hurl himself higher, flipping over the next rank of defenders. He landed in a crouch, his boots skidding against the marble but his balance unshaken.

Shouts filled the chamber, armoured feet clanging as reinforcements poured in. A sword arced for his head— Eryx dipped beneath it, spinning past, brushing the weapon as though mocking the strike. He leapt again, hands catching the edge of a tall plinth. Using it as a springboard, he twisted his body mid-air and came down behind another guard, shoving him aside without a strike.

The shield glimmered ahead, runes etched along its rim like a beacon calling him. His breath came steady despite the storm of steel and shouting around him. The world narrowed to a single point: the pedestal.

A final defender stepped forward, broad-shouldered and braced for impact. Eryx surged toward him, feinting left, then darting right, slipping through the narrowest gap in the man's guard. His hand brushed the man's gauntlet as he slid past, then he was free.

At last, he reached the pedestal. The Thearonite shield gleamed under the lamplight, flawless, ancient, powerful. He stretched out his hand, fingers trembling as they hovered over its surface.

And then—

The glass dome overhead shattered with a deafening crack.

Shards rained down in a glittering storm. The air shifted, sharp alongside dust and broken stone. Eryx froze, half-crouched before the shield, his heart hammering.

On the balcony he had leapt from moments ago stood a
figure cloaked in menace: a slender, masked woman. Her
eyes glowed, slits aflame with an unnatural green
essence, and at her belt pulsed the unmistakable radiance
of Verdacryl.

The hall fell silent. The guards who moments ago had
fought with desperate ferocity now stood rigid, weapons
slack in their hands. Even Eryx, still reaching toward the
shield, felt the heat in his chest cool to ice.

Ξ

Fallax, Bard, Rannax, and Eroge crested the ridge as the
town revealed itself—a cluster of stone and timber
buildings huddled around a central well, its moss-
darkened stones glinting faintly in the sinking sun. To
men who had wandered across barren stretches of scrub
and dust, the sight was more than welcome; it was a
beacon, a reminder that civilization still existed beyond
the endless march of wilderness.

They threaded through the narrow streets, the smell of
iron and ash lingering in the air. Eroge's sharp eye was
drawn almost immediately to a squat building near the
well—its iron sign still faintly gleaming: a blacksmith's.
He drifted toward it, curiosity written all over him.

Inside, two smiths worked, their tools clanging half-
heartedly against the metal. Both bore injuries—
bandaged arms, bruised faces, cuts that hadn't quite
healed. Their eyes narrowed as they noticed the
strangers. The older of the two straightened, wiping
sweat from his brow, and barked, "Move along. We

don't need your kind sniffin' around here." His words were followed by a string of profanity spat with such venom that even Bard, usually quick with a reply, chose to say nothing. The resentment in the room was thick as forge smoke.

Fallax lingered only a moment, his mind mapping the town against scraps of knowledge he'd collected from his study of Thearon geography. The local leader was no noble of note, merely a town official, but that was the man they needed to reach. Still, the sun was already sliding toward the horizon, streaking the sky with copper light. Rest—and ale—came first. Tomorrow would bring the politics.

They found a tavern tucked between two leaning buildings. It was small, with four tables, one harried server, and an atmosphere thick enough to choke on. Locals turned as they entered, eyes following them with open suspicion. Every whisper, every half-hidden glance, told the four they were intruders.

The only empty table sat in the corner, scarred with knife marks and stained with old drink. They claimed it without a word. Four Yelast bitters were ordered, the mugs clattering onto the table a few minutes later. The taste was harsh, bitter, but welcome all the same.

For a time, they sat in silence, the aches of travel settling into their bones. Their legs throbbed from the march, their skin still stung from sun and wind, but listening— listening was what mattered.

Rannax leaned back, half-turned as though casual, ears straining toward the conversations around them. Bard's loud belches and muttered curses threatened to drown the room, but Rannax tuned him out, focusing on the murmur of voices. Snippets came: talk of the blacksmiths' injuries, mutterings of an attack. Then the words blurred into tavern-noise again—until another fragment cut through, sharp as a blade.

"…soldiers, asking… two men… glowing ores…"

Rannax stilled. His pulse quickened as he pushed deeper into the noise, listening harder, straining to pull the words from the muddle of voices.

"…tall one, scarred… the other… younger… eyes like flint, hair dark…"

The description was unmistakable. Eryx.

Before his mind could stop him, Rannax shot to his feet and strode across the room. The locals flinched back, muttering, but he ignored them, his attention fixed on a stout woman clutching her drink. He leaned in, voice urgent. "Describe the second man again."

The woman's eyes widened, but she spoke, her voice sharp with the thrill of gossip. Each word painted the image clearer—Eryx's face, his manner, his bearing. By the time she finished, there was no room for doubt.

Rannax turned, throat tight, and saw his companions watching him. They had heard enough. The truth settled like a lead weight in the air between them.

"Eryx…" Eroge muttered, his voice cracking slightly, "working with Romius." His heart sank as though stones had been dropped into it. Was his friend caught in Romius's storm, or had he become a storm himself?

Bard swore under his breath, shaking his head. Rannax sat heavily, jaw clenched. The tavern seemed colder now.

Fallax, as always, was the first to speak. His voice was measured, but it cut clean. "If the boy is with Romius, then he is lost to us. Whatever friendship, whatever bond you thought remained—bury it. From here on, he is the enemy."

The words struck like hammer blows. None of them wanted to believe it, but the truth was there, staring them in the face. Emotion would cloud their judgment and that could mean death.

And so, in that dim little tavern, over mugs of bitter ale, three soldiers of Barrack Thirteen wrestled silently with the possibility that one of their own had already slipped beyond saving.

Ξ

The museum trembled as silence gave way to the crackle of power.

Eryx's hand lingered on the Thearonite shield, the cold metal sending a rush of energy spiralling into his veins. Silvery-blue smoke bled from his skin, curling like ghostly flame around his arms. His heartbeat pounded in his ears. The guards froze, eyes wide, as if instinct told them this fight was not theirs.

Above, the masked woman stepped forward from the shattered balcony. Her boots crunched against glass as she dropped lightly to the museum floor. A sickly dark-green aura bled from the Verdacryl crystal at her hip, crawling up her arms like veins. The mask revealed only her eyes—slits burning with malevolent flame.

"You touch what isn't yours," she said, her voice sharp, metallic. "And you don't leave alive."

Eryx snarled, rolling his shoulders. His skin rippled as patches of it hardened, glinting into polished steel. He was pondering if this was a part of Romius' plan or not

In a heartbeat he launched forward. His speed blurred the space between them, floor tiles cracking under the force of his stride. He swung the shield like a battering ram, silvery smoke flaring with the impact. The woman caught the blow on a wall of stone she pulled from the floor itself—marble bending like clay at her command. The shield slammed against it, sparks spraying, but the wall morphed mid-strike into jagged spikes aimed for his chest.

Eryx twisted aside, flipping over the razors of stone, landing low with feline grace. With a thought, the steel braces of the nearby display stands screeched to life, bending and snaking toward her like living chains.

She didn't flinch. With a flick of her hand, smoke shot from her fingers, engulfing the metal as they turned liquid black, losing its form and splattering uselessly to the floor. In the same breath she spun forward, her hand morphing into a serrated blade of obsidian that slashed toward his throat.

Steel rippled across Eryx's neck and jaw—her blade screeched against him, sparks flying. His fist, now a silver gauntlet of living Thearonite, hammered into her side. The impact blasted her across the hall, smashing her into a column.

The woman stood, coughing, her mask cracked but still intact, villainous green smoke pouring out. She pressed a palm against the column, and suddenly the marble twisted—its veins glowed green, flowing up like liquid. It stretched and sharpened into a spear she hurled with impossible precision.

Eryx caught it mid-flight, fingers digging into the shaft. His power surged; the spear liquefied, silver-blue smoke swirling as he strained against the force of the throw. With a gritted teeth, he spun and swung a fallen weapon back at her in a deadly arc.

She met it head-on, shifting her own weapon from stone into metal, from metal into glass, adapting faster than most men could breathe. Each clash rang like thunder. Sparks of silver and green lit the hall, their powers bleeding into one another, twisting the air itself.

But she was more disciplined. Her movements were precise, almost surgical. Eryx fought like a storm—raw, relentless, fuelled by youth and fire. His strikes cracked the floor, shattered cases, tore gouges through stone walls. Her counter-strikes wove through his rage, deflecting, redirecting, turning his power back against him.

At last she feinted low, then caught him across the ribs with a blade of jagged crystal, sending him sprawling through a display. Shards rained down. Blood trickled down his side, steaming where it touched the steel of his skin. He was not quick enough.

But Eryx only rose, eyes blazing, silver smoke billowing now in thick torrents. He raised his hand, and from every corner of the museum the Thearonite—nails, ornaments, fragments, hidden veins in the architecture—glowed and the power converged around him in a storm.

The woman narrowed her eyes, dark-green glow flaring. The world itself seemed to ripple around her. "This only ends with death."

Eryx refused to respond. This was not what Romius had planned. This was all linked to the attack at the carriage, his exile. He had all the pieces but couldn't see the picture. He needed Romius and he needed him now.

The air exploded as the two forces collided again— Verdacryl's green flame against Thearonite's silver storm, shaking the very foundation of Thearon.

The museum was wreckage. Displays lay in ruin, walls cracked and bleeding dust, the air a war of silver smoke and green fire.

Eryx's storm of Thearonite mist howled around him, hundreds of shards spinning like a cyclone. He hurled forward in a wave, a tsunami of living metal. The masked woman planted her feet and raised both hands. The floor itself obeyed. Tiles tore free, glass reshaped into shimmering shields, wood and stone twisted to her will. He crashed into her defence, silver sparks against green flame. He stumbled to the floor.

Her body blurred with unnatural grace. She slipped past his feeble attempts like water through cracks, every swipe bending just slightly out of her path. She closed the distance in a heartbeat, hand reshaping into a jagged obsidian claw.

Eryx barely had time to harden his chest into steel before she struck. The impact sent him flying into a wall, ribs groaning under the force even through his armoured flesh. He coughed blood, silver smoke spilling from the wound like steam. His legs trembled as he rose, but she was already upon him again—her strikes ruthless, each blow guided with deadly precision.

A green glow flared in her palm, and suddenly the steel skin on his arm softened, turning brittle and chalky under her manipulation. Her next strike shattered it, leaving flesh exposed.

Eryx cried out and staggered back, the fight being dragged out of him blow by blow. His powers flickered, the silver-blue smoke thinning. She loomed over him, mask cracked but eyes burning brighter than ever.

"You fight well," she hissed, voice low, dangerous. "But not well enough."

She raised her arm, obsidian blade forming, ready to plunge through his chest—

When a *roar* split the hall.

A massive battle axe, black as midnight with veins of silver fire, crashed between them, forcing her to stumble back. The weapon buried itself into the marble floor, its sheer weight cracking stone. The green glow of her Verdacryl faltered for the first time.

From the shadows at the shattered balcony, a figure dropped—towering, broad, eyes blazing silver. Romius. His presence was suffocating, power rippling from him in waves that made even the walls groan. He extended his hand, and the axe—*Domir*—tore itself free from the floor and flew into his grasp.

The masked woman froze. Her eyes, once aflame with Verdacryl's glow, narrowed in something close to fear.

"You..." she breathed, voice sharp with recognition.

Romius levelled Domir at her, the silver glow lighting the museum with ghostly fire.

For a heartbeat, the tension stretched thin. Eryx stood, clutching his side, struggling to draw breath. He'd never seen Romius like this, not so utterly unshakable. The woman tilted her head, silent, then with a swirl of green smoke, she leapt back into the shadows. In seconds, she was gone—vanished.

The silence left behind was deafening.

Romius turned, the glow in his eyes dimming slightly. He extended a hand to Eryx, pulling him to his feet with surprising gentleness.

"You've stirred a hornet's nest, boy," Romius muttered, steadying him.

Eryx wiped blood from his lip, wincing. "Where on Warrah were you?"

No response.

Without another word, the two slipped out through the ruined side of the museum, Domir's glow lighting the rubble-strewn path. The streets outside were already stirring with alarm, guards rushing toward the chaos. Romius led them through back alleys, Romius carried Eryx as they burst into the open expanse.

At last, the crooked silhouette of Romius's shack came into view—its wooden frame a jarring contrast to the town's pristine stone.

Eryx exhaled, every muscle screaming. For now, at least, they had escaped.

Ξ

The tavern grew quieter as the night stretched on, locals slipping out one by one until only a handful remained, shadows thrown long across the wooden walls by the guttering lamps. The server yawned, polishing mugs more out of habit than care, but the four men of Barrack Thirteen still sat in their corner. Their mugs had long since emptied, the dregs bitter at the bottom.

The silence between them was no longer companionable. It was heavy, brittle, ready to splinter at the wrong word.

Eroge shifted restlessly, elbows on the table, hands scrubbing across his face. Every so often he opened his mouth as though to speak but closed it again. His leg bounced beneath the table, the nervous energy of a man fighting with himself. When at last he did speak, his voice was low, raw.

"Eryx wouldn't betray us. He wouldn't. Not by choice." His eyes burned as he looked at them, seeking something—anything—in their faces to anchor his hope.

Bard snorted, loud, slamming his mug down so hard the table rattled. "People change, boy. You think you know someone, then war, fear, power—" he jabbed a thick finger toward the door, toward the dark streets beyond "—and suddenly they're not the lad you remember. They're a stranger. Maybe worse." He belched afterward, the drink taking effect. His shoulders slumped, but his words lingered like smoke.

Rannax leaned back in his chair, arms folded, gaze distant. His jaw flexed, the muscle working as he mulled over what he'd heard, what he'd seen. "We don't know enough," he said finally, voice level but taut with tension. "Descriptions, gossip, rumours in a tavern—that isn't proof. I'll not condemn the boy until I see him with my own eyes." His tone made it clear he was already preparing to do just that, no matter what the others decided.

Fallax, as ever, remained still. His expression unreadable, his eyes sharp and steady. When he spoke, it was without hesitation. "You're all letting sentiment cloud the truth. Romius is chaos. If Eryx walks with him, whether willingly or not, he is dangerous. That makes him an enemy. We can't afford to pretend otherwise."

Eroge's chair scraped loudly as he pushed back, anger flaring. "He's my friend. My brother-in-arms. You'd throw him away without even trying to save him?"

Fallax's gaze cut to him, cool as steel. "I'd throw away a thousand friends to keep you alive tomorrow."

The words hung in the air, sharp and merciless. Eroge clenched his fists but didn't reply. His anger had no outlet; it churned inside him, threatening to eat him alive.

Bard waved a hand, reaching for another mug but finding none. "All this talk's poison. Best we sleep. Maybe the morning will make sense of it all."

But sense did not come.

Later, when they finally settled into the cramped, rented room above the tavern, the truth of their divisions deepened. Bard snored heavily, the ale dragging him into uneasy dreams. Fallax sat in silence by the window, sharpening his knife by lamplight, his mind already calculating, stripping emotion away piece by piece. Rannax lay awake staring at the ceiling, every instinct telling him to track Eryx down and find the truth himself.

And Eroge—Eroge stood alone by the shuttered window, watching the quiet street below. He thought of laughter shared in the markets, of playing games, having each-others back in a life where every man fought for himself. He thought of Eryx's smile, his recklessness, his loyalty. And he wondered if that boy still existed—or if he was already gone.

CHAPTER 24- DIVISION

The shack groaned as Romius shoved the door shut behind them, the warped wood rattling against its frame. Domir resting against the far wall like a sentinel.

Eryx paced the uneven floor, fists clenched, chest still rising and falling hard from the fight. His silver-blue smoke lingered faintly around his shoulders, as though his body refused to let the rage settle.

"You left me." His voice was sharp, cutting the silence.

Romius dragged a chair into the centre of the room and sat heavily, the floorboards creaking beneath his weight. He didn't look up. "You handled yourself."

"Handled myself?" Eryx snapped, spinning toward him. "That woman nearly *killed me*! She shattered my skin, tore me apart piece by piece. If you hadn't shown up when you did, I'd be lying in a pool of my own blood!"

Romius's eyes flicked up then, silver glow simmering faintly. His tone was flat, a hammer striking cold iron. "Exactly, I arrived and you're still breathing."

Eryx slammed his hand against the table, the wood warping under the sudden strain of Thearonite energy. "You don't get it! You don't know what it's like to be left behind—to watch someone walk away and wonder why you weren't enough for them to stay." His voice cracked on the edge of the word. "I was left for dead and you were nowhere to be scene. I am still waiting for an explanation." He jabbed a finger at Romius, smoke curling from his fingertips. "You're no different to the rest of the scum."

For the first time, Romius leaned forward, his massive frame casting a shadow across the boy. His voice carried the weight of stone and years of bitterness.

"You think you're the only one who's been left? My king rots in chains, my brothers-in-arms turned their backs, my family cast me out like filth. I begged for mercy once—just once—and they spat on me. Don't stand there and whine about abandonment as if you own it."

The words hit like a forge hammer. Eryx's chest heaved, his jaw tightening, tears threatening but lost in the fury boiling inside.

"You were supposed to fight beside me," Eryx growled. "Not chase your vengeance while I bled!"

Romius rose slowly from the chair, towering, his presence filling the shack like a storm. His expression was carved from stone, but his eyes burned brighter. "Vengeance is all I have left. You want me to cradle you, boy? To soothe your fears like some doting father? I am not your father. If you can't stand alone, you'll never survive."

The words slashed through what little restraint Eryx had left. His skin shimmered, patches of steel crawling over his arms, smoke billowing heavier from his mouth and eyes, mixing with the tears. He stepped forward, closing the distance until he was chest-to-chest with Romius.

Romius didn't flinch. His own silver glow flared, smoke rising like battle-fire, every breath searing the air.

The two stood nose to nose, unyielding, the room trembling with the clash of their power. Silver and blue smoke coiled together, mingling, choking the space with raw energy. The shack creaked as though it might split apart under the pressure of their fury.

Ξ

The barracks office was heavy with stale. Gremallax stirred in the chair he had slumped into the night before, the weight of his armour cast aside in a heap near the wall. His head pounded, his throat raw as if he had swallowed ash. For a moment he considered letting the blackness claim him again, to sink into the numbness— but duty called. He would travel north with the army soon.

On his table lay the previous days parchment, edges still crisp. He blinked against the blur in his vision, forcing his trembling hand to drag it closer. The bold ink bled together, but he made out enough.

**THEFT IN THE CITY.
SUSPECTS AT LARGE.**

His heart gave a painful thud. The words twisted further down the page, and there it was—**Captain Gremallax's name.** The City Lord had begun his hunt.

Alicius.

His vision sharpened with the name, the haze burning back just enough to bring his thoughts together. She had taken shelter somewhere, hidden in the labyrinth of the tenth tier. He had painted a target on her without even realizing.

He tried to stand. His legs betrayed him, buckling, sending him crashing against the edge of the desk. He hissed through his teeth, gripping the wood hard enough to splinter it. His body screamed to sink back into the chair, into the oblivion flax promised.

But he fought it.

"Not her," he rasped, dragging himself upright. Sweat slicked his brow, his breath ragged. His reflection in the steel mirror across the room was unrecognizable— sunken eyes, sallow skin, the husk of the commander he once was.

He forced himself to the wash basin, plunging his face into the icy water. The shock ripped a gasp from his lungs, clearing the fog for just a heartbeat. He clung to that clarity, gripping it like a weapon.

If the City Lord's men reached her first, Alicius would be no more than another pawn, another crushed soul. He couldn't let that happen.

He pulled on his cloak, fingers fumbling with the clasp, and belted on his sword. The weight nearly pulled him down, his muscles screaming from neglect and poison. But he bore it. He had to.

Gremallax staggered toward the door, caught sight of Urasmus and Holiax. He gave them orders to ready the troops and begin the march. Gremallax would follow later. Now he had to fight.

maybe, just maybe, he could save *her.*

Ξ

The first fingers of dawn stretched across the cracked shutters of the inn, painting the room in pale gold. The four soldiers stirred on their straw mattresses, the stale smell of ale still clinging to their breaths. Silence held for a moment—until Fallax spoke.

"Eryx isn't just lost in Romius' shadow," Fallax said coldly, buckling his sword belt. "He's part of this now. This criminality. Whatever he was to you, Eroge, that boy is gone."

The words landed like a blade through Eroge's chest. He shot upright, fists clenching. He had spent all night toiling with this notion. "You don't know him like I do. Eryx wouldn't betray us—he wouldn't betray *me!*"

Fallax didn't even flinch at the outburst. "I know enough. He's working with Romius. That makes him our enemy. You can shout all you want, but facts don't bend to your feelings, soldier."

Eroge's chest heaved, his jaw locked tight. He stepped forward, rage burning through the fatigue in his limbs. He towered over the general, "Say. That. Again."

Fallax turned slowly, his eyes sharp and unyielding. "If you're about to throw a punch at your superior," he sniped through gritted teeth, "then be ready to accept what comes after."

The air thickened, the space between them about to snap—until two voices cut in.

"Enough!" Bard shoved Fallax back with a heavy hand. "Don't pour oil on the fire, Fallax. You've said your piece."

At the same time, Rannax moved swiftly, gripping Eroge's arm before the younger man could lunge. "Outside. Now." His voice was calm, steady, but it left no room for argument.

Eroge's breath came ragged as Rannax dragged him toward the door. The cool morning air hit them like a rain storm, though Eroge's fists still shook with fury.

"Why don't they believe me?" he snapped, pacing, eyes hot with unshed tears. "Why does everyone think Eryx is lost? He's my friend. My brother! He wouldn't—he couldn't—" His voice cracked, the anger slipping into pain. "I just… I miss him. I miss them all. My family. My friends. And now he's gone too."

Rannax leaned against the wall, arms folded, his eyes softening. "I know. I haven't seen my family in years either. Decisions pulled me away, and the world didn't care if I wanted to go or not. Life takes you in directions you don't choose. Some you dream of. Some you curse. But the only thing you can control is yourself."

Eroge turned his face away, swiping roughly at his eyes. The silence stretched, broken only by the clatter of shutters being opened across the town.

"You stay cool, Eroge," Rannax continued. "Because if you lose yourself, then Romius wins. Then Eryx is truly gone. And I know you're stronger than that."

Eroge drew a shaky breath. The fire in his chest dulled, not gone, but manageable. He looked at Rannax, finally meeting his gaze, and gave a short nod. "Yeah… I'll try."

"That's all any of us can do," Rannax replied.

Ξ

Alicius tugged firmly at Oliax's hand as they pushed through the crush of the early morning rush. The streets of Tydell buzzed with vendors setting up stalls, labourers hurrying toward unfinished structures, the rumble of cartwheels carrying stone and supplies. To anyone else it was ordinary, but to her, every noise felt sharpened, every glance a potential threat. She had spent the night in Horoge and Glorius' home, but sleep had never come. Instead, she'd lain awake, staring at the ceiling, replaying the headlines of the parchment and imagining what might already be moving against her.

Now she had what she needed. She just had to escape before the City Lord's hand closed around her.

She turned down a narrow lane—and froze.

Two guards stood planted outside *Horoge & Sons*, their uniform catching the pale morning light, their postures stiff and deliberate. Between them, Horoge himself, collar bunched in a guards fist.

"Tell us where she went," the first guard snarled, yanking him forward. His partner, a wiry man with a cruel smirk, delivered a hard punch into Horoge's stomach. The sound was sickening, the kind of hit that could fold most men in half.

But Horoge was not most men. He was broad and barrel-chested, years of hammering iron giving him a body more like stone than flesh. He absorbed the blow with a grunt and straightened to his full height, glaring down at the two smaller men. His silence was louder than words, his glare a wall they couldn't climb.

The guards shifted uneasily. They puffed their chests, spat more threats, even slung insults at his family name—but they knew better than to press further. To draw steel against the town's most respected blacksmith would stir trouble they couldn't afford. Eventually, with a shove and a final warning, they left, muttering to each other as they vanished into the street's tide of bodies.

From her hidden place amongst the crowd, Alicius exhaled, her pulse pounding so loud it filled her ears. She tugged Oliax closer, crouching low, waiting until the last trace of the guards disappeared.

Only then did she move. Swift and silent, she darted down the alley and slipped through the back entrance of the forge. The air inside was thick with heat and soot, but safer than the open street. Horoge was already waiting. He reached behind her and yanked the heavy fabric curtain shut, draping it over the forge entrance to block curious eyes.

"You shouldn't be here," Horoge rumbled, voice low and urgent. His hands were still trembling faintly from the encounter outside.

"I don't have a choice," Alicius whispered, holding Oliax tightly. "My time is running short."

The words hung in the air, heavy with unspoken meaning. Both of them knew she couldn't linger here much longer. The net was tightening.

Ξ

The City Lord stood on the wide terrace of his mountain manor, the early sun crowning the jagged peaks in molten gold. From here, the world stretched before him like a conquered map. He could see in every direction— the ribbon of the river winding through the valley, the clusters of towns brimming with industry, the glimmer of Tydell's spires—and beyond, the faint haze of the borderlands that divided Thearon from its enemies.

This was his kingdom now, even if the King still technically drew breath.

The mountain air was sharp, biting at his throat, but it filled him with a sense of dominion. Every breeze that stirred the banners on his walls reminded him of the puppets dancing at the pull of his strings. The King— useless, sentimental, blinded by tradition—had been neatly pushed aside, confined where his words no longer mattered. Others fell in line as if it had been their will all along. Nobles, generals, merchants—each one bent, broken, or bribed into his web.

Now his designs could unfold unhindered.

Already his men had been dispatched to seal Gremallax's girl's fate. A loose thread that needed cutting. It was only a matter of time before the streets whispered the same fear across the entire country: resist, and be wiped away.

His army was larger now, hardened by preparation and strengthened by the Kings own army being funnelled into his war machine. With Leax out of the way and dissenters silenced, he could unleash it at last.

Thearon would not stumble forward in chaos—it would march under *his* banner, through fire and steel, until every enemy was ash at his feet.

But more than borders, more than crowns, his true purpose burned in his chest: the eradication of Ellomancers.

The gifted. The cursed. Those who bore the touch of Warrah in their veins.

They had twisted his world once—warping loyalties, disrupting order, unbalancing everything with their chaos. He would not allow another to gain an upper hand. They would be hunted, torn from their hiding places, slaughtered without mercy. He would cleanse Thearon of their taint and leave nothing but obedient men and women, bound to his will.

As the wind shifted, he smiled faintly. A smile without warmth.

Yes. Thearon would be reborn by his hand.

And in the depths of his mind, the thought flickered—he was not just saving the realm. He was shaping it into a legacy that would never be forgotten.

Ξ

Jaimius tore across the Exia Desert like a phantom, his body low, arms outstretched as streams of sand curled and surged beneath his command. The barren sea of gold bent to his will, propelling him forward with astonishing speed. Behind him, a tail of whirling dust stretched for leagues, a storm of his own making. The desert's silence was shattered by the hiss and rush of shifting grains as if the land itself had become his steed.

Beside him, a cart of files and records skimmed across the sand, held aloft by a twisting column that writhed like a serpent. Every so often, it dipped, weaving in time with his movements as if the desert itself was protecting his work. At his hip, Auracite pulsed with golden light, each thrum searing against his ribs, fuelling the boundless energy that coursed through his veins. He was alive in the sand, freer here than anywhere else. Out here, there were no watchful eyes, no suspicion—he could embrace his gift without fear of discovery.

The dunes rippled endlessly, waves frozen in time, but Jaimius carved through them with fluid mastery. He darted over ridges, slid down slopes, spun around rising spires of sandstone, every movement seamless, natural. He was the storm, the shifting desert incarnate.

But as the horizon broke, so too did his rhythm.

A wall of banners. A forest of spears. The glint of armour in the unrelenting sun.

A Thearonite army, vast and bristling, stretched across the border like a dam of iron and flesh, waiting for the flood. Jaimius skidded, sand cascading around him, and veered sharply toward the jagged outcrop of a lone rock formation. He dove behind it, the sand swallowing him whole before spitting him out into its shadow.

Heart pounding, he crouched low and stilled the shifting currents around him. His hand tightened around the glowing Auracite, drawing in another pulse of energy. His eyes sharpened, his hearing stretched across the dunes like spider-silk. The murmurs of the soldiers reached him—fragmented words of anticipation, of orders to brace for Karathi blades, of confidence that the invasion was imminent.

But Jaimius knew better.

Karathal had no intention of war. He had seen the documents, heard the speeches prepared by diplomats who carried no swords but promises of alliance, of treaties meant to "save Thearon" from its decay. His time spent with many Karathi provided all of this. The soldiers here weren't protectors. They were bait, strung like a trap for enemies who weren't coming.

His duty was clear. He had been tasked to return to the King, to hand over years of research and reports, to bow to the old order. But his heart—his heart burned for Karathal, for the people who had welcomed him, for the brilliance of a civilization that had given him purpose beyond being a tool of the crown.

The Auracite at his hip pulsed harder, its golden glow flaring like a heartbeat. He clenched his jaw.

If he let the diplomats walk into this, they would be slaughtered, and war would consume both nations. If he obeyed his orders, he would betray the very place that had become his home.

Jaimius pressed his palm into the sand, feeling it stir and bubble under his touch, ready to carry him wherever his choice demanded. He stared toward the horizon, where the Karathi caravan would soon crest the dunes, banners fluttering in the desert wind.

He couldn't let them reach the Thearon line.

Ξ

Eryx abandoned Romius' shack without protest from the brutish man. The silence between them had said enough.

For once, Romius did not argue, and Eryx did not look back. He set out toward the first town he had reached when he came to these lands, the weight of his decision pressing against his chest.

He needed to find a place to live. To work. To set down roots and build a life that wasn't shackled to theft and violence. He had to escape the cycle of criminality that seemed to cling to him like sand on a hot day. He wanted to make amends, to start afresh.

The town rose in the distance, its morning bustle stirring to life as smoke curled lazily from chimneys. Eryx swung south to avoid the blacksmith's shop, wary of recognition. He kept to the alleys, head low, steps brisk but measured, until he slipped from a narrow passage onto a broader street.

That's when the doors of a government hall burst open.

A dozen soldiers stormed out in unison, boots hammering stone, armour catching the light of dawn in cold flashes. Their formation was too precise for ordinary patrolmen—these were Garraw soldiers. Eryx recognized them instantly, the sight snapped a jolt of fear through his veins.

Without hesitation, he made himself scarce. His body flowed into movement, quick and quiet, a single breath carrying him up the wall and onto the roof above. His fingers dug into stone for leverage, his boots finding purchase with ease born of strength and instinct.

From his vantage point, he looked down at the soldiers spreading into the streets, their voices cutting sharp commands, their presence a net cast wide across the town. The crowd thinned as townsfolk pulled away, whispering, staring, hurrying their children indoors.

Eryx crouched low, forcing the silver-blue smoke of Thearonite to fade back beneath his skin. He couldn't risk a glow, not here—not with eyes everywhere. The Garraw were hunting and if they had come for him, then this was no mere patrol.

The rooftops stretched ahead, narrow spines of clay and stone, each one a step toward either freedom or exposure. His heart hammered as he weighed the path. He had wanted to begin again. He had wanted to find peace. But already, before his first step into a new life, the past had closed its jaws around him.

Still crouched, breath steadying, he whispered to himself like a vow:

"Not this time. I won't run forever."

Then he sprang forward, vanishing into the shifting maze of rooftops, a shadow slipping above the waking town.

CHAPTER 25- IMPACT

Romius leaned against the porch railing, Domir propped beside him, as he watched the distant shimmer of movement across the sands. An army. Too large to be a wandering garrison, too disciplined to be raiders. Probably Fallax's. An army gathered to slaughter him at last.

They had been creeping across the desert since the moment Eryx stormed out, a slow, inevitable tide of steel and banners. Romius told himself he didn't care—that boy wasn't his responsibility. And yet, somewhere beneath the scars and bitterness, something gnawed at him. He wasn't Eryx's father, but the thought of the boy alone, angry, and hunted struck a chord he didn't want to admit existed. Years of solitude had cracked his armour, left him more vulnerable than he liked to believe.

The soldiers drew closer, the sun flashing off helmets and spear tips, until they halted barely fifty feet from his shack. Dust drifted lazily between them, the silence thick and oppressive. Romius wrapped his hand around Domir's shaft, the axe already humming with anticipation, ready for Thearonite to course through his veins. He set his feet in the sand, every muscle tensed, prepared to die swinging if that was the end fate had dealt him.

A horn blared. A single, low call that rolled across the dunes like thunder.

Romius braced, jaw clenched. But instead of charging, the formation shifted. With military precision, the entire host wheeled north, banners snapping in the wind, cavalry surging at the flanks to guide the column. Within moments, the army was marching away, leaving Romius standing in the desert heat, staring at the line of dust they trailed behind.

They weren't here for him.

His grip on Domir loosened, the axe resting heavy at his side. He watched them march, a thousand questions clawing at his mind. He had collected secrets all his life—names of traitors, caches of Auracite, the shadow dealings of lords and thieves—but this? This was beyond him.

Why march north? Why now?

Karathal. They had to be pressing the border. Perhaps his self-imposed isolation had dulled him more than he realized. Politics had shifted while he rotted away out here in the sands. He hated the thought, but he could not ignore it.

Romius turned back toward the shack. He grabbed a worn bag from inside, stuffed it with what supplies he had left, and slung it across his shoulder. If the world was moving toward war, then hiding in his shack would mean dying in ignorance. He had no intention of letting the truth pass him by.

He would follow the army from a distance, track their movements like a wolf in the dunes, and uncover what storm was gathering at the border.

And perhaps—just perhaps—he would find where Eryx had run off to.

Ξ

Fallax, Rannax, Eroge, and Bard pushed through the dusty streets toward the town official's building. A column of dishevelled soldiers marched past them in the opposite direction, boots dragging, armour scuffed, eyes hollow. As they passed, several men stared the four down, sizing them up with suspicion—or resentment. The Barrack Thirteen soldiers held their gazes for only a moment before brushing past. None of them spoke, the heat of their earlier argument still hanging heavy in the air.

The group ascended the steps of the town hall, its stone walls weathered by sandstorms and sun. Fallax pulled out his general's identification parchment at the doors. The guards hesitated only briefly before stepping aside, clearly unsettled by the presence of the scarred, battle-hardened outsiders.

Inside, the cool air of the upper floor was a welcome relief. They climbed a narrow staircase and entered the official's chamber. The woman at the desk spun to face them, her expression already sharp with frustration.

"I have just spoken with your soldiers," she blurted. Her voice was strong, not shrill, but edged with tension. "The two men are gone. They attacked my people—why would I harbour them?"

Fallax blinked, momentarily thrown by her directness. He had come expecting evasions, excuses, perhaps cowardice. Not this.

"I have no reason to accuse you," he said calmly, steadying his tone. "But it seems we are searching for the same men. Tell me—why were those soldiers after them?"

The official straightened. She was striking—beautiful, elegant, her posture commanding yet weary. While it was not unheard of for a woman to hold such a post, it was still uncommon enough to be remarked upon. She wore it well.

"They were involved in the theft in Garraw," she explained, her voice tight. "Violence followed in their wake. My concern is not only for what they stole, but what Garraw itself is hiding."

Fallax narrowed his eyes. "Go on."

She exhaled slowly, folding her arms. "Twice a year, maybe more, we see it. People—half-starved, scarred, in broken chains—stumble through here. They never stop. They just keep running south, as if the very sands behind them were aflame. Always from the direction of Garraw."

Silence fell over the chamber. Fallax turned his head toward Rannax, who met his gaze with the same grim weight. This puzzle was twisting into something far darker than either of them had expected.

The official continued, "As for your fugitives, they left with such haste my people couldn't trace them. By now, they could be anywhere."

Fallax inclined his head in thanks. "Your honesty is noted. And appreciated."

With that, the four men turned and left the chamber, their boots echoing across the stone floor.

Outside her door, they slowed their pace down the stairwell. Bard broke the silence first, his voice a low rumble. "If those chains are true, Garraw isn't just hiding thieves. It's hiding monsters."

"Or breeding them," Fallax muttered. He adjusted his cloak. "Our mission just shifted. We can't keep chasing shadows. We need to decide: do we hunt Romius and the boy… or head north, toward Garraw, and uncover the truth?"

Eroge's jaw clenched, but before he could speak, Rannax raised a hand. "Let's weigh it carefully. Thearon is bleeding in places we don't yet see. One wrong step, and we're part of the rot instead of stopping it."

They reached the main doors. Fallax exhaled through his nose, tired but firm. "Then we weigh it outside. Fresh air, and perhaps a plan."

Rannax pushed the doors open—

And froze.

Standing in the sunlight, framed by the dust-bright street, was Eryx. His posture taut. He didn't move, didn't speak—he just waited.

The four soldiers halted in the doorway, silence pressing in like a blade's edge.

Ξ

The streets of Tydell still carried the chill of early morning, though the sun was beginning to burn its way through the haze. Alicius tugged Oliax by the hand, weaving through the shifting crowds, her heart pounding harder with every step. She could feel the walls of the city closing in on them, each corner, each passing soldier, a threat waiting to swallow them whole.

They ducked into a narrow alley, shadowed and damp, far from the bustle. Alicius pressed her back against the cold stone, her breath quick, her hand still wrapped tightly around her daughter's. Oliax looked up at her with wide eyes, trusting and uncomprehending.

Alicius crouched down, pulling Oliax close so they were face to face. Her hands cupped the little girl's cheeks, and her voice trembled as she spoke, trying to sound strong but failing to mask the crack of fear.

"My sweet one… listen to me," she whispered, eyes brimming. "You must promise me something. Promise me that if—if anything happens—you will run. You will not look back, no matter what you hear, no matter what happens to me."

Daniel Berrisford © 2021

Oliax frowned, confusion tightening her little brow. "But, mother—"

"No." Alicius pressed her forehead against her daughter's, tears slipping down her face. "You *must*. Even if I fall, even if they catch me—you run. You keep running until your legs give out, until the sand takes you. Do you understand? I would rather the world take me than lose you."

Her words came faster, sharper, as though speaking them might carve them into Oliax's soul. "You are everything I have left, Oliax. Everything. If they hurt me, I can bear it. But if they take you—" her voice broke, a sob tearing free, "—I could not survive that."

Oliax clutched at her mother's shoulders, her small hands trembling. "I don't want to leave you."

Alicius forced herself to smile through the tears, brushing her daughter's hair back, kissing her forehead with desperate tenderness. "And I don't want to let you go. But love—sometimes being a mother means choosing pain so that you might live without it. If I cannot shield you with my hands, then I will shield you with my sacrifice. Do you understand me?"

The girl nodded, slowly, reluctantly, tears welling in her own eyes. Alicius pulled her close and held her as if the embrace might fuse them into one. For a long moment, mother and daughter clung to each other in the quiet of the alley, the noise of the waking city a distant hum.

Then Alicius stood, wiping her face, pulling Oliax up beside her. Her grip on her daughter's hand was iron. Her heart screamed with every step, but her mind stayed sharp, repeating the same command over and over.

Ξ

Jaimius infused the sand surrounding his cart, threads of golden light from the Auracite at his hip spiralling into the grains. The desert obeyed him as if it were an extension of his own body, rising to swallow the cart and bury his files deep beneath protective dunes. With a final wave of his hand, the surface smoothed flat, leaving no trace of what lay hidden beneath. Safe.

Then, without hesitation, he turned toward the horizon. The Karathi caravan crept steadily across the golden wastes, but so too did the Thearon troops, disciplined lines of steel and banners already setting their formation. The gap between predator and prey was closing fast.

Jaimius' boots barely touched the sand as he propelled himself forward, the desert itself pushing him like a tide. A plume of fine dust trailed behind him, spraying in a great serpent's tail, marking his passage.

His figure was unmistakable—tall and lean, his sun-scorched skin bronzed by years by the desert, his hair black and flowing loosely behind him. His eyes burned a fierce gold, flecked with shifting motes of sand, reflecting the power that coursed through him. A dark cloak streamed out behind, its hem frayed from countless dunes, yet his movements remained graceful, even elegant, as though he and the desert were one.

The Thearon soldiers spotted him first. Confusion rippled through their ranks, then tension. A figure racing across the desert at impossible speed could only mean one thing—an Ellomancer.

Jaimius didn't slow. He skidded into place between the two forces, raising his arms.

A Karathi ambassador stepped forward, robes billowing, his voice carrying across the dunes, "We come to parley! We are here to—"

The words were cut short. A horn blast, a shouted order, and arrows screamed into the sky, cutting through the ambassador's plea.

Auracite flared. The golden stone at Jaimius' hip burned hot, light spilling like fire through the seams of his skin. The sand beneath his feet erupted upward in a towering wave, curling overhead in a shield. The arrows struck, splintering harmlessly into the wall of sand, falling like rain at his feet.

The Karathi scattered, cries of alarm carrying across the wind as their caravan began its retreat. But the Thearon troops did not falter—their orders were clear. No witnesses. No survivors. They surged forward in disciplined lines, blades drawn, determined to cut down the fleeing diplomats.

Jaimius clenched his fists. His jaw tightened. He could hear the voice of his king whispering in the back of his mind, the oath he'd sworn to the throne. Yet before him lay the only home he had chosen for himself.

The sand answered his turmoil with violence. Shards of hardened glass-like grit erupted from the ground, slicing through armour and shields alike. Soldiers screamed as the desert ripped into them, their formations breaking under the assault. Jaimius moved like a storm—sliding low, twisting high, arms carving great arcs as torrents of sand obeyed his every command. Spears shattered. Helmets split. Men were thrown from their feet as waves of desert swallowed them whole.

The soldiers faltered. Fear rippled like a plague through their ranks. They had been told the old bloodlines were dead, that Sandshifters were nothing but stories whispered to children. Yet here he was—one man, standing against an army, the very earth bending to his will.

"Sand demon!" one soldier cried, the name carrying like wildfire.

Then horns blared again—this time in retreat. The Thearon soldiers broke, scattering back across the dunes, abandoning their attack.

Jaimius stood alone, chest heaving, the desert quiet once more. He looked down at his hands, the Auracite still glowing faintly, the weight of his choice pressing down harder than the sun itself. He had turned his blade on his own people.

He knew what that meant.

With a final gesture, he slammed his palms into the sand. The ground beneath him roared, exploding upward in a spiralling pillar that hurled him skyward. In a burst of golden light and dust, Jaimius vanished into the endless horizon, leaving only whispers in the wind—

—whispers of a legend made real.

Ξ

The City Lord sat behind his great blackwood desk, the mountain sun spilling pale light across its polished surface. Across from him, his daughter lingered, shoulders slumped. Caelius, normally sharp and poised, looked more like a chastened child than the ruthless hunter she had become.

The silence between them was heavy, broken only when he finally spoke, his voice low, controlled, yet biting. "You let the boy escape."

Caelius lifted her head, eyes flashing as she tried to salvage herself.
"Father, I—Romius was with him. The man with the steel skin. An Ellomancer. You cannot—"

The City Lord's face twisted with disgust at the word. His hand clenched on the desk as though even speaking of such creatures stained the air.
"Another abomination. Another blight. And you let them both slip away."

She faltered, lips parting then closing again, no defence strong enough to withstand his fury.

He leaned back, fingers steepled, staring past her. He had a grip tighter than iron on the Thearon hierarchy, the nobility, the soldiers, the coin-lords of the trade houses. But his problem lay in the shadows—street urchins, vagrants, outlaws, and now these cursed Ellomancers who resurfaced like weeds between the cracks of his empire. They meddled unseen, and for all his control, they disrupted his design.

A sharp metallic screech cut the silence. Both heads turned as a bronze-winged bird crested over the balcony and glided into the chamber, its wings clattering with each beat. It alighted on the desk, talons clicking, and delivered its scroll. The City Lord tore it open, scanning the script in a heartbeat.

His face darkened.

A Sandshifter. At the border. Interfering.

The message crumpled in his fist as he surged upright, slamming both hands down upon the desk. Dark green mist poured from his skin, seeping into the wood. With a sickening crack, the surface crumbled to dust beneath him, collapsing under the force of his wrath.

Caelius recoiled, her chair skidding back against the stone floor as she shielded herself from the falling fragments.

The Lord closed his eyes, breathing slow and deep. When they opened again, calm calculation returned. He extended one hand, and before Caelius' wide eyes, the desk reformed itself, green light knitting splinters back into seamless shape. The gesture was deliberate—reminding her of his power, his control.

He sank back into his seat, his tone measured but seething with purpose.

"No more hesitation. No more mistakes. This… we use to our advantage."

His gaze cut into Caelius like a blade.

"Summon the scribes. Call every Craekee. Word will spread from here to the farthest village. We will set this nation aflame with fear. They will see the truth I give them—that Karathal consorts with Ellomancers, that these poisonous creatures crawl back from the dirt to destroy us. And when the people believe…"

A thin, cruel smile curved his lips.

"…they will unite. Under me. Against a common enemy."

Caelius swallowed, trying to steady herself as the weight of his plan unfurled before her. His voice was a sermon and a sentence all at once.

"Any who show signs of connection," he continued, his voice a cold decree, "will be slain. No exceptions. No mercy. We will cleanse Thearon."

The silence that followed was absolute. The City Lord leaned back, fingers drumming lightly on the freshly reformed desk, already three steps ahead in his mind. Caelius bowed her head, knowing better than to challenge him, even as unease coiled in her chest. She went off to carry out her orders.

Ξ

Fallax's body lunged forward like a predator, claws of authority ready to strike, but Eroge's hands gripped his arms with restraint. "Fallax! Wait!" he barked, his strength enough to hold the general back just long enough.

Rannax ignored the commotion, pulling Eryx into a protective embrace. "Talk to me," he urged, his voice calm amidst the rising tension.

Eryx exhaled sharply, gathering himself. He began to explain—words tumbling out in fragmented sentences, a stream of fear and desperation lacing each one. But before his story could reach clarity, a cry pierced the dawn.

"There's the boy!"

The guards—those same dishevelled soldiers from earlier—spun around, their faces twisting in recognition. Barrack Thirteen was surrounded: twelve to five.

Eryx's silver-blue eyes flared. He let go of Rannax's grip, hands closing around the bow staff Eroge threw to him—a finely crafted piece of Thearonite wood, light yet unyielding, polished to a deep bronze sheen. The staff hummed faintly in his hands, as if aware of the power coursing through its new wielder.

With a swift pivot, he sent a whirling arc of Thearonite energy up the staff. Silvery-blue smoke coiled around it like living steel, amplifying every strike. The first guard lunged—Eryx spun, staff arcing, catching the man on the side of the jaw. The soldier crashed to the ground, stunned.

Beside him, Rannax was a storm. He darted forward, fists coated in light Thearonite sheen, each strike precise, incapacitating guards without mercy. Bard moved like a shadow, slashing with twin daggers, disarming one opponent and spinning to trip another. Eroge's strength was a wall—he intercepted attacks aimed at Eryx, sweeping guards aside with controlled, terrifying force. Fallax, a man with experience but years away from the front lines darted to protect his men.

Eryx leapt onto a guard's shoulders, swinging the staff down in a crushing arc. The weapon bent and flexed under his control, wrapping around the man's torso, hurling him into another. Silvery-blue smoke hissed against the sunlit morning as he twisted, spinning the staff to deflect arrows, redirecting their flight harmlessly into the street.

One guard tried to flank him, dagger raised. Eryx stomped the ground, channelling Thearonite through the soles of his boots. The street erupted with a wave of force, knocking the man off his feet. Another charged from behind, but he twisted mid-air, the staff extending unnaturally, striking the attacker across the ribs, forcing him back into the throng.

Rannax moved like liquid steel, ducking low under a swinging baton, then spinning on the balls of his feet to deliver a rapid series of elbow strikes. Each movement was economical, deliberate, and deadly. One guard lunged with a dagger—Rannax caught his wrist, twisted it, and sent him tumbling into the wall with a sickening thud. Not a single wasted motion.

Bard was a blur of motion above them. He barrelled through crates and walls, his daggers a streak of silver in the dim alley light. He didn't just strike; He anticipated. Every lunge, every swing, every pivot was premeditated. A guard attempted a swing at him as he landed on his shoulder, spinning around to kick him squarely in the chest, sending him crashing into two others like a domino effect. He landed with a thud, already spinning again to intercept another attacker.

Eroge was pure power incarnate. When two soldiers attempted to flank Eryx, Eroge's fist caught one in the jaw, sending him sprawling into a stack of crates that splintered under the impact. Without missing a beat, he pivoted, grabbing the second soldier by the shoulders and slamming him backward into the wall, cracking stone and wood alike. His movements were brutal but controlled, every strike calculated to disable without wasting energy. As the smoke from Eryx's Thearonite staff curled around them, Eroge used the momentum to sweep his legs through a third attacker, sending the man tumbling into his own comrades, creating chaos in the enemy ranks. Every guard that dared approach felt the full force of Eroge's raw, unrelenting strength, leaving space for Rannax, Bard, Fallax, and Eryx to exploit with lethal precision.

Fallax kept the rhythm of the battle anchored. He wasn't the flashiest, but his precision meant no strike was missed. He created openings for the others, herding the guards like a chess master controlling the board. Even as exhaustion began to whisper at his limbs, his mind remained unshakable, calculating the next sequence with cold clarity.

The fighting moved as one organism. Eryx's Thearonite whirled in tandem with Rannax's strikes, Bard's slashes, and Eroge's crushing blocks. Each move complemented the other, their cohesion honed through shared battle experience.

By the time the smoke of exertion and power cleared, the twelve guards were either on the ground, incapacitated, or retreating. Eryx's chest heaved as silver-blue mist curled from his skin, his staff resting lightly in his hands but still humming with energy. Rannax clapped a hand on his shoulder, steadying him.

"We need to move," Rannax said, voice low. "They'll be back with more to follow."

Eroge glanced around, scanning for reinforcements. Bard wiped a streak of blood from his dagger, smirking. Fallax, finally gaining his breath back, gave a curt nod of approval.

Ξ

Romius watched the fight from above, his eyes narrowing as he tracked every movement. Pride swelled in his chest at the sight of his protégé—Eryx—wielding the staff with a fluid elegance that belied his raw power, each strike a calculated blend of speed and force. But that pride twisted into a knot of betrayal and sadness as he saw his childhood friend, Fallax, moving in perfect synchronization alongside the boy. Memories of shared training, of youthful laughter and unspoken loyalty, clashed violently with the present reality.

He lingered until the five of them bested the opposition, darting into the wilderness, their figures disappearing toward the direction of Garraw. Romius's jaw tightened; part of him ached to intervene, to call out a warning, yet another part—hardened by years of survival—knew he could only follow from a distance.

Ξ

Alicius and Oliax moved cautiously through the narrow streets of Tier Ten, the market still waking to the morning sun. Stalls were bustling, vendors shouting half-hearted greetings to customers. The scents of baked bread, fresh vegetables, and livestock mingled with the dust of the cobbled roads. Alicius kept her eyes sharp, scanning every shadowed alley and open doorway.

Their pace was quick but careful, slipping past carts and weaving through the many townsfolk. Every clang of a metal pot or shout of a vendor made her heart leap—she knew the guards could be close, hidden among the crowd. For now, they were unseen, shadows among shadows.

But the peace was fragile. From the corner of her eye, she caught a flash of green and gold—a uniform too deliberate to be coincidental. Guards, moving with practiced precision, were fanning out, eyes sweeping the market. Alicius froze for a heartbeat, then tugged Oliax's hand. "Run," she whispered, and they darted into the narrowest alley they could find, weaving between stalls, scattering crates and startled merchants.

The guards spotted them almost immediately. Shouts pierced the morning air: "There! Stop them!" A chase erupted, boots pounding against the cobblestones, voices shouting orders. Alicius and Oliax vaulted over overturned crates and carts, twisting down side alleys that opened into the farmlands beyond the city, along the river's edge. The market became a blur behind them as the fences and fields of Tier Ten's outskirts stretched ahead.

Alicius's heart hammered in her chest as she sprinted through the tier ten farmlands, Oliax clutching her hand, stumbling over uneven earth and stray roots. The sun burned through the mist, highlighting the flashes of guards barrelling after them, shouting and raising their weapons.

She zigzagged through the crops, ears straining for every footstep and shout. A scythe glinted in the sun as one guard swung, narrowly missing her. Dirt sprayed beneath their boots, Oliax whimpering with each stumble. Alicius's mind raced, calculating the path ahead— through the irrigation ditch, past the broken wagon, towards the barn at the far edge of the fields.

The tall grass loomed ahead like a green ocean. Without hesitation, she dove in, dragging Oliax with her. The stalks swayed around them, masking their shapes, hiding their frantic breaths. Behind them, the guards slowed, shouting in frustration, scanning the sea of green. Alicius forced herself to remain still, every muscle coiled tight, ears straining to detect any movement.

After what felt like an eternity, she shuffled forward on hands and knees, the grass brushing against her face, until she reached the storage barn. She slipped inside, her small frame pressing into a shadowed corner behind stacked bales of hay. Oliax pressed against her side, trembling, and she wrapped an arm around the girl, whispering through ragged breaths, "It's okay… we're safe, just for now. We have to stay hidden."

The sounds of pursuit faded slightly as the guards moved past the barn, unaware of the two fugitives pressed into the shadows, hearts still racing, the faint smell of hay mingling with the sweat of their narrow escape.

Ξ

Gremallax stormed through the bustling market, the shouts of merchants and clatter of carts fading behind him. His eyes scanned frantically, searching for the familiar emblem on a guard's cloak—the unmistakable mark of The City Lord's hunters. Spotting one, a lone figure moving with purpose and stealth, Gremallax's blood boiled.

Without hesitation, he seized the guard, his strength unmatched, and dragged him toward a nearby carriage. The startled figure struggled, shouting, but Gremallax's grip was unbreakable. He flung the man into the carriage, slammed the door, and barked to the driver with a voice that refused argument. The horses leapt forward, kicking up clouds of dust, taking them away from the crowded market.

They rattled down hidden lanes and narrow paths, away from prying eyes, until they reached a remote outhouse tucked behind overgrown hedges—a place only Gremallax knew. He flung open the carriage door, dragging the guard out with force that left no room for resistance. The man struggled, eyes wide with fear, but Gremallax's glare was enough to silence any defiance.

"You will tell me everything," he growled, his voice low and dangerous, "or you'll wish you had never drawn breath today."

The guard swallowed hard. Gremallax would not relent until he had the answers he sought.

Ξ

The sun dipped low, painting the horizon in streaks of gold and crimson. Finally, far enough from the town that the distant clang of bells or shouts of guards couldn't reach them, the group set down to rest. Smoke curled lazily from a small fire, the smell of roasted meat mingling with the crisp evening air. For the first time in weeks, the members of Barrack Thirteen felt complete.

Eryx, seated on a fallen log opposite the fire, exhaled slowly, the tension in his shoulders easing. The others gathered around, their faces softening as they took in the sight of him—alive, unharmed, and back with them.

"Didn't think you'd ever show," Eroge said, his voice roughened by relief, though a small grin tugged at the corner of his mouth.

Eryx smirked, leaning back against the log. "I had to. Even a rogue like me needs his team. I've been... surviving," he said, his steel-blue eyes flicking to each of them. "Learning things. Avoiding people who would rather see me dead than live. Romius... he's not just a brute. He's... complicated."

Rannax nudged him gently. "Complicated, yes. But at least now you're here with us. That matters more."

Fallax, ever the steady presence, passed him a mug of ale. "And if you've been surviving, I'm expecting details. Exile doesn't make itself—how have you been keeping alive, boy?"

Eryx chuckled softly, a sound that carried a mix of pride and weariness. "I've been... learning. Thearonite manipulation, tracking, avoiding soldiers." He gave a half-smile, glancing at Bard. "I guess I owe the girl in the armoury a thanks for the staff."

Bard raised an eyebrow, snorting. "A girl in the armoury, huh? You soft-hearted rogue." The group laughed, the sound ringing across the clearing.

Eroge rolled his eyes but couldn't hide a grin. "Better soft than dead. Now spill everything. We've been busy too."

Fallax leaned in, speaking quietly as he shared what they had learned from the town official and the whispers in Garraw. Rannax added the intel he had overheard, every word weighed carefully, every clue logged in his mind. Bard interjected with colourful exaggerations, mimicking the guards and locals in ways that had Eroge slapping him on the back and laughing aloud.

Eryx listened intently, nodding. "So Romius, he took me to Garraw. It is a huge pit filled with the glowing ores and slaves. The king has been monopolising three precious minerals as they are the power source to ellomancy."

Fallax was still cautious but recent events have shown that anything could be possible and anyone could be evil. He spread a worn map over a flat rock, pressing his fingers to the marked points. "We can't fight all this at once. We need a plan. Small, precise strikes. Information first, confrontation second. We hit only when we are ready—and together."

Eroge leaned forward, resting his elbows on his knees. "Together, huh? That's something I haven't said in a long time. I've missed this. You lot, your… chaos."

Bard snorted, raising his mug. "Chaos and me? Don't forget me! I bring the finesse!"

Rannax smirked, shaking his head. "You bring loud noises and bad smells."

Eryx finally let himself relax, the tension in his chest melting slightly. "Alright, so we move together, carefully. Each step deliberate. But tonight…" He gestured to the fire and the food. "Tonight, we eat, we drink. Tomorrow, we fix this mess."

The group erupted in laughter again, voices mingling with the crackling fire. Stories were swapped, teasing thrown back and forth, the camaraderie and loyalty of Barrack Thirteen knitting itself tighter. For one night, at least, the world outside could wait. Romius watched it all unfold from the cover of a large rock.

Ξ

The first light of dawn barely filtered through the tent flaps when Fallax shook Eryx awake. His grip was firm, insistent. "We need to talk. Now," he said, his voice low but edged with urgency.

Eryx stirred, blinking against the weak sunlight. "Fallax… what—?"

"No time," Fallax interrupted. "Tell me about Romius. Everything. No omissions."

Eryx swung himself to a sitting position, rubbing the sleep from his eyes. "Romius… he's no ordinary man. He found me when I was—" He hesitated, swallowing memories that still cut. "When I was alone. He fed me, sheltered me… trained me. Showed me how to fight, survive."

Fallax's eyes narrowed. "Survive what?"

"Ellomancy," Eryx continued, going into detail about the rise and fall of Poltan, how Renaesius' reign collapsed, and the corruption of Leax. Everything he had been told he shared.

Fallax sat back, silence falling like a weight between them. Pieces he had overlooked, moments that had seemed odd or trivial, began clicking together. The strange disappearances, the whispers of Ellomancers in hiding, the subtle manipulation of events—it all aligned.

"You… you trained with him," Fallax said finally, voice tight. "And I… I thought he was the enemy." His fingers clenched into fists, a mixture of guilt and regret pressing into his chest. "I abandoned him, didn't trust him. All this time, when chaos and deception reigned, I—" His voice cracked, eyes glistening in the early morning light. "I treated my old friend like a threat instead of seeing the truth."

Eryx reached out, placing a hand on Fallax's arm. "We've all been misled. But the past can be corrected."

Fallax shook his head, bitterness and sorrow mixing. "Where is he now? Why aren't you with him?"

Eryx's jaw tightened, memories flashing across his mind. "Romius… he chose his own path. When I needed him most. He went after vengeance instead of staying. I couldn't follow. I had to leave, to survive, to fight my own battles. Sometimes you can't fight alongside someone who's chasing their own fire."

Fallax's expression softened, understanding and regret mingling. "So, you left him… even though you knew the risk?"

Daniel Berrisford © 2021

Eryx nodded slowly. "Yes. Ellomancy is far more widespread than we realize. There are others like him, others like us. I needed to step back, gather myself, and face what's coming."

Fallax closed his eyes, drawing a slow, steadying breath. The weight of his past mistakes pressed down, but he also knew there were problems to face—together. "Then we move forward. Together."

Eryx's lips curved into a faint, determined smile, the tension between them easing. "Together."

Outside, the wind whispered through the camp, carrying a sense of quiet resolution. For Fallax, the day had begun not just with interrogation, but with revelation, reflection, and a resolve to correct the course of what had once been lost.

CHAPTER 26- MAKING AMENDS

Gremallax had spent the night extracting every secret the soldier knew. Blood coated the floor, smeared across the walls, and soaked his clothes, sticky and warm against his skin. The man had barely breathed by the time he revealed the truth: The City Lord planned to kill Alicius. The words hit Gremallax like a blade to the chest, sharper than any wound he had inflicted.

He lingered for a moment, staring down at the broken, trembling figure, the scent of blood heavy in the air. Half of him wanted to finish the job, to leave nothing behind but silence—but the other half was already moving, pulling him toward a far grimmer purpose. He left the soldier where he lay, broken and gasping, in the shadowed outhouse, and stepped back into the chill of the early morning.

The farmlands along the River Tyde awaited him, sprawling and wild, fields glistening with dew and shadows stretching long across the soil. Flax still coursed through his veins, sharp and bitter, a lingering fire that made his hands twitch and his vision narrow. Some would call what he had done last night a drug-fuelled rage, a mindless frenzy—but he knew better. It had not been rage. It had been love twisted with guilt. Pure, ferocious, and unrelenting.

Each step toward the river felt heavier than the last. The wind whispered through the tall grasses like ghosts, and somewhere in the distance, a craekee called out, a hollow note that seemed to echo his own heart. He clenched his fists, feeling the grit of blood and dirt under his nails, the ache in his muscles, the burn in his lungs. Everything he had done—everything he would do—was for her. Time was slipping away. Alicius's life hung in the balance, and he would not fail. Not now. Not again.

Ξ

The King received the message at the same moment the entire nation of Thearon did: Ellomancers had returned. A poison to society, they had been thrust upon Thearon by the Karathi. He knew he had to act—and fast. He needed to claim ownership of the narrative before Sallomannax gained momentum, before the rival could amass followers and seize the throne from under him.

Without hesitation, the King summoned his advisors and set them to work. Their task: create an Ellomancer eradication force, a relentless network to scour the land. Utilizing the endless reserves of Thearonite, Verdacryl, and Auracite mined from the Pit of Garraw, they were to detect any trace of connection to Warrah, ensuring no Ellomancer could hide or ally with potential threats.

Leax's mind was stretched thin, waging too many wars on too many fronts. The people had to see a ruler in control, decisive and unshakable. To falter here—over the return of these dangerous creatures—was to invite chaos.

Every decision, every command, had to reinforce his image: a king vigilant, unyielding, and always two steps ahead of those who would challenge him. Failure was not an option—not now, when the very soul of Thearon hung in the balance.

Ξ

Alicius crawled out from her hiding space in the barn, her muscles stiff and aching from the hours of crouching. She scanned the surrounding fields, relief washing over her when she saw no guards in sight. Moving cautiously, she approached a farmhand nearby, keeping her voice low and calm. He directed her to the farm manager, and with the coins she had stolen clutched tightly in her hand, she secured a small boat and a cache of supplies for her journey. Her plan was simple: row west, out toward the sea, and begin a new life along the coast—a fragile echo of the childhood she had longed to reclaim.

At the wooden jetty, she began loading the boat, moving swiftly, with Oliax hidden beneath a heavy blanket. Each motion was precise, practiced, born of desperation. Her heart pounded with anticipation and fear, a drumbeat in her chest urging her onward.

But further down the river, at the edge of the Tenth Tier Markets, five guards appeared, marching steadily in her direction. A cold dread sank into her stomach. Her pulse accelerated, each beat hammering painfully in her ears. Her hands trembled violently, spilling some of the supplies she had just secured. Her breath became shallow and rapid, as if the air itself had turned thick and unbreathable. The world around her seemed to narrow, colours dimming and sounds distorting into a muffled roar.

Her vision blurred; she felt lightheaded, the ground tilting beneath her. A tightness gripped her chest, as if invisible hands were squeezing, making every breath a struggle. A ringing buzz filled her head, thoughts scattering into frantic, jagged pieces—*they're coming... I'll be caught... I won't make it...* Her stomach churned violently, nausea rising in waves. She staggered, the boat rocking slightly under her shaking hands. Sweat beaded on her forehead, dripping into her eyes, stinging and blinding.

Her mind screamed for her to run, to move, yet her body refused to obey. She froze, trapped in the crushing grip of panic, every second stretching into eternity. The guards were closer now, their boots thudding against the cobblestones, echoing into the valley behind. Her chest heaved, her fingers curling into trembling fists as she tried—desperately—to summon control. But the terror had her in its grip, raw and unyielding, and all she could do was stand frozen at the edge of freedom, on the brink of being caught.

Ξ

As Barrack Thirteen packed their belongings, a hulking figure emerged from the shadows of the makeshift campsite. The five of them froze. Fallax, still reeling from the revelations of the previous night, was stunned. His childhood friend now stood before him, a ghost from a past he had barely dared to remember.

Rannax, Bard, and Eroge shifted into defensive stances, ready to fight if necessary. Eryx, ever composed, stepped forward with measured calm and asked, "Why have you come after me?"

Romius's voice rumbled like distant thunder as he explained the truth: Thearon was on the brink of war with Karathal. Fallax, still piecing together the fragments of his thoughts, interjected. "We have had scout reports indicating that the Karathi intend to invade. Months of them."

Romius's eyes narrowed. "Who signed off on these reports?"

The question struck Fallax like a dagger. He felt naïve, blindsided. Slowly, the pieces began to fall into place: the king had sent him to guard the borders on the word of the City Lord. Yet, during his entire watch, no troops had been sighted. No engagements had occurred. Every order, every report—lies.

Rannax's voice cut through the mounting tension. "The City Lord wants war. I don't know why, but he intends to confront Karathal head on."

The five of them exchanged grim glances. They didn't yet know why, but they knew they wanted answers. The air between them was thick with resolve, their shared purpose driving them on.

Finally, the six men reached a silent consensus. The corruption, the lies, the manipulation—all of it converged in Tydell. That was where they needed to be. That was where the answers awaited.

Ξ

Gremallax downed another gulp of Flax-concentrated water from his canteen and powered down the dirt path, muscles coiling with every step. In the distance, he could see them—the five men moving fast, relentless in pursuit of her. He had to reach them before they did.

He gritted his teeth, forcing his legs to move faster, the earth tearing beneath his feet as he sprinted, lungs burning and heart hammering like war drums. Dust kicked up around him, the scent of dirt and sweat clinging to his throat.

As he closed the distance, the trailing man glanced back, only to find himself on the receiving end of Gremallax's fury. With a roar, he swung, fists like hammers, and struck squarely across the man's nose. Bone cracked, blood spattering, the man crumpled, stunned, while the others faltered just long enough for Gremallax to surge in front of them.

Ξ

Alicius clutched the edge of the wooden boat, her knuckles white, eyes darting between the riverbank and the approaching figures. Five soldiers, moving with deadly precision, were closing fast. Her heart raced—not just from fear, but from the sight of him: Gremallax. Seeing him brought a flurry of emotions; love, anger, fear, passion, distrust.

He appeared suddenly, bursting from behind like a wild animal, muscles coiled and eyes blazing with purpose.

One of the soldiers reached for her, but Gremallax was faster, swinging a heavy fist that connected with the man's jaw. A sickening crack echoed over the river, and the soldier staggered, hands clutching his face. Alicius flinched, a part of her wincing at the violence even as relief surged through her chest.

The second soldier charged, weapon raised, but Gremallax pivoted, catching the man's wrist mid-swing. He twisted with a practiced precision, sending the soldier sprawling to the muddy ground. Alicius's stomach knotted at the ease with which he dispatched them, at the raw, unrestrained power he wielded. She loved him for protecting her—but the fear in her gut whispered, *he is dangerous, too.*

A third soldier lunged from the river's edge, blade glinting. Gremallax met him head-on, blocking the sword with his padded forearm, gritting his teeth, pain from the impact. The soldier's eyes widened and Gremallax shoved him back into the shallow water, the man gasping as he splashed and scrambled to regain his footing. Alicius's heart clenched as water sprayed over her, cold and pungent, reminding her that nothing here was safe—not even her feelings.

The final two soldiers hesitated, circling, eyes calculating. Gremallax's chest heaved, muscles taut with effort, yet there was no hesitation in his movements. With a roar that made her flinch, he slammed his shoulder into one, sending him into the other. They crashed to the ground together, a tangle of limbs and armour. Alicius bit her lip to keep from crying out, torn between admiration and terror.

When the fight was over, the five men lay groaning and broken in the dirt and shallow river mud. Gremallax stood over them, chest heaving, hair matted with sweat and blood. He turned toward her, and for a heartbeat, the fury in his eyes softened. "Go," he said, voice low and rough. "Get in the boat."

Alicius's hands trembled as she moved, every nerve screaming both to trust him and to run from him. She climbed into the boat, Oliax still hidden beneath the blanket, and watched him step back, a predator and a protector all at once. She loved him—but love alone wouldn't keep her alive.

Ξ

The City Lord stepped down from his carriage, robes brushing the dust of the riverbank. Beside him, his daughter Caelius followed with practiced grace, her sharp eyes scanning the scene. They approached Gremallax, who stood breathless, body still trembling from battle as Alicius's boat drifted farther into the current, her silhouette vanishing into the horizon.

The City Lord's voice was calm, measured, as if the chaos of the past moments meant nothing to him. "I was informed of your absence at the front lines, Captain. You know well that disobedience is punishable by death."

Gremallax said nothing. The Flax that had fuelled his strength now ebbed, leaving him hollow. His limbs felt heavy, his breath shallow, the sharp edges of exhaustion cutting into every nerve. He stared at the ground, jaw tight, unable to summon a word in his own defence.

The City Lord tilted his head, almost pitying. "You thought saving her would heal the wound left by your wife and child. But you could not save them, and you cannot save her. That is your truth."

A flicker of pain crossed Gremallax's eyes, but he remained silent. The City Lord sighed as though disappointed in a stubborn servant, then drew a blade from his side. It was long and gleaming, more ornamental than practical, its gilded hilt a symbol of authority rather than a weapon of war. Yet in his hands, it promised death.

"If you want something done," the City Lord murmured, "you do it yourself."

With no hesitation, he drove the blade into Gremallax's chest. The breath tore from the captain's lungs in a ragged gasp. His body arched, then faltered, collapsing as the steel withdrew. He toppled down the bank, landing in the shallow edge of the river. Water lapped against him, rushing red as it carried his blood downstream.

Above him, the sky stretched vast and blue, uncaring. His vision blurred, then burned bright with unbearable light. Shapes emerged within it—his wife, her smile soft as he remembered, and his daughter, arms outstretched, laughter carried on a wind only he could hear. Tears welled in his fading eyes as he stepped forward into their embrace. Warmth enveloped him at last.

On the bank, the City Lord wiped the blade clean with a flick of his wrist, then turned. Caelius climbed back into the carriage at his side. Without sparing another glance at the body, he climbed in as well, the door closing with a hollow thud.

The horses pulled them back toward the city. War awaited. It was time to finish his plans.

CHAPTER 27-KNOWLEDGE IS POWER

Jaimius reached Tydell with a cart creaking under the weight of files. He slowed at the city gates, then dismounted, choosing to walk the rest of the distance into the empty barracks. His boots echoed across the stone floors as he made his way toward Barrack Thirteen.

Once, this place had been alive with shouts, laughter, the clang of steel, and the restless energy of men preparing for war. Jaimius remembered his visits here, always brief, always for business—collecting Auracite. Now, the halls lay hollow, stripped of sound, their residents scattered across the Exia Desert, erecting war camps in grim anticipation.

Inside the barrack, dust clung to abandoned bunks and discarded gear. Jaimius knelt beside a rough-hewn table, setting down his satchel of documents. He would use Craekees to deliver the files quickly and quietly. Once the task was done, he would return to Karathal and leave Thearon's intrigues behind. He imagined himself living freely, finally unshackled from duty and deception.

But as he spread the parchments across the table, a faint noise reached his ears—boots scuffing, voices low outside the door. His heart gave a sharp kick. Slowly, he rose and edged toward the window slit.

Familiar faces came into view. Bard. Rannax. And with them, the boy who had joined not long before Jaimius' last departure. Their expressions were hard, their steps purposeful.

Jaimius called out, his voice carrying across the empty yard. If he played this right, he could use them—trusted hands to deliver the information for him—freeing him to return sooner than planned. He trusted Rannax and Bard more than most, and when they turned at the sound of his voice, the old familiarity was there.

Bard broke into a grin, bellowing, "Aye! Look, it's the bloody weirdo!" His laughter shook the silence, and though Jaimius had always been reluctant to speak much during his brief visits, the men had managed to pry words from him before.

Behind them came the boy who had joined just before Jaimius left, followed by three others he didn't recognise. The group carried the weight of men who had seen too much in too little time.

Rannax, ever direct, pressed him. "Why have you returned, Jaimius?"

He explained quickly—about the files, the delivery, and the truths he had pieced together. As he spoke, he saw their expressions shift, determination hardening. The fears they carried matched his own: Thearon was moving toward war.

Fallax stepped forward, snatching up the files, rifling through them with impatient hands. His brow furrowed. "There's barely anything here on Karathal's intent to invade." His voice sharpened. "These reports speak of

something else. A technologically advanced country—
one ready to bring Thearon up to speed."

A silence fell. Fallax swallowed hard, the realization
plain in his eyes. "I've spent the last few days realising
how little I actually know."

Jaimius' voice was quiet but steady. "The King wants
this information."

Fallax slammed the parchment down. "No. We keep it. If
this reaches him, it will give Thearon the excuse it needs
to invade Karathal. That is exactly what the City Lord
intends."

Jaimius opened his mouth to protest, then shook his
head, his words tumbling out. "Most of the files I've ever
sent—every word, every detail—they all went through
the City Lord's Craekee. Even the King's parchment,
signed and sealed, instructed me to use his."

Romius, who had stood silent until now, finally spoke.
His voice carried the weight of truth. "Sallomannax. The
City Lord" He said the name like a curse. "He is the
hand behind this. He has been pulling every string—this
siege, this deception—just as he once controlled it all
back in Poltan."

The weight of revelation pressed over the group. None
argued. They didn't need to.

At last, Jaimius gathered himself. He left the files in their
hands. Turning from them, he stepped back into the open
air. Sand swirled around his boots, carried on a dry wind.

He did not look back. For the first time in years, the path ahead was his alone. A future not of duty or deceit— but of freedom.

Ξ

Barrack Thirteen, joined by Romius, rifled through the stacks of files Jaimius had left behind. Pages covered every detail of Karathal—its education, its housing, its culture, its financial systems. Jaimius had been meticulous, leaving behind the work of years, maybe decades.

The six men did not have the luxury of time to study it all, but even the briefest glances told them what they needed to know: Karathal had no desire for Thearon's barren lands. No ambition for conquest. No hunger for its cities or people. There was only one thing Karathal might covet—the Pit of Garraw.

That was the truth. Generation after generation of kings had fought wars and cloaked Thearon in isolation, all to guard the pit. While the world moved forward, Thearon fell behind—technologically, culturally, politically—its monarchy tightening its grip in the name of preservation. The gifts of the pit had been hoarded, not shared, not traded, jealously guarded as the kingdom's one true crown jewel.

Fallax slammed a fist against the table, the files scattering. "All of this," he growled, "every death, every lie—it has always been about Garraw."

The others said nothing, but their grim faces spoke for them.

They rose and made for the armoury, its doors heavy. Inside, rows of discarded weapons and half-forgotten armour filled the gloom, remnants of soldiers who had long since marched for the desert. Eryx drifted from the others, a quiet pull drawing him deeper into the chamber. There, in the far corner, he found a small stack set apart from the rest. His breath caught.

It was his.

The gear he had been forced to abandon when the city cast him into exile—his sword, his shield, his worn leather satchel. Dust clung to them, but they had been cared for, not discarded. Someone had kept them safe. Charliax had kept them safe.

Eryx's hand lingered on the bow staff, memories flickering in his mind. Even in his absence, even in his disgrace, someone had thought he was worth remembering. He strapped the satchel to his back, the weight familiar, grounding, and returned to the others with his head held higher.

They gathered the rest of the weapons and armour— breastplates dented from old battles, shields battered and scarred. When they emerged from the barrack, the path was clear in their minds. The City Lord's manor loomed far above, perched on the heights of the top tier like a vulture overseeing its feast.

Their ascent would begin at once.

CHAPTER 28- DECISIONS

Alicius and Oliax drifted down the Tyde River, the current pulling them steadily toward the sea. The gentle rocking of the boat should have been calming, but Alicius's mind wandered restlessly. She found herself thinking of Eryx. Was he safe? Had Fallax found him? He was nearly a man now, old enough to choose his own path, but still young enough to need protection. She had to believe in him—just as Horoge had told her.

A tear slipped down her cheek before she could stop it. She quickly wiped it away, unwilling to let Oliax see her fear. Then she caught her daughter's smile—bright, unguarded, innocent—and the weight on her chest loosened.

"Look, Mama!" Oliax pointed across the dark waters.

Alicius followed her gaze and froze. The girl was describing a stone tower, a beacon with a bright flame blazing from its peak. A sailor's guide to shore. But they were still hours from the sea. No such beacon should exist here. And Oliax… Oliax had never seen one before.

Confusion gnawed at Alicius, but she swallowed it, forcing a gentle smile for her daughter's sake. "Yes, I see it."

The child's eyes sparkled as if she truly did, and in that moment, Alicius noticed how the darkness seemed to fall back from Oliax, how her very presence seemed to glow faintly with hope.

Alicius turned her face toward the current and let the river carry them onward. Whatever the truth of what Oliax had seen, she clung to the comfort of it. A light in the dark. A promise that there was still something worth reaching for.

Ξ

Urasmus sat in the officers' tent, the stale heat of the Exian Desert pressing down even through the canvas walls. Across from him sat Holiax—newly promoted, the ink on his captain's commission barely dry. Together, they had led their men into the desert on Gremallax's command. Now, the most recent message from Tydell declared Holiax as Captain… and Gremallax executed for crimes against Thearon.

Urasmus's jaw tightened. He had fought beside Gremallax long enough to know the man's flaws—his temper, his addictions, his reckless disregard for his own life. But he also knew this: Gremallax had always put Thearon first, to a fault. To brand him a traitor felt like a cruelty too neatly packaged, too convenient.

Holiax rose, his voice steady as he addressed the officers gathered in the tent. "Orders are clear. We prepare an assault forward at dawn. If we catch the Karathi off guard, we gain a strong foothold before they can mobilise. No hesitation."

Urasmus listened in silence. The younger man spoke with confidence, with fire, but there was something brittle beneath it—a sharpness that belonged more to ambition than experience. The years had calloused

Urasmus; he had long since learned that orders were followed, not questioned. Yet a quiet unease gnawed at him.

As the meeting ended, he stepped out into the desert night. The air was dry, carrying the faint sting of sand on the wind. He looked across the rows of tents, the dim glow of campfires, the weary soldiers preparing for yet another war they did not understand. He thought of Barrack Thirteen, scattered but alive, he hoped—digging for truths he could not reach from here.

Urasmus squared his shoulders and walked on. He would carry out his orders, as he had been trained all his life. But deep down, he knew obedience had its price. And sooner or later, Thearon would have to pay it.

Ξ

A panicked messenger burst into Sallomannax's office, her breath ragged, hair plastered to her face with sweat. The City Lord sat unmoving at his desk, fingers steepled, eyes sharp as glass as he listened to the girl stammer out her report.

"Six men… they entered the barracks…" descriptions followed.

Sallomannax cut her off, his voice calm, almost bored. He needed no portrait painted to know who they were. Fallax. Rannax. Bard. Eryx. Romius. Eroge. Barrack Thirteen had rallied—and with them, the boy. His lip curled into the faintest sneer. Of course, his daughter's failure would return to haunt him. How foolish he had been to believe the general would simply roll over and accept his fate.

Rising from his chair with deliberate slowness, Sallomannax's shadow stretched long across the marble floor. He turned to his scribe, the weight of his words striking like a blade.

"I want every guard in the city. Every tier. Seal the streets. Barricades, blockades, walls of steel and stone—turn this manor into a fortress. I do not want excuses. I do not want questions. I want action. And you will kill on sight."

The scribe nodded furiously, quill scratching before he bolted for the door.

Sallomannax turned, his gaze settling on Caelius. His tone shifted, soft but poisonous. "And you—finish the job you started. Or you will face the same fate as Gremallax."

The words hung in the air like a death sentence. Caelius met his gaze only for a moment, then gave a single nod. Without hesitation, she stepped onto the balcony's edge and leapt. Her boots struck the stone courtyard below with a sharp crack, her cloak flaring behind her as she landed. She did not look back.

Sallomannax watched her disappear into the dark, his expression unreadable. This war had come to his doorstep, but the city was his. And he would not surrender it—not to Barrack Thirteen, not to Leax, not to anyone.

CHAPTER 29- JUSTICE

The group split into three pairs: Fallax and Eroge, Rannax and Bard, Eryx and Romius. The plan was simple but perilous. The first task fell to the others: to clear a path, draw attention, and create space for Eryx and Romius to reach the City Lord.

They began their trek around the foot of the mountain, each step careful, measured. The City Lord's manor loomed above them—a jewel carved into the jagged rock, gleaming even as the sun sank behind the peaks. From their vantage point, the rising streets were choked with soldiers, a dark tide stretching from the city gates to the doorstep of the City Lord. Sallomannax had prepared meticulously, every avenue and stairway a potential trap. The air itself seemed heavy with anticipation, the kind that makes the skin prickle and the heart hammer in the chest.

The six men exchanged a brief, synchronized nod, the kind forged from countless battles and silent trust. No words were needed. Each knew their part. Without hesitation, they separated, slipping into the shadows and moving with purpose. The night air bit at their faces, carrying the faint clamour of distant patrols. Every corner, every stone, could conceal danger—but their eyes were sharp, their resolve sharper.

Up the mountain they went, each pair weaving through the chaos of Sallomannax's defences, converging ever closer on the heart of the enemy's stronghold. The battle to come would demand everything they had—and more—but in that moment, united in intent, they felt the pulse of certainty: they would reach the City Lord, one way or another.

Ξ

Sergeant Polaris was one of the few left in Tydell to monitor and police the tiers while the bulk of the army marched toward Karathal. His orders were clear: protect the City Lord's manor at all costs. With only one hundred and fifty men at his disposal, he moved with calculated precision, herding civilians into their homes, barring doors, and erecting makeshift blockades along the narrow streets. Every barricade, every shuttered window, was another line of defence against the chaos he knew was coming.

From his vantage point on Tier Four, Polaris surveyed the streets below. They were unnervingly empty, save for the disciplined ranks of his men. Lanterns burned along the eaves and corners of the streets, casting long, flickering shadows that danced like ominous phantoms across the cobblestones. The warm glow belied the danger it illuminated, turning every alleyway into a potential killing ground.

Polaris did not know exactly what to expect. He had faced battles before, but never like this—never defending a city from within its own veins, never knowing if the enemy was already upon them. Still, he felt a grim determination harden within him. He would fight, and he would not falter. The city was his responsibility, its people his charge, and he would wield that duty like a blade against whatever came.

The night held its breath. The streets waited. So, did he.

Ξ

Caelius perched on the crumbling stone wall of a stairway that wound down toward the third tier, her figure cloaked in the shadows of the lanternlight. She sat poised, eyes fixed on the narrow street below, waiting for the boy to appear. Eryx. The moment she saw him, she would strike. She had failed once, and failure was a weight her father would never allow her to carry. This time, she would finish the job. This time, he would see her worth.

The knife in her hand pulsed with a sickly dark-green haze as she fed it Verdacryl from the stone at her side. Smoke coiled around the blade, hissing as it warped, reshaping itself with every shift of her intent—knife, star, knife, star—an endless cycle of indecision. Did she want to see Eryx's eyes widen as steel slid into him, or would she rather watch his body crumple from afar, pierced before he could even register her presence?

Her gaze flicked briefly to the broader path beyond. Romius. She had not forgotten his name or his deeds. The butcher of Poltan. A man who had cut his way through armies, left villages in ruin, and never once faltered. His power was legend, his resolve a sharpened edge. He was the unknown in this game, and the unknown made her wary.

But she reminded herself of what she was—what her father had made her. From childhood she had been moulded, shaped in the Verdacryl's image, until its touch was second nature. An Essencrafter before she was even grown. Her father had turned her into a weapon, and she would prove to him that his weapon was flawless.

The knife shimmered in her grip, Verdacryl twisting eagerly in her palm. Caelius smiled faintly, cruelly. The boy would come. And when he did, she would be ready.

Ξ

Rannax and Bard crept low through the shadow of the crumbling stone wall, the distant echo of orders and clashing steel rumbling through the city tiers above them. The ninth tier loomed ahead, its staircase narrowed by wooden barricades and jagged iron spikes. At the foot of it, ten guards stood in formation, shields raised, their helms catching the flicker of torchlight. Every other route they had scouted was barred or collapsed — this was the only way up.

Bard let out a sharp breath through his nose. "Ten against two. Sounds fair."

Rannax gave him that crooked smile, the one that had always meant trouble. "Bard's Bait?"

Bard groaned, already knowing where this was going. "Don't even start. You remember the last time? Back in the east pass, you said *just stand there, wave your arms about, I'll do the rest.* I still have the scar."

Rannax's grin only widened. "And yet, here we are — alive. Go on, give them the old Bard bait trick. One more time."

Bard scowled, but the warmth in Rannax's eyes pulled him in like it always did. Reluctantly, he straightened, rolled his shoulders, and stepped out into the torchlight.

"Listen lads, we—"

The hiss of bowstrings cut him off. Arrows whistled, a deadly rain aimed straight at his chest. Before Bard could blink, Rannax's arm clamped around his collar and yanked him back into cover, an arrowhead grazing his torso.

Bard's heart thumped in his throat. "Well. That went well."

Rannax's smirk was gone now, replaced with calculation. He peeked around the edge of the wall, noting the archers behind the shield line, the staggered formation. Too tight to slip through. Too disciplined to scatter.

"How about," Rannax murmured, eyes glinting, "the Tree Trunk?"

Bard's face lit up despite the danger. "Now that I like."

They crouched together, Bard planting his heavy shield in front of them like a great slab of oak. Shoulder to shoulder, they hunched low and shuffled forward, the scrape of boots the only sound. Arrows thunked into the wood, splinters bursting near Bard's knuckles, but he held firm, teeth clenched. Step by grinding step, they pressed forward, the enemy shouting in confusion.

At ten paces, Rannax whispered, "On three."

Bard tightened his grip on his axe, muscles coiled.

"One."

Another arrow slammed into the shield.

"Two."

The guards raised their spears, preparing for the rush.

"Three!"

They exploded apart, rolling opposite ways, the shield left standing between them like the trunk of a fallen tree. The guards' focus stayed on the barrier, and in that heartbeat of hesitation, Bard and Rannax surged around it — flanking, blades drawn, battle-cries breaking the silence of the tier.

Bard came barrelling from the left, axe raised high, bellowing like thunder. Rannax darted from the right, blade low, his movements sharp and precise.

The guards scrambled to adjust, their formation fracturing.

Bard's sword smashed down on the first man's shield, the impact rattling bones and forcing him backward into his comrades. With a savage grunt, Bard hooked the blade back and drove his shoulder into the staggered line, breaking their stance.

On the other side, Rannax slipped under a thrusting spear, his sword flicking up to carve a deep line across the exposed thigh of its wielder. The man cried out and collapsed, clutching at his leg as Rannax spun past him, slicing another guard's arm before he could recover.

"Keep moving!" Rannax barked, already pressing forward.

Bard swung wide, cleaving a soldier's helm with enough force to send him crumpling into the dirt. An arrow sang past his cheek, close enough to shear off a lock of hair. He turned and spotted the bowman just behind the shield wall, already nocking another shaft.

"Not this time," Bard growled. He hurled his knife end-over-end. It spun through the air and struck the archer square in the chest, dropping him like a sack of stones.

Another soldier lunged, spear driving toward Bard's ribs. Bard barely twisted in time, the iron tip raking his side. Pain flared, hot and sharp, but his fist came crashing down on the man's jaw, sending him sprawling.

Meanwhile, Rannax wove like a wolf through a herd. Every step was measured, every strike meant to cripple rather than clash. A quick cut across the knee here, a stab into a shoulder there — never giving the enemy a chance to reset their stance. Two more fell in his wake, groaning and bleeding on the stone.

"Five left!" Bard roared, yanking his knife free from the archer's corpse.

The remaining guards regrouped, tightening their circle, shields up, spears thrusting in deadly rhythm. Their leader barked an order, and they moved as one, pressing toward Rannax to pin him against the wall.

But Bard wasn't having it. With a battle-cry that shook the lanterns, he charged straight into their flank, axe chopping down like a woodcutter on kindling. The first shield splintered, the guard behind it thrown off balance. Rannax seized the moment, his blade flashing to pierce under an armpit, the man crumpling before he could scream.

Three left.

The man in charge swung at Bard, a heavy blade clanging against his. Sparks showered, both men straining, teeth bared. Rannax darted in and slashed the leader's exposed wrist, forcing him to drop his weapon with a howl. Bard finished it, driving his knee into the man's gut before burying his axe in his chest.

Two more tried to run, panic overtaking discipline. Rannax hurled his sword, the blade spinning end over end until it caught one between the shoulder blades. The man pitched forward, lifeless. The last didn't make it three steps before Bard's knife came down from behind, ending the fight.

Silence fell. Only the rasp of their breath and the dripping of blood onto stone remained.

Bard rested his sword on the ground, leaning on it with a grin. "Tree trunk, eh? Not bad for an old trick."

Rannax retrieved his sword from the fallen man, wiping it clean on a tattered cloak. "Not bad at all. Now let's keep moving. That was just the first blockade — and you know it won't be the last."

Bard groaned, but his grin widened. "Good. I was starting to get warmed up."

Ξ

Whilst Rannax and Bard's clash thundered in the distance, Romius led Eryx, Eroge, and Fallax along a shadowed stairway, climbing with the silence of wolves stalking prey. Every step up the stone felt heavier, the weight of Tydell's fate pressing on their shoulders.

Domir's blade hummed faintly as Romius drew it in and out of the darkness, the ancient weapon cutting through hastily erected barriers with deliberate care. Timber supports cracked and split like kindling beneath its edge, and where stone reinforced the walls, Romius carved precise wedges until Eroge heaved boulders aside with brute strength.

The four kept to the unlit edges of the tier. Lanterns glowed like watchful eyes on the streets, casting tall, searching shadows across the cobbled paths. Every time soldiers passed, their boots hammering in ordered rhythm, the group flattened against walls or ducked behind wreckage, holding their breath until the patrol faded into the distance.

Eryx's ears rang with the clash of steel and the shouts of
men below — Rannax and Bard were holding the line.
The sound filled him with both dread and reassurance.
They were strong enough to survive. They had to be.

He brushed against the wall of a home as they passed,
people stirred. From within came muffled whispers:
mothers shushing children, elderly men cursing softly at
the City Lord under their breath, prayers whispered to
gods Eryx had never heard. Citizens of Tydell, trapped in
their homes, listening to the city they once trusted tear
itself apart.

For a moment, Eryx hesitated. He could feel the pulse of
fear inside the building as keenly as if it were his own
heartbeat. His hand twitched at his side, but Fallax's
voice cut through the stillness.

"Eyes forward, boy. You can't save them all. Not
tonight."

Romius didn't even look back. "Fallax is right. Our
purpose is ahead. The City Lord falls, or none of this
matters."

Grinding his teeth, Eryx pressed on, forcing himself to
focus. He was no use to anyone if he faltered now.

The stair to the seventh tier loomed closer. This one was
wider, sturdier — reinforced with layers of rock and
metal plates that gleamed faintly in the torchlight. It
would not fall quietly.

Romius rested Domir across his shoulder, testing the barrier with its tip. Sparks hissed as the blade kissed steel. "We won't pass this one without noise," he muttered.

Eroge gave a grim smile, already rolling his shoulders. "Noise is fine. Let's just make sure it's worth it."

Ξ

Rannax and Bard crouched at the foot of the staircase to tier eight, the stone steps stretching upward into shadow. The air here was heavy with smoke, the smell of oil burning somewhere above. Lanterns flickered, but the light was thin, leaving great pools of blackness that could hide anything.

"Strange," Bard muttered, resting his battered shield against the ground. "No guards? I don't like it."

"Nor do I," Rannax agreed, scanning the dark rise above them. "Keep sharp."

They waited, patient hunters at the foot of the stone slope. But no movement came, no clatter of boots. Only silence, and the soft hiss of wind between tiers. Finally, Rannax gave a sharp nod. "We go. Slow."

Halfway up, the silence shattered. A dull *thump* above, followed by the roar of fire. Two barrels, already blazing, came hurtling down the staircase, bouncing, spitting sparks as they struck the walls.

"Down!" Rannax barked, grabbing Bard's shoulder and hauling him flat to the steps. The first barrel thundered past, flames licking their boots as it crashed into the street below and burst into a spray of burning oil. The second smashed hard against the railing, splintering wood into jagged shards before tumbling on.

Bard coughed smoke, swatting out a smouldering ember caught on his sleeve. "Oh, brilliant. Fire barrels. Why not just roll boulders like normal people?"

"Because we're facing cowards," Rannax growled. His sharp eyes caught the figures above — two scrawny soldiers, laughing harshly as they wrestled another barrel toward the steps.

"We'll be cinders if we stay here," Bard said, shifting his shield onto his arm.

"Then we don't stay."

The next barrel came tumbling. This time Bard stood his ground. He crouched, raised his shield, and braced. The impact shook his arm to the bone, the metal ringing like a bell. Fire washed around him as the barrel split and spilled burning oil, but the shield turned most of it aside, creating a narrow path.

"Go!" Bard roared through the smoke.

Rannax darted forward, leaping through the flames with reckless speed. He scaled the last dozen steps two at a time, cloak singed, eyes locked on the pair above. One soldier's face twisted in shock as Rannax burst from the smoke. He swung low, his sword smashing the boy's knee out from under him. The man shrieked, collapsing on the stone as the barrel he was guiding rolled free.

The second guard fumbled for his torch, trying to set another barrel alight. He barely raised it before Rannax slammed into him, shoulder-first. The impact drove the air from his lungs and hurled him back against the wall. Before he could recover, Rannax's pommel struck his temple, dropping him into a twitching heap.

Meanwhile Bard trudged up through the fire, smoke-blackened, shield glowing faintly from the heat. He gave Rannax a look equal parts anger and admiration.

"You might've told me you planned to charge straight through!" Bard barked, stamping out a smouldering spark on his trousers.

Rannax only grinned, dragging the groaning, half-conscious guards away from the barrels. "And rob you of the surprise? Where's the fun in that?"

Bard shook his head, but there was a reluctant smile tugging his beard. "One day, Rannax, your mad plans will kill us both."

"Maybe," Rannax replied, hefting his sword as he peered up at the next stair. "But not today." The path to tier eight was theirs.

Sounds from further up interrupted their conversation. They had to press on.

Ξ

Sallomannax stood in the courtyard of his manor, the jewel of Tydell perched high upon the mountainside. The torches around him burned bright, their flames licking at the cold night air, but his gaze stretched downward into the darkness below. He could barely make out the figures moving tier by tier, but the echoes carried their tale clearly enough — steel clashing, wood splintering, men screaming as they fell.

His men were dying. His carefully placed defences were being stripped away one after another.

Still, Sallomannax did not allow fear to touch his face. His features were a mask of calm, but beneath it, adrenaline surged like a raging tide. His pulse hammered in his throat, his fingers twitching near the hilt of his blade as if hungry for what was coming.

"The thorns," he muttered, half to himself, eyes narrowing as he strained to see the shadows climbing toward him. "Persistent, sharp little thorns… drawing closer with every breath."

Behind him, servants scurried like frightened mice, reinforcing barricades, dragging fresh weapons from the armoury. Soldiers stood in formation at the edge of the courtyard, silent, restless, their eyes flicking between their lord and the dark valley below. Sallomannax could feel their unease, but he offered no words of comfort. Instead, he drew in a slow breath, steadying himself.

"They think me cornered," he whispered, his voice steady despite the storm building within. "But they forget… I built this city. I forged its walls and filled its pockets. I shaped its armies with my own hand."

He clenched his fist.

"And I will not die while thieves and traitors scratch at my gates."

Sallomannax turned sharply, his gown snapping at his heels. He moved with purpose toward the centre of the courtyard, where his chosen guard waited — the finest blades still loyal to him. Though shadows of doubt lurked at the edge of his thoughts, he buried them deep. He would meet these intruders head-on, not as a cornered animal but as the master of Tydell.

Adrenaline burned hot in his blood now, heightening every sense. The night no longer felt cold. His lips curved in something between a snarl and a smile.

"Let them come," he growled. "Tonight, Tydell will drown in their blood."

Ξ

The four had barely reached the narrow ledge between tier six and tier five when the noise they had made alerted the soldiers. Steel boots thundered on stone above and below, the shadows of soldiers pouring from hidden watch posts. They were cut off, pressed in from both sides. Torches flared against the rock, spears glinting in the orange light.

"Ten to a man," Fallax muttered grimly, his hand going to his sword. "We'll carve them space."

Before Eryx or Romius could protest, Eroge was already moving. The giant of a man drew in a deep breath, braced himself, and launched downward toward the wave of guards below. His shield met the first line with the crash of a battering ram.

The soldier's body folded under the impact, bones snapping like brittle twigs. Eroge didn't pause—he swung his mace in a brutal arc, the spiked head catching another guard at the shoulder and pulverizing bone, the man crumpling as if the weight of the weapon had stolen the strength from his body.

Another lunged, spear thrusting for Eroge's side. He caught it on his shield, the wood splintering but holding, then twisted his whole body and slammed the soldier back into the stone wall. The man's skull cracked against the rock, the torchlight flickering as blood splattered in its glow.

The men tried to circle him, but Eroge was a mountain in motion. Slow, yes, but every swing landed with devastating finality. One guard's arm shattered under his shield edge; another was caught in the stomach by the mace and lifted from his feet, hurled backward into two comrades. Their cries echoed as they tumbled down the stairs, colliding in a heap of blood and broken steel.

A spear grazed Eroge's thigh, but he ignored it, his face twisted with raw determination. He caught the shaft in his massive hand, wrenched it from the soldier's grip, and snapped it over his knee. With the broken halves, he drove both ends into the man's chest, pinning him screaming against the wall before moving on.

The soldiers tried to overwhelm him with sheer number, piling in, blades hammering against his shield, but each one that came too close was smashed aside. Eroge's shield crashed down like a falling gate, crushing skulls and collarbones alike. His mace rose and fell with steady rhythm, and every time it did, another scream was silenced.

Ξ

Fallax didn't hesitate. He grabbed Eryx by the shoulder, pushed him forward, and barked to Romius: "With me— through them!"

They surged up the stairs. Romius tore Domir through the first line like parchment, the great blade shrieking as it split stone and flesh alike. Sparks spat from the stair wall, soldiers screamed, and in the chaos Eryx followed, weaving his power in bursts—flaring arcs of force that hurled men aside, clearing Romius' flanks.

Steel rang in a furious tempo. Romius swung wide, scattering guards like straw dolls, and Eryx drove forward, every motion fuelled by raw survival. One soldier lunged from the side, spear aimed for the boy's ribs—Eryx's instincts flared, a shockwave burst from his palm, and the man was ripped off his feet, hurled screaming into the darkness below.

Together they carved a bloody line through the blockade. The way up to the next tier opened before them, lantern light flickering wildly in the wake of destruction.

Fallax turned once they broke through, planting himself between his men and the soldiers who rallied to give chase. His voice was raw as he roared:

"RUN! I'll hold them!"

Romius caught his eye for the briefest moment, and though he said nothing, the nod he gave carried the weight of respect—and of farewell. Then he shoved Eryx onward, the two disappearing up the stone stair.

Fallax drew both blades, his stance broad, every muscle tensed like a bowstring. The soldiers advanced warily, regrouping, a dozen at least pressing up from below, their torches casting jagged shadows across the blood-slick steps.

He spat, wiped sweat and blood from his brow, and snarled:

"Come on, then. You'll not touch them while I still draw breath."

They charged.

Ξ

Eroge did not move quickly—his steps were deliberate, heavy, like an avalanche working its way down the mountainside. But what he lacked in speed, he made up for in raw endurance. Still, the tide pressed harder.

Blades scraped against his shield, spears jabbed from angles he couldn't cover, and though his mace landed with bone-crushing finality, for every man he felled another seemed to step in. His arms burned, his breath came ragged, and a spear tip carved a shallow line across his ribs.

Fallax shouted above the clash, rallying him: "Hold them, Eroge! Just a little longer—hold!"

The giant bared his teeth, roared, and surged forward, but the press of soldiers finally slowed him. His shield splintered further, his mace heavy with blood. He crushed one man with a shield- swipe only to take a blow to the back of his knee, dropping him for a heartbeat. The guards swarmed, smelling weakness.

And then—shouts from behind.

Steel flashed in the torchlight as Rannax and Bard crashed into the enemy's rear. Bard's laughter boomed through the chaos, his shield slamming a soldier against the stair rail before his axe cut him down. Rannax moved like a phantom, his blade finding the gaps in armour, striking quick and precise.

The sudden attack threw the soldiers into panic. Half turned to face the new threat, and in that heart-beat Eroge found his strength again. He rose with a guttural roar, swinging his mace in a brutal arc that smashed through two men at once.

Between the three of them, the press broke. Bard bowled a man clean off the stair edge, his scream trailing into the darkness below. Rannax cut another's hamstrings, leaving him writhing as he leapt forward to drive his blade into a second foe. Eroge slammed his shield down like a hammer, crushing a skull into the stone.

The enemy line wavered, cracked, and finally collapsed under the combined fury. Within moments, the stairs below were slick with blood and scattered with broken bodies.

Eroge stood amidst them, chest heaving, shield barely more than a ruin of wood and iron, mace dripping red. But when he looked up at Rannax and Bard, a weary smile cracked through his bloodied face.

They turned upwards.

Ξ

Fallax met them head-on, blades flashing, each strike delivered with grim precision. He was no brute force like Eroge, nor spectral dancer like Rannax—Fallax was a storm contained in steel, fury controlled and honed. He cut the first man down with a thrust through the throat, parried another's axe into the wall, and drove his second blade through the man's gut. A shield slammed against him, but he twisted, ducked, and slashed low, spilling blood across the stone.

Still, they came, climbing over the bodies of their own, forcing him step by step back. Fallax's arms burned, his breath ragged. His blades dripped red, his boots slipped on blood-slick stone, but still he fought. Three men remained, circling him like wolves, waiting for the old general to falter.

One lunged from the right—Fallax caught the strike, steel screeching against steel, but another slammed into his back with a shield, forcing him to his knees. The third raised his sword high, ready to split him in two.

Then a bellow roared through the stairwell.

"RAAANNAX!"

The soldier's head snapped up just in time to see Bard barrel into him like a charging ox, shield-first. The man flew back, smashing against the wall before crumpling lifelessly.

Rannax slid in low, his twin blades flashing. In one fluid sweep he felled the soldier behind Fallax, then drove his knife up into the man's chest before the cry left his lips.

The last soldier turned to flee—but his escape was cut short by Eroge. Bloodied, battered, but still unbroken, the giant grabbed him by the collar and slammed him face-first into the stair wall. Bone cracked. The man went limp.

Silence.

Fallax, panting, stared at them, half in disbelief. Rannax offered a hand to pull him up. Bard leaned on his shield, chest heaving. Eroge stood behind them, the faintest grin hidden beneath the blood streaking his face.

"You looked like you could use a hand," Rannax quipped, his grin sharp even through exhaustion.

Fallax clasped his forearm, their grips tight, steady. "You took your time."

Bard barked a laugh, almost delirious. "We were busy dancing with barrels of fire."

For a heartbeat, even amidst the corpses and ruin, there was relief. They were together.

Fallax straightened, sheathing one of his blades. "Romius and Eryx are ahead. We continue behind them until they reach Sallomannax."

The others nodded, the weight of their mission pulling them back into focus. With no more words wasted, the four men gathered themselves, turned toward the looming ascent, and pressed on—upward, toward the City Lord's manor.

Ξ

Caelius glided down. The noise of battle had become a beacon, a trail of blood and fire leading her straight to her prey. The stone itself bent to her will—dark green smoke pouring from the Verdacryl at her hip, solidifying beneath her feet in fleeting steps that dissolved the moment she passed. To watch her descend was to see a phantom sliding effortlessly through the air, a figure unbound by the laws of men.

Her eyes glowed in the half-dark, not with life but with fury—fuelled by years of neglect, by desperation to earn the love of a father who had never truly seen her as more than a weapon. Rage sharpened every line of her face as she got lower and lower, the stairways coiling like a serpent around Tydell's mountain tiers.

Then she saw them.

The boy. Eryx. Standing in the dim glow of lantern-fire, his hand tight to his staff, his posture raw with determination and fear. Beside him stood Romius, silent, heavy, his presence as foreboding as the axe he carried.

Caelius slowed her descent, each step of smoke cracking faintly beneath her boots. She gripped her weapon, its form flickering—knife to throwing star, star to spear-tip—her will undecided on how to end him, only that she would.

She whispered to herself, voice breaking, trembling with hate and longing all at once:

"Father will see me. He will see me."

The air seemed to hum with the gathering of her power. The stone walls around her twisted, shuddered under the Verdacryl's influence, ready to shatter at her command. She stepped into their path, her silhouette cutting through the lantern-glow, smoke curling at her feet.

Ξ

Romius and Eryx surged forward, blades flashing in the lantern-light, the clash of steel ringing up the narrow stairwells. More men gathered behind than ahead, their shouts echoing through the tiers, but the two pressed on, cutting a path upward. Each level was steeper than the last, the climb more brutal, the walls closing in. Sweat and blood streaked down their faces, but the City Lord's manor loomed closer, its silhouette like a crown of stone against the night sky.

Then—she dropped from above.

Caelius.

She landed in front of them in a swirl of green smoke, the stone beneath her boots cracking under the force. Her weapon writhed between shapes in her grip. Her eyes glowed with that unnatural light, fixed on Eryx with venomous certainty.

Eryx froze. His breath caught in his throat. Memories of their last encounter burned in him like fire—how she had dismantled him without mercy, how her power had made him feel like a child swinging a stick at a storm. His body wanted to move, but fear held him rooted.

Romius's hand clamped on his shoulder, steady and firm. The old warrior turned him, his face etched with battle scars and a rare, almost fatherly softness in his gaze.

"Lad… this one is mine," Romius said, voice low, gravel steady even over the chaos around them. "I owe you one. You go. End this. Save this city."

Eryx's lips parted, trembling with protest, but the words didn't come.

Romius gave a small, almost imperceptible smile. "I believe in you."

The weight of those words sank into Eryx's chest.

Eryx bolted upward, forcing his legs to move, forcing himself to trust. His boots pounded the stone, his breath ragged, each step carrying him closer to the City Lord's gates.

Behind him, Caelius hissed in fury and lunged, her weapon lengthening into a spear, aimed to pierce through his back—

—but Romius was there, intercepting, arms locking around. With a roar he dragged her off her feet, momentum carrying them both toward the edge.

Eryx glanced back just as the two tumbled from the stair, their figures vanishing over the wall of tier four, swallowed by the abyss below. The last thing he saw was Romius's hand still clutching Caelius, ensuring she would not escape.

The sound of their fall was lost in the clash of battle.

Eryx's throat tightened, but he didn't stop. He couldn't stop. Romius had given him the only thing that mattered—time.

Ξ

Steel clashed, shields cracked, and blood slicked the stone steps as Rannax, Bard, Eroge, and Fallax battled their way upward. Every breath burned in their lungs, every strike was slower than the last, but still they fought on, shoulder to shoulder, determined to break through. The guards kept pouring in, desperate to hold their ground, but Barrack Thirteen was relentless.

Rannax's blade flashed, cutting a man down with practiced precision. Bard shoved another soldier back with his shield, teeth bared in a grim smile. Beside them, Eroge fought like a wounded bear, his mace swinging in wide, devastating arcs, each impact splintering bone and sending bodies reeling. Fallax was a storm unto himself—his blade swift, unyielding, his voice rising above the violence to rally them onward.

Then the sky cracked.

A thunderous *boom* shook the stone beneath their boots. All four staggered, looking up just as a streak of silver-blue collided mid-air with a whirl of dark, poisonous green. The storm of colours spiralled downward, twisting like two furious serpents entwined, before crashing into the tier below them.

The explosion lit the mountainside like dawn—searing light, shards of energy spraying outward, dust and stone flying into the air. The shockwave rippled up through the staircase, forcing the men to shield their eyes. For a heartbeat, it was as if the night had been torn apart.

Ξ

They fell together, crashing through air and dust, until Romius forced their descent onto a lower terrace. Stone split beneath their impact, the shock shuddering through the mountain. For a moment, both rose in silence—two titans poised, the air between them trembling with tension.

Caelius' eyes burned with a poisonous green glow. In her hands, a dagger melted into a spear, then a cluster of jagged shards, each spinning around her like orbiting stars. "You're far from your boy now, old wolf," she hissed. "This is where your story ends."

Romius flexed his shoulders, his chest heaving as his skin rippled to steel. Plates of silver-grey sheen slid across him like armour being forged in an instant. He stepped forward, boots cracking the stone. "Then let's finish it."

She struck first.

The shards shot forward in a rain of green-lit blades, whistling through the air like a storm of razors. Each one carried enough force to skewer a man clean through, yet Romius did not falter. He lowered his head and charged straight through, his body ringing with the metallic clang of steel upon steel as the projectiles shattered against him. Sparks burst in every direction, a fiery halo marking his advance.

A few shards pierced through the gaps where flesh still showed, blood streaking down his arms and legs, but he didn't slow. His momentum was thunder itself.

Domir came around in a crushing arc, the great axe howling as it cut the air. The weight of it seemed to drag the very wind with it, pulling dust and fragments of stone in its wake. The blade struck with the force of a siege ram, aiming to cleave her in two.

But Caelius moved with inhuman grace. Her feet barely touched the ground as she twisted aside, Verdacryl light flaring around her like a cloak. The weapon struck the earth where she had stood, and the terrace split open with a deafening crack, sending chunks of rock flying skyward.

She retaliated instantly, seizing the debris mid-air. With a thought, the shattered stones warped into jagged spears, each infused with the sickly green glow of her essence. They whirled toward Romius in a spiralling barrage.

Romius roared, wrenching Domir free from the ruined ground. He spun the axe in a defensive arc, steel skin glinting as he knocked one spear after another aside, the clash ringing like temple bells. Shards that slipped past embedded into his body, scraping and biting against his hardened flesh. He ignored them, stepping forward through the storm.

Every movement of his was deliberate, monstrous, his strikes like falling mountains. Every movement of hers was fluid, unpredictable, her power reshaping the battlefield with each heartbeat.

And as Domir came down again, whistling like the judgment of gods, Caelius didn't retreat this time. She raised her hands, and the ground itself surged upward to meet the axe, stone hardening into a barricade infused with her will.

The clash was apocalyptic. The barricade shattered into dust and fire, but Domir's swing was slowed—enough for Caelius to dart in close, her hand wreathed in twisting green smoke.

Ξ

Eryx bobbed and weaved past the final few guards, his breath ragged, his body aching, but his focus unbroken. Every strike, every sidestep was driven by the vision of what waited at the top. He broke through, at last the grand oak doors of the City Lord's manor loomed before him, iron-bound and immovable.

He slowed only for a heartbeat, chest heaving, the weight of the night pressing down. Then he closed his eyes and pulled deep. Light surged through him, burning his veins like fire, gathering at his core until his skin glowed and his eyes blazed with raw brilliance.

With a cry that shook the night, he hurled himself forward. The staff in his hands ignited with radiant force, and he drove its point hard into the seam of the doors.

The explosion was thunderous. Oak splintered, iron twisted, and the massive doors burst inward as if struck by a storm. Dust and shards rained down into the vaulted entry.

Eryx staggered across the threshold, his staff blazing, and his eyes widened.

The grand hallway stretched out before him—pillars of white stone, banners of Thearon's crest hanging heavy in the silence.

And waiting for him were three soldiers unlike any he had faced before.

They stood in formation, giants clad in plated armour blackened with age, each holding a weapon that looked as though it had felled a hundred men already. Shields as tall as a man braced before them, faces hidden behind helms adorned with jagged crests. They did not move, but their presence radiated menace—these were the chosen, the elite of Tydell, bred and trained for this very moment.

And behind them… Sallomannax.

The City Lord stood elevated, his delicate robes shimmering with silver thread, his hands clasped before him. His eyes—cold, merciless, burning with contempt—fixed on Eryx. No fear. No hesitation. Only loathing.

Eryx's pulse thundered in his ears. He tightened his grip on the staff, the glow of light humming louder in his bones.

He knew he should be afraid. He knew he was outmatched. But in that moment, all that remained was the fire in his chest and the promise he had made to his family, to Barrack Thirteen, to the city itself.

With a defiant roar, Eryx lunged forward.

Ξ

Caelius leapt, twisting the ground itself. The stone below Romius buckled and rose like jagged teeth, forcing him off balance. She landed behind him, her hands slamming to the earth. A wave of the staircase tore free and surged upward like a tidal wave, threatening to bury him.

Romius roared, his muscles bulging, steel flowing through his veins. He smashed his shoulder into the rising stone, shattering it to rubble, then spun with inhuman speed. Domir cut through the debris and through Caelius' defences, clipping her shoulder. She cried out but answered with fury—her blood dripping onto the ground, instantly infused, sprouting into writhing green spines that lashed at him like whips.

One caught his arm, sinking deep. Another wrapped around his leg. Caelius tightened her fist, and the spines constricted, aiming to crush and tear.

Romius gritted his teeth, steel overtaking his limbs entirely. His body gleamed silver-blue, unbreakable. With a bellow, he ripped himself free, chunks of glowing spine still embedded in his flesh, and hurled Domir straight at her.

Ξ

The three elites moved as one. Shields slammed down in unison, their boots pounding the marble as they advanced. Their weapons—two halberds and a colossal hammer—caught the torchlight, gleaming like executioner's tools.

Eryx's staff flared as he raised it. Light pulsed outward in a wave, striking the shields with a deafening crack.

The soldiers staggered but held, digging their heels into the floor.

The first elite surged forward with his halberd, a sweeping strike that could have cleaved Eryx in two. Eryx ducked low, rolling beneath it, his staff spinning in his hands. He rose with a burst of light, slamming the butt of his weapon into the soldier's chest. The blow rang out, denting the plated armour and sending the man skidding back several steps.

But the second was already on him. The hammer crashed down, splintering the marble where Eryx had stood. He darted aside, sweat stinging his eyes, his lungs burning. The sheer force rattled through his bones—one hit from that, and it was over.

The third came from his flank, halberd spinning like a whirlwind. Eryx lifted his staff, catching the strike, sparks exploding in a cascade of light and steel. He twisted, channelling power through the weapon, and a radiant shockwave blasted outward, forcing the soldier to stumble back.

For every step he gained, they pressed harder. Their coordination was perfect, honed by years of battle. One pressed, two covered. One struck, two flanked. It was like fighting a single beast with three heads.

Eryx bared his teeth, refusing to yield.

Light surged hotter inside him, spilling from his skin in radiant arcs. He spun his staff in a blur, parrying the halberds and deflecting the hammer, his movements faster, sharper, driven by desperation. His eyes glowed like twin moons, his voice raw.

He broke forward, slamming his staff into the ground. The marble beneath their feet cracked and erupted, a column of light shooting upward, throwing two of the elites into the pillars. The third—the hammer-bearer—charged through, unrelenting.

Eryx met him head-on.

The hammer swung down, but this time Eryx caught it. His hands shook with the effort, arms burning, knees buckling, but he held. The weapon rang as if striking an unbreakable wall of light. With a cry, Eryx wrenched it aside and drove his staff into the man's helm. The glow flared brilliant white, and the soldier collapsed, armour crashing against the stone like thunder.

The other two rose, battered but alive. They rushed him together.

Eryx spun his staff, the light surging brighter than ever, and vaulted forward. He struck one across the jaw, shattering his helm and sending him sprawling. The last came at him, halberd raised, screaming.

Eryx thrust his staff forward, a beam of pure radiance glowing at its tip. It struck the soldier square in the chest, lifting him off his feet and hurling him across the hall. The man's armour smoked, and he did not rise.

Breathing hard, Eryx stood alone amidst the wreckage. The three elites—Tydell's finest—lay defeated at his feet.

The hall fell silent, save for the ragged sound of his breath. His body shook, his limbs heavy, but his spirit blazed brighter than ever.

At the far end of the chamber, the City Lord's doors loomed.

Eryx staggered toward them, staff still glowing faintly, his chest swelling with defiance. He pushed them open—

And the world betrayed him.

The ground beneath his feet erupted in a swirl of dark green smoke. Marble cracked and warped, reshaping itself like clay. Tendrils of stone, glowing with that sinister hue, shot up and coiled around his limbs. His arms were wrenched wide, his legs pinned, his staff clattering uselessly to the floor.

The light inside him flared against the bindings, but they only tightened, squeezing like the grasp of a giant's hand.

A low, mocking laugh filled the chamber.

From the shadows beyond, Sallomannax stepped forward, his delicate robes shimmering, his hands raised in casual command. His eyes burned with triumph.

"You came all this way," he said softly, his voice like poisoned silk, "only to kneel."

Ξ

She reacted instantly. The stone floor liquefied, swallowing the blade before it reached her. But Romius was already behind it, closing the distance like a thunderbolt. He tackled her with the force of an avalanche, both of them crashing into the wall.

The impact was cataclysmic—stone exploding outward, dust filling the air. Caelius spat blood but slammed her palm against his chest. Matter warped beneath her touch, his steel shell groaning as cracks spread. For a terrifying heartbeat, Romius felt her power threaten to kill him from the inside.

He responded with raw strength. His forehead smashed against hers, staggering her, and he wrapped both arms around her waist. Muscles straining, he lifted and hurled her across the terrace, her body breaking through a pillar before skidding to a stop.

But she rose again. Bleeding, trembling, eyes wild with fury and desperation. The ground behind her rose into twisted spires, dark-green light spiralling upward. Weapons, whips, chains—all conjured at once. They lunged at Romius in a torrent.

He answered with a war cry, Domir back in his grip, his body glowing brighter with every heartbeat. He swung, cut, shattered. Each strike demolished one of her creations, the ground itself screaming in protest as their powers tore the terrace apart.

When they finally clashed again, it was steel against smoke, muscle against willpower. Neither gave ground. Neither yielded. Their blows shook the mountain, their blood painted the stones.

And then—silence.

They broke apart, both staggering, both barely standing. Romius's steel skin was fractured, jagged cracks leaking blood beneath. Caelius' body trembled, her left arm limp, her breath ragged.

They had given each other everything.

Neither had won. Both had been broken.

As dust drifted between them, Romius lifted Domir weakly, and Caelius raised a hand trembling with dark light. The next move could have ended either one of them—
But the mountain itself groaned, collapsing under the strain of their war, forcing the two masters to retreat, broken but alive.

Ξ

Rannax's blade cleaved through the last soldier before him, the man's body tumbling lifeless down the stairs. He barely had time to breathe before he caught sight of her—Caelius. She was broken, bloodied, limping away into the shadows, her once-proud stride now a jagged stagger. The Verdacryl still hissed around her like smoke from dying embers, but her defiance burned even as her body betrayed her.

Rannax's instinct was to finish it—to chase her down and put an end to her poison. But then he saw Romius.

The Steelmancer was on one knee, one hand buried into the cracked stone for balance, Domir heavy at his side. His chest rose and fell in ragged bursts, every breath drawn with the sound of metal grinding against metal. His skin flickered between flesh and steel as though his body no longer knew which form it could sustain. In his other hand, the Thearonite cube glowed faintly, pulsing in rhythm with his heart, feeding him just enough to remain upright.

"Romius!" Rannax barked, rushing to him. He slid an arm under the older man's shoulder and hauled him to his feet. Romius was a mountain even in his weakness, his weight near impossible to support. But Rannax bore it, teeth gritted, his arm trembling with the strain.

Romius's eyes opened, steel-grey and bloodshot. "I'm not… done," he rasped, though his body told another story. Every scar, every wound from the battle with Caelius and the endless climb through Sallomannax's gauntlet had left him fraying at the edges. Without the cube feeding him, he would have collapsed long ago.

"Don't speak," Rannax growled. "Save your strength. We'll hold them."

Above and below, the chaos of battle roared. Bard's shield was dented and bloodied, but he stood his ground against the flood of soldiers still pouring up the tiers. Eroge, though battered and limping, swung his mace with raw fury, each strike like a hammer blow that crushed men to the stone. Fallax fought with the calm precision of command, every thrust and counter a reminder that he had once led armies.

Barrack Thirteen closed ranks around Romius.

Romius coughed, blood flecking his lips. He tried to push Rannax away, to stand on his own, but his knees buckled. The cube pulsed again, its light dimming, then strengthening, then dimming once more like a candle guttering in the wind.

"Rannax…" Romius's voice was low, urgent despite its weakness. "You must hold… until the boy finishes it. If Sallomannax lives… none of this matters."

Rannax tightened his grip, his jaw set. "Then you rest. We'll see it through."

The sound of boots thundered from above—more soldiers descending, blades and shields flashing in the torchlight. Bard swore under his breath and raised his shield, planting his feet. Eroge roared, his voice echoing like a beast's, and swung his mace in a wide arc.

The enemy came crashing down upon them.

Barrack Thirteen stood their ground, forming a wall around Romius. Every strike, every block, every cry was for him—for the man who had carried them through hell and still stood, even when broken.

Rannax's sword whirled. Romius tried to rise again, the cube's glow flickering, but Rannax pressed him down.

"Not yet, old friend. You've done enough. Now let us carry you."

Ξ

Eryx strained against the binding green smoke that coiled around his limbs like living chains, each tendril infused with the City Lord's mastery. The more he fought, the tighter they squeezed, digging into his skin like hot iron. His staff lay just out of reach, taunting him on the polished stone floor.

Across the hall, Sallomannax descended the steps from his throne with the slow, measured pace of a man utterly in control. His delicate robes shimmered faintly in the firelight, a mockery of refinement. His eyes, cold and sharp as a predator's, never left Eryx.

"You look just like the rest of them," Sallomannax mused, his lips curling into a cruel smile. "Defiant even when caught. But defiance only delays the inevitable."

He circled the boy, hands clasped behind his back, savouring the moment. Then he laughed—a dry, humourless sound. "I suppose it is fitting. That you, a mere child stumbling from one miracle to the next, should be the one to hear my truth before you die."

Eryx glared up at him, chest heaving. "Truth? Or just another lie to cover your filth?"

Sallomannax's smirk widened. "You'll see soon enough." He stopped in front of the boy, his voice turning sharp, theatrical. "It was I who helped Leax. The 'honorable king' you so despise? He could never have turned the realm without my guidance. Together, we twisted the tale, pinned every shadow, every betrayal, every unspeakable crime on the old king. The people begged for a saviour, and Leax became their beacon. My beacon."

His hand flared with green smoke, and he gestured wide, as though painting his grand achievement in the air.

"And Poltan?" He chuckled, shaking his head. "A city of fools. I turned them against Romius with but a whisper. A forged tale here, a staged betrayal there. They saw a monster because I gave them one to see. A Steelmancer cast down by his own people—delicious irony."

Eryx's jaw clenched, but he forced words through gritted teeth. "You destroyed lives. Families. Whole cities—for power."

Sallomannax ignored the accusation, his eyes bright with the joy of confession. "Garraw was my true triumph. The Pit—ah, such beauty in cruelty. Slaves working until their bodies broke, digging, bleeding, dying, all to ensure the three precious elements would never fall into the hands of Ellomancers. A steady stream of suffering to keep my dominion intact."

He leaned in close, his whisper venomous. "And then, of course, there was my daughter. My perfect weapon. I sent Caelius into Thearon, into the wilds, into the villages, to cut out your kind before you could ever bloom. It did not matter if you were man, woman, or child. No spark would survive."

Eryx's stomach turned, bile rising in his throat. "You…
you turned her into a monster."

"Monster?" Sallomannax scoffed, standing tall again. "I
turned her into purpose. Into strength. Unlike you." His
gaze hardened. "You were nothing. A boy with a string
of lucky mistakes. Do you know how many times I tried
to erase you? The carriage—the strike that should have
split you in half. My daughter's blade. Yet somehow you
slithered free each time. Do you know what Damiax told
me? That your blade curved in the air. A fluke. A trick of
chance."

His voice rose, echoing across the vaulted hall. "But fate
cannot save you forever. You've delivered yourself to
me. And now I will savour ending you, knowing you
crawled all this way just to die at my feet."

The tendrils of smoke squeezed tighter, and Eryx cried
out in pain. But through the agony, he found his voice.
"Why?" His eyes burned, not with fear but with fury.
"Why do you hate Ellomancers so much? Why do you
want us gone? You are one yourself."

For a heartbeat, Sallomannax was silent. Then his
expression darkened, and a terrible grin spread across his
face.

Ξ

Caelius stumbled into the shadows of an abandoned
building, the stone walls cold against her bloodied limbs.
The dark green smoke of her power still curled faintly
around her hands, but it no longer obeyed as it once

had—her strength was spent, her body trembling with exhaustion.

She sank to the floor, pressing her forehead against the cracked wood of a shuttered window. Her breaths came ragged, each one a reminder of how close she had come—and how completely she had failed. The boy… Romius… Eryx… they had slipped through her grasp again.

For a moment, she let herself feel the weight of it all: the pain, the rage, the desperate longing for her father's approval. But even that pride was poisoned. The lessons he had taught her, the power he had pushed her to master, had not secured his love—they had made her a weapon, a tool, a failure in the end.

She curled into herself, the dim light of the room catching the streaks of blood on her skin. She had survived, but only barely. And the gnawing thought remained, sharper than any blade: she had failed her father… again.

The silence pressed down on her, broken only by the faint creak of the building settling and the distant echoes of battle outside. Somewhere in the city, the world moved on. And for her, there was only the hollow ache of defeat and the cold, lingering doubt of what kind of monster she had truly become.

Ξ

Sallomannax's eyes glimmered as he stepped closer, the dark green smoke coiling around Eryx's limbs quivering with his every heartbeat. His voice was calm, almost tender, but carried the weight of decades of cruelty.

"Do you want to know why I despise your kind, boy?" he asked, pacing slowly across the chamber. "Why I will see every Ellomancer wiped from this world?"

Eryx glared at him, his muscles straining against the binding smoke, but remained silent.

Sallomannax continued, voice dripping with venom and memory. "I was not born to this cruelty. No, I was taken—snatched from my family as a child, sold into the hands of Ellomancers who saw potential, who saw a blank canvas. They beat me, abused me, bent me until I learned the ways of Essencecrafters. They forced me to master powers I barely understood, to warp the world to their whim. They stole everything from me—my home, my family, my childhood. And when I became strong enough... I killed them. Every last one. And in that moment, I swore I would eradicate every living soul who carries that curse of power, every Ellomancer, so no child would ever enslave another like I was."

His voice rose with each word, shaking the walls of the chamber. The smoke binding Eryx trembled and twisted, the green tendrils retracting from the boy and lunging back toward Sallomannax as if drawn by the fury in his veins. The marble beneath his feet cracked, the dark energy coiling around him like a living extension of his anger.

Eryx felt the shift immediately. The tendrils constricting his limbs loosened, giving him room, just enough. With a roar that shook the stone and firelight, he hurled every ounce of strength into his arms and legs. Muscle and spirit ripped him free.

Stone and smoke screamed as chunks of marble and twisted Verdacryl exploded outward. Eryx's body flew backward, tumbling across the floor before he landed in a crouch, his staff clattering to the ground nearby. His breath came in ragged gasps, but his eyes burned brighter than ever, blazing with defiance.

Sallomannax staggered, taken aback by the sheer force of Eryx's escape. The green smoke writhed around him, still alive, still dangerous, but no longer holding its captive.

Eryx rose fully, muscles trembling, eyes locked on his foe. The binds were gone, but the weight of the fight ahead pressed heavy. Still, he stood tall.

"You took everything from others to protect nothing but your anger," Eryx growled. "I won't let your hatred decide the fate of Thearon—or of Warrah."

Sallomannax's laugh was low, dark, and filled with malice. "Oh, boy… the real lesson begins now."

Ξ

Caelius dragged herself forward, every step a battle against the pain screaming through her body. Her arms shook, her hands cut and scorched from the previous fight, yet she forced herself onward. The glow from the City Lord's shattered entrance pulsed ahead—blue from Eryx's Thearonite energy, green from the power

Verdacryl gave her father. It called to her, igniting a flicker of fury and desperation within her.

Romius saw her stumbling, bloodied and trembling, and instinctively moved to intercept. He limped, one leg bruised and bleeding, his own exhaustion evident in every laboured step, but he refused to let her reach Eryx. He closed the distance carefully, reading her movements, anticipating her next shift of weight, her every subtle attempt to regain balance. He placed a firm hand on her shoulder.

She yanked, trying to push past him, and he countered—not with brute force, but with precision. He shifted his stance, pivoting and using her momentum to redirect her sideways, guiding her away from the glowing doorway. His steel-like reflexes met her Verdacryl-infused strikes with a measured deflection, catching the edges of her green smoke without allowing it to lash uncontrolled.

They moved in a careful dance of restraint. Romius blocked, parried, and nudged; Caelius twisted, feinted, and lunged. Each motion was subtle, almost elegant, but loaded with the power of two seasoned combatants, each measuring the other, neither able to fully dominate due to fatigue and injuries. Every strike carried the weight of their exhaustion—muscles burning, joints stiff, lungs ragged—but they relied on skill, leverage, and instinct over raw strength.

Romius's voice cut through the tense silence. "I won't let you hurt him—don't force me to stop you by breaking you!"

Her green smoke writhed around them, a living extension of her anger and determination, and Romius responded with controlled gestures, channelling his own essence to disrupt the tendrils without harming her. He held her back gently but firmly, grounding her as much as restraining her, each move calculated to conserve both of their dwindling reserves.

Caelius' chest heaved; she glared at him, torn between her father's expectations, her exhaustion, and the glimmer of respect for his skill. For a moment, they locked eyes, the fight pausing in the unspoken understanding that neither could give their all—not yet— and that any misstep could be fatal.

Finally, Romius stepped aside just enough to guide her to the floor, keeping her off balance while ensuring she could not surge forward toward Eryx. Both leaned heavily on each other, breaths ragged, faces smeared with blood and dirt, their bodies screaming in protest.

They were battered, bruised, and exhausted—but still masters of their powers, still alive, still measuring every move in a delicate balance of control and restraint.

The glow from the doorway flickered and pulsed ominously.

Ξ

Rannax, Bard, Eroge, and Fallax staggered forward over the debris-strewn tiers, each step heavy with fatigue and pain. Blood streaked their armour, bruises blackened their skin, and every breath was a reminder of how close they had come to death. The few remaining soldiers they faced had fallen, leaving only the echoes of battle and the acrid scent of smoke and blood.

Eroge's mace hung low at his side, arm trembling from the exertion, but his eyes burned with unyielding determination. Bard's shield bore dozens of dents, and Rannax's sword hand ached with every movement, yet they pressed on. Fallax scanned the horizon, calculating the path to the manor, the distant glow of blue and green light pulsing ominously from the shattered entrance.

The sounds of chaos grew louder with every step: crashing marble, the roar of unleashed energy, and the faint cries of men inside. They moved as one, silent nods passing between them, each aware of the stakes—every second wasted could cost lives, could tip the balance of the war.

Though battered, they were unbroken. Every wound, every drop of blood spilled, had tempered them further, sharpening their reflexes and resolve. With grim determination, the four warriors approached the threshold where the battle raged brightest.

Ξ

The chamber shook with the reverberations of their powers. Stone splintered, pillars cracked, and the air hummed with energy as Eryx faced Sallomannax, the master of Verdacryl and Essencecraft, at last fully unleashed.

Eryx's body glowed, veins coursing with Thearonite light. Every muscle coiled, every movement precise. Sallomannax stood opposite, dark green smoke writhing around him like serpents, his hands crackling as he bent the environment to his will.

Without warning, Sallomannax struck first. The floor beneath Eryx erupted into jagged spires of green-infused stone, lancing toward him from all directions. Eryx dove, staff spinning in a blur, slashing through the spikes and sending shards flying into the walls.

Sallomannax laughed, a cold, cruel sound that echoed off the marble. "Do you think you've grown enough to challenge me, boy? I've shaped the world, and you... you are nothing!"

The City Lord slammed his hands into the ground. The smoke surged into massive tendrils, whirling toward Eryx like living chains, each seeking to crush, strangle, or impale him. Eryx ducked, rolled, and slammed his staff into the ground, unleashing a shockwave of light that shattered the green tendrils before they could strike.

With a roar, he surged forward, closing the distance. Steel and light collided with smoke and stone as the two clashed. Eryx struck with the staff, every blow a fusion of strength, speed, and unyielding endurance. Sallomannax countered by reshaping the stone around him, weapons and barriers forming in an instant to deflect each strike.

The chamber became a storm. Pillars exploded, fragments raining down. Eryx spun, dodged, and swung, carving paths through the living architecture Sallomannax conjured. The City Lord retaliated with bursts of green smoke, smashing the floor, walls, and ceiling as if to crush the entire chamber upon the boy.

Eryx's eyes blazed with determination. He surged upward, vaulting over a collapsing column, and struck Sallomannax across the chest. The impact hurled him backward, but the City Lord laughed, reforming instantly, smoke wrapping around his limbs like whips.

"You think brute strength will win this?" Sallomannax sneered. "It is my mind, my mastery, that will end you!"

Eryx didn't answer. Instead, he channelled every ounce of his Thearonite light, his staff glowing like a sun in miniature. He leapt high, twisting in the air, and brought the staff down point-first onto the centre of the floor. Light erupted in a blinding explosion, the force radiating outward.

Sallomannax staggered but did not fall. His smoke surged in a desperate flurry, trying to bind Eryx mid-strike. But Eryx pressed forward, every strike following in rapid succession—swinging, stabbing, smashing, blinding his foe with the sheer speed and precision of his assault.

The green smoke recoiled under the brilliance of his power. Sallomannax's defences faltered, cracks appearing in the ground and in his own control. He roared in frustration, summoning everything he had left, the smoke wrapping tighter, sharper, forming a massive claw aimed to crush Eryx.

Eryx gritted his teeth, muscles screaming, veins burning with light, and met it head-on. The two forces collided, an explosion of green and silver that ripped through the hall. Stones tumbled, windows shattered, and the very walls groaned under the pressure.

With one final, desperate surge, Eryx planted his staff into the centre of the smoke tendril. Light pulsed outward, searing through the corrupted Verdacryl, shredding Sallomannax's control. The City Lord screamed, his body writhing as the very essence he had twisted to power him began to unravel.

The ground buckled, the smoke convulsed, and with a final, ear-splitting roar, Sallomannax was flung backward. He landed against the shattered wall, smoke dissipating, robes torn, body broken. Eryx approached cautiously, every nerve alert, staff ready.

The City Lord struggled, coughing, eyes wide with disbelief. "No… this cannot… I am…"

Eryx raised his staff, the glow of Thearonite light bathing the chamber. "Your tyranny ends here."

With a decisive strike, Eryx drove the staff through Sallomannax's chest. Green smoke hissed and evaporated, his life extinguished instantly. The City Lord's body slumped to the floor, utterly still. Silence fell.

Eryx dropped to his knees, breathing heavily, limbs shaking from exhaustion. The chamber was a ruin—

stone shattered, smoke lingering in curling tendrils, and the echoes of their clash fading.

Ξ

Caelius burst through the shattered doorway, every step driven by desperation and exhaustion. Her eyes fell on her father, slumped and broken on the cold stone floor, the life and arrogance that had defined him now gone. A surge of grief, rage, and lingering loyalty propelled her forward.

She dove to him, cradling his body against her chest. The last remnants of her Verdacryl essence flared around her, twisting the ground beneath into living green smoke. The floor shivered and cracked, and with a final, shuddering breath, she sank into the stone, dragging her father's body with her. The chamber seemed to swallow them whole, leaving only silence and the faint echo of Verdacryl energy dissipating.

Romius followed closely behind, limping from his wounds, the Thearonite cube in his hand still glowing faintly. He reached Eryx, who sat exhausted and bruised, body heaving from the fight but eyes sharp and aware. Romius rested a hand on the boy's shoulder, a gesture heavy with relief and unspoken pride.

For a moment, the chaos outside seemed to fade. The battle had claimed much, yet here they were—scarred, battered, but still alive. Together, they sat in the dim glow of the ruined manor, catching their breath, hearts still pounding, aware that the war had shifted, but the cost had been steep.

Eryx looked to Romius, and though words were unnecessary, the understanding passed between them: they had survived the storm, but the world was far from safe, and their fight was far from over.

CHAPTER 30- THE NEXT STEP

Eryx sat on the shattered edge of the balcony, the beautifully crafted railing now lying in ruin below, twisted remnants of once-proud stone and iron. His legs dangled over the drop as he stared out across the sprawling city. The first light of dawn crested the mountains, golden and warm upon his face, yet the valley beneath still drowned in shadow. It felt fitting. He had saved his home—or at least, what was left of it. But he knew this was only one battle. The war had only just begun.

Though the City Lord was gone, his ideology lingered like smoke in the lungs, choking and stubborn. Ellomancers like Eryx would never be free—not yet. They would be hunted as beasts, branded as curses, blamed for every misfortune until the last of them was ash or memory.

Romius lowered himself beside him, the balcony groaning beneath the weight of his hulking frame. He said nothing at first, simply watching the sunrise alongside the boy. The warmth painted his scarred features, softening the grim lines carved by years of betrayal and blood. For the first time in decades, he allowed himself to just… admire the view.

He had completed what he set out to do. Vengeance was his. Every man and viper who had conspired to kill his king lay dead by his hand. But as he turned to look at Eryx—still young, still burning with questions, still carrying the weight of a future not yet written—Romius knew his own journey was not truly over.

Ξ

Caelius knelt on the cold stone deep in the mountain, clutching the lifeless body of her father. Her injuries preventing her from moving. The weight of him pressed down, but not with love but oppression. He had never seen her as a daughter, only as a weapon. Every lesson, every harsh word, every manipulation had been designed to mould her into something formidable, something dangerous—capable of wielding Warrah's touch.

Now he was gone, leaving her adrift in a world that had never embraced her for who she was. The man who had been both her teacher and tormentor, the only figure she had ever leaned on, was gone, and with him vanished the fragile thread that had tethered her to the remnants of humanity she had clung to.

But grief twisted quickly into something darker. Because of the toxic ways of her father, she was now a target—a villain in the eyes of King Leax's new regime. The very power he had forced into her veins made her a threat, a weapon to be hunted and destroyed.

And so, in that quiet, cold chamber, a new resolve began to harden within her. She would not crumble. She would not beg for mercy. She would seek vengeance—not just for herself, but for the life that had been stolen from her, the love that had never been given, and the father who had taught her the art of power and cruelty alike.

Her tears fell freely, but beneath them burned a fire, one that would no longer be guided by anyone's hand but her own.

Ξ

Eroge, Rannax, and Bard stepped into the City Lord's office, their bodies battered, clothes torn, and blood streaked across their faces. Every breath they drew was heavy with exhaustion, but they had survived through sheer grit and determination. The room was quiet, the weight of their journey hanging between them.

Eryx moved forward first, a smile breaking through the grime, and embraced them. The relief was mutual, if fleeting. Behind them, Fallax entered, his eyes scanning the group until they landed on Romius. For a long moment, they simply regarded each other, old wounds and unspoken truths suspended in the air. Then, in a gesture of reconciliation, they clasped forearms—a silent acknowledgment of respect and a past left behind.

The silence lingered only briefly before Eryx broke it with a question, tentative yet eager: "What now?"

Rannax, ever ready with a plan, stepped forward. "We travel to Karathal. Eryx will be targeted here for the rest of his days. Karathal will have answers, and there we will find Jaimius. Once we do, we return to save Thearon."

The group nodded in agreement, resolve hardening within them.

Fallax shifted his stance, the weight of responsibility pressing down. "I will not be venturing with you," he said, his voice steady but tinged with regret. "I will take charge of Tydell. I need to build a force capable of matching King Leax and preventing this situation from spiralling further. You go, gather information, form alliances. I will hold the fort."

Barrack Thirteen exchanged uneasy glances, reluctant to leave their general behind. But Romius stepped forward, voice firm yet understanding. "It's what he must do." He caught Fallax's eye and saw the echoes of betrayal mirrored there, the sting of lies and manipulation they had both endured. "Fallax needs to take charge. He cannot allow anyone to deceive him again. This is his fight now, just as ours continues elsewhere."

The room fell into a quiet understanding. The plan was set, the paths diverging, yet their purpose remained united. Each of them carried the same determination: to uncover the truth, to protect what remained, and to save Thearon.

EPILOGUE

Oliax sat on the beach, toes buried in the cool sand as waves hissed and rolled against the shore. Behind her, her mother busied herself scrubbing the sea-front shop, the scent of salt and fish clinging to the air. Oliax barely noticed. Her attention was fixed on the small golden cube she clutched in her hands.

She had taken it from a drawer in the captain's house before everything changed. Through the long journey, across river and road, she had carried it with her, hidden close. It was more than a keepsake—it was precious. The cube made her feel safe, warm, as if unseen arms wrapped gently around her. And when she held it just so, when she listened carefully, she could hear and see things—things that helped her mother.

Smiling softly, Oliax pressed her palm into the sand. A golden glow spilled from her fingers, light rippling outward like sunlight through water. Grains of sand stirred, lifted, and swirled into delicate shapes. Slowly, a structure began to rise before her eyes, mountains forming in miniature.

It was Tydell. The city she looked back on from the boat as they drifted away, another place she had once called home. Its peaks rose in the sand, its tiers formed in perfect detail, each tiny grain held together by the golden light of the cube. She tilted her head, watching the city grow taller under her touch, her face half lost in awe, half lost in memory. Memory of her brother.

Printed in Dunstable, United Kingdom